# ANOTHER WOMAN'S DAUGHTER

D0957031

# ANOTHER WOMAN'S DAUGHTER

## FIONA SUSSMAN

WITHDRAWN

BERKLEY BOOKS, NEW YORK

## BERKLEY

An imprint of Penguin Random House LLC
375 Hudson Street, New York, New York 10014

Copyright © 2015 by Fiona Sussman.
"Readers Guide" copyright © 2015 by Penguin Random House LLC.
Penguin supports copyright. Copyright fuels creativity, encourages diverse voices,
promotes free speech, and creates a vibrant culture. Thank you for buying an authorized
edition of this book and for complying with copyright laws by not reproducing, scanning, or
distributing any part of it in any form without permission. You are supporting writers and
allowing Penguin to continue to publish books for every reader.

BERKLEY® and the "B" design are registered trademarks of Penguin Random House LLC.
For more information, visit penguin.com.

Library of Congress Cataloging-in-Publication Data

Sussman, Fiona.
[Shifting colours]
Another woman's daughter / Fiona Sussman.—Berkley trade paperback edition.
p. cm.
"Previously published in the UK as Shifting Colours
by Allison & Busby / May 2014"—Verso title page.
ISBN 978-0-425-28104-8 (paperback)
1. Birthmothers—Fiction.    2. Adoptees—Fiction.    3. Racially mixed
people—Fiction.    4. Family secrets—Fiction.    5. South Africa—Fiction.
6. England—Fiction.    7. Domestic fiction.    I. Title.
PR9639.4.S923S55 2015
823'.92—dc23
2015014273

PUBLISHING HISTORY
Previously published in the UK as *Shifting Colours* by Allison & Busby / May 2014
Berkley trade paperback edition / October 2015

PRINTED IN THE UNITED STATES OF AMERICA

10   9   8   7   6   5   4   3   2   1

Cover art: "Woman" by Joana Lopes / Shutterstock; "Bird" by Kichigin / Shutterstock;
background by iStock / Thinkstock.
Cover design by Lesley Worrell.
Interior text design by Laura K. Corless.

This is a work of fiction. Names, characters, places, and incidents either are the product of
the author's imagination or are used fictitiously, and any resemblance to actual persons,
living or dead, business establishments, events, or locales is entirely coincidental.
The publisher does not have any control over and does not assume any responsibility
for author or third-party websites or their content.

Penguin
Random
House

*For my family, whose love and support bind the pages of this book.*

## AUTHOR'S NOTE

As I embarked on the writing of *Another Woman's Daughter*, I was acutely aware of the challenge ahead—the challenge of writing in the voice of characters whose life experiences and culture were so different from my own. I hope I have not unwittingly caused offense to anyone. In the end I have drawn on my experiences as a mother, daughter, wife, and sister, and I hope that the common denominator I share with my characters is our humanity.

While the first twenty-five years of my life provided me with personal knowledge of life in South Africa during the apartheid era, I am also indebted to the authors mentioned at the end of this novel, whose works supplemented my knowledge of the world my characters would inhabit.

If this book inspires you to explore other works set against the backdrop of Africa, you may wish to read *Under Our Skin* by Donald McRae, *We Need New Names* by NoViolet Bulawayo, *Tsotsi* by Athol Fugard, *Cry, the Beloved Country* by Alan Paton, or *The Grass Is Singing* by Doris Lessing.

# PROLOGUE

She stands in front of the stove, her black frame erect and proud, wooden spoon poised over a battered preserving pan. She is completely still, seemingly mesmerized by the rise and fall of the sugary sea. It is a hot African morning and the air is thick with the sweet smell of fig jam.

Just when I think she'll never move again, she scoops up a spoonful of the scalding liquid and drops it onto a saucer, then, tilting and rotating the blob of gold, she checks for fine creases in the sample.

I cross my fingers, hopeful for one more saucer to lick before the golden sweetness is locked away in squat glass jars with shiny brass lids—treasure that will belong to someone else.

This is the first memory I have of *Mme*, my dearest mother, the first sweet memory. But it remains tangled with the other events of that dreadful day; I've never been able to tease the two apart.

Many years have passed and still this picture slides into my mind uninvited, the edges polished, the lines clearly defined. I can almost smell her—a comforting cocktail of Sunlight soap and wood smoke—and touch the beads of perspiration hiding in the creases behind her knees. Sometimes her laughter bursts into my head or I hear her call me—my name full and round in her mouth. Frustratingly, though, as with all the memories I have of *Mme*, her face always blurs under the pressure of my focus.

# PART ONE

# CHAPTER ONE

## 1959

## Miriam

*Mme* teetered on tiptoes under the low ceiling beams, placing the last jars of fig jam on the shelf beside the other preserves—a fantastic collection of peaches, cling stone plums, deep purple mulberries, tightly packed apricots, mango chutneys, and lemon achar. I counted one, two, three, four . . . nine fat jars of jam transformed by the fingers of morning sunlight into pots of amber.

As she balanced there on the three-legged stool, I inspected the soles of her big black feet. They were white on the underside and black on top. I examined mine. They were pale on the bottom too, but not rutted with the same gullies and canyons of hard, dry skin. *Mme* said one day, when my journey had been longer, my feet would look more like hers.

She jumped down off the stool and landed with a thud, her bottom wobbling under the taut fabric of her maid's uniform.

I jumped up and down trying to make mine jiggle too, but I couldn't see far enough over my shoulder to know if it did. Gideon, the garden boy from next door, said *Mme* had the biggest, most beautiful bottom in the whole of Johannesburg. He would peer over the garden wall whenever she passed and shake his head in admiration. I hoped my bottom would grow round and wobbly like *Mme*'s.

A cool breeze swept over the open stable-type door and into the kitchen, diluting the morning heat. *Mme* shifted her gaze to the kitchen clock, its faded hands edging around the small white face. "*Hau*, Miriam! Ten o'clock. Still so much to do."

She scooped me up and pressed me to her. I loved all her big bits—her bosom, her bottom, her shiny black calves. She had no angles or peaks, just gentle hills and gradual valleys. "Today is a special day, child. The Madam, she will come home with a new baby. We must make everything good." *Mme* was excited, so I was too.

Sitting me down at the kitchen table, she secured a tea towel around my neck, picked a plump mango from the fruit bowl, and, with a small paring knife, began to strip away the thick orange skin. She did this with maddening skill, leaving scarcely a trace of sweet flesh on the peels for me to gnaw at while I waited.

The fragrance of the ripe fruit blended with the smell of caramelized sugar still hanging in the air. I breathed in a hungry breath. Mangoes were even better than jam. Then I was chasing the slippery orange ball around my plate, wrestling with it and shrieking each time I lost hold. Finally, *Mme* secured it for me with the stab of a fork, and at last I was able to sink my fingers into the flesh of my favorite fruit.

It wasn't long before all that was left of my treat was a pale, hairy pip, which *Mme* rinsed under the tap so I could add another member to my Mamelodi mango family.

"This is Baby Mamelodi," I said, teasing the long, stringy fibers into a frizz.

*Mme* frowned as she wiped clean my sticky mustache. "Babies do not have big hair when they are born. You will see the Madam's baby. Maybe it will have no hair."

No hair? My skin prickled. I didn't like the thought of that. It sounded like a snail without its shell.

"My baby *will* have hair," I said defiantly, putting Baby Mamelodi out on the back step to dry.

*Mme* shrugged.

Later I would draw on eyes, a nose, and a wide-open mouth; *Mme* said babies could cry a lot. But the hair thing kept bothering me like an annoying fly, and later, when no one was watching, I chopped off Baby Mamelodi's hair.

As *Mme* moved through the rest of her chores, I drove a cotton reel between her busy feet, watched as a tribe of ants swarmed over a blob of jam, and arranged a circle of pebbles around the giant pine tree in the garden. *Mme* said it had once been a small *piccanin* of a Christmas tree the Madam had tossed out. Now it stretched to the sky, its roots lifting the slate paving into crooked ripples.

By the time the sun was high in the sky, a honeyed smell of furniture wax filled the huge home. Bathroom basins boasted gleaming white bowls, wooden floors shone, and the brass reflected all the funny faces I pulled. The house was ready.

"Everything done," *Mme* said, sinking onto the kitchen stool with a mug of hot tea. I leaned in against her. Her skin was shiny and her uniform damp and strong smelling.

She poured some tea into an egg cup for me, added a drop of milk and two cubes of sugar, then stirred. Now we could drink tea together like grown-ups.

I stirred again—*clink, clink, clink.* Then the room was quiet, except for the refrigerator humming in the corner like a hive of bees. I was just about to take my first sip of tea when the neighbor's dogs began to bark, then the doorbell screamed, cracking open the afternoon stillness.

I shot under *Mme*'s skirt.

"The Madam is here," she whispered, her words steady and reassuring.

Taking my hand, *Mme* started toward the front door. "Remember, we must not upset the new baby."

"Celi-a!" The Madam's voice forced its way through the open louvers into the entrance hall. "Celia!"

"Coming, Madam."

As *Mme* turned the key, the dark panels of wood lunged toward us. I ran and hid behind the umbrella stand, a hollowed-out elephant's leg. It smelled of sour milk and damp clay. I wished I hadn't hidden there. I didn't like the leg. Somewhere in the veld was an elephant hobbling around on three legs.

Peering out from behind it, I saw the Madam standing in the doorway, her wide shape silhouetted by the afternoon sun.

Rita Steiner wasn't pretty like *Mme*. She had a curiously flat face, with black button eyes and purplish-colored lips, and her big body was draped in loose skin like an elephant's slack hide. She had long brown hair, which she kept twisted in a knot at the nape of her neck. *Mme* said it fell right to her bottom when it was let out. I wished the Madam would let it out. Every night I pulled at my frizzy black curls till tears of pain squeezed out of my eyes, but still I couldn't get my hair to reach below my ears.

The Madam rested her hand on the shiny brass knob—a smooth white hand, which didn't belong to the rest of her lumpy body.

She moved out of the bright light into the cool darkness of the house. Behind her, hidden until now, was the Master—Michael Steiner. I liked him. He was long and thin like a stick insect, with a nest of brown hair confusing his straight lines, and kind gray eyes that smiled when he spoke. Today his eyes were red and his shoulders curled inward, like a piece of wet paper that had dried awkwardly.

*Mme* looked down. She said it was rude to look a white person in the eyes, but my eyes were very disobedient and kept creeping up.

Sunlight forced its way into the entrance hall. An African afternoon clamored to be let in—the smell of frangipani, the cricking of crickets, a furious blue sky. My mind began to wander to acorn houses, pet lions, and painted warriors.

The wooden door banged shut. The Steiners were standing in the hallway, their arms empty. I peered out through the louver slats. The car was empty.

No one said anything. No one moved. An awful gloom

coiled itself around the room like a snake squeezing out all the air and light.

I smiled at the Master. *Mme* frowned at me.

"Bring us tea in the sunroom, then get the bags out of the car." The Madam's voice cut a hole in the afternoon.

"Yes, Madam."

I wondered why the Madam was walking in such a funny way. She looked as if she were balancing a ball between her legs. Once I made it all the way to the bottom of the garden with a tennis ball gripped between my knees. I didn't drop it once.

"Hello, Miriam." Michael Steiner stepped out of the shadows and rested a warm hand on my head. I wasn't sure whether to smile or not, so I did a quick up-and-down one.

The Madam disappeared into the sunroom and the Master quickly followed.

"Come, child," *Mme* whispered, ushering me back to the sunlight and sweetness of the kitchen, and we left the entrance hall to the dark tambuti table that lived there and the wrinkly old elephant leg balancing in the corner.

For the next few days the Madam stayed upstairs in her bedroom with the blinds lowered and the thick drapes drawn. *Mme* took her meals up on a tray, and later collected them, barely touched. Once, when I followed *Mme*, the Madam complained that just seeing me sent pains through her swollen bosom and tugged at her collapsed belly. From then on I was confined to the kitchen as *Mme* moved through her jobs on tiptoe and voices were kept to a whisper.

The days that followed were slow and tedious, unless the

Steiners were fighting. Then their angry words would burst open the long silences and I'd yearn for the boredom of before.

"No, Michael, we won't try again. That's it! You hear me? Enough!"

"Reet, I know how you feel. I—"

"You have no idea! I can't go through it again. Not again! Two miscarriages, and now . . . now my daughter stillborn!"

So the Madam's baby had missed two carriages and was still waiting to be born.

The Madam's voice rattled and shook as if she were about to laugh, then she started to cry. "I can't do it anymore, Michael."

I covered my ears, but still her voice found its way into my head.

"And besides, I don't really want a child. This has been about you all along. What *you* want."

"That's unfair, Rita. You know it is. You've longed for a child as much as I have. You're hurting—I understand that. Just don't let it come between us. We can—"

"Leave me alone! Get out!"

Master Michael asked *Mme* to make up a bed for him in the spare room, and after that he and the Madam slept in separate beds. It must have been lonely. I would have hated to sleep in a big bed all on my own. What if the *tokoloshe* came?

The long hours turned into long days, and then long weeks. Darkness skulked in every corner and lived under every floorboard. It hid beneath the roof tiles and pushed down on all of us, making our minds heavy and our bodies sluggish. It was a relief to escape into the sunshine.

Then one morning, as the leaves on the trees began to fall, no longer able to hold on to autumn's gold, the Madam came downstairs, had breakfast, and left for work. Life in the big house returned to the way it had once been, and no mention was ever made of the day the baby didn't come home.

# CHAPTER TWO

## 1959

## Celia

It was easy to forget what lay beyond, living in Saxonwold—the leafy, white man's suburb, where the engines of large cars sung deep-voiced hymns, the lawns were grasshopper green, and the *thwop* of tennis balls being hit back and forth infected us all with a lazy calm.

The street where I worked was lined with jacarandas, and in spring the road was covered with a carpet of purple petals, which softened the sound of tires on the tarmac and filled the air with the scent of summer.

I was one of the lucky ones. I had a pass permitting me to live on my employers' premises, far from the townships and compounds where smoke and corrugated iron traced a different landscape. I could walk down the quiet, shady streets, even when a police van prowling for illegal overstayers appeared from nowhere, sending other black people scattering like pigeons. I didn't have to wake at four in the morning, wash with cold water from a communal tap, then dress by the shy light of a candle. Nor did I have to catch a train into the city, followed by several buses into the suburbs, sharing the journey with *skelms* and *tsotsis*—township thugs who harassed, robbed, and raped. For eight years I had managed to escape this reality.

The best part of my day was lunchtime, that precious half hour when I could sit on the grassy verge with the other maids and houseboys in the street, talking, laughing, and sharing—a salve for the pain of faraway families and demanding madams.

One of us usually had a baby strapped to our back. Rarely it was our own; more often it was one of our white charges. Regardless, the child always seemed content, wrapped close to a mother's flesh and rocked by constant movement and chatter.

My Miriam started life in just such a way—on my back—her warm, pudgy body pressed hard up against mine. Fearful of losing my job, I had worked until just before the pains came, and returned from the hospital up north only hours after pushing my daughter into the world. I was back at work before the stream of blood sapping my strength ceased to flow.

When Miriam grew too big to be carried, she would potter about nearby, foraging for insects and treasures, and at night snuggle up close, her small body molding itself to mine. Miriam— my big little shadow.

For a time I managed to ignore the day looming like a storm cloud on the horizon—the day I would have to send my only daughter back to the homelands. She couldn't stay in the white suburbs. The law decreed that, like her brothers before her, she must return to her place of birth just outside of Louis Trichardt, a small farming community in the Northern Transvaal. And once again I would have to suffer a separation that would leave me with a deep *donga* in my heart and an emptiness in my soul. What rhino deserts her calf? What elephant leaves her young? Can a mother turn away from her child simply because she is told to do so? So I clung to my Miriam for as long as I dared.

With time this became harder to do—juggling my job, the law of the land, and the needs of my cheeky little sprite. Miriam was conspicuous; she had energy. No longer content to simply follow me around on my daily chores, she wanted to play and yearned for the company of others. Sometimes, out of frustration and panic, I would find myself chiding her for just being a child who ran and wriggled and laughed and breathed. In the end I realized I could not contain her and therefore could not keep her.

Like a beautiful song that eventually draws to a close, so the last handful of weeks passed, and a full orange moon hung once again in the sky. I lay awake wrestling with what was to come; the next day I would have to book a taxi to transport my last born away and out of my life.

"Sorry, Madam." I hovered behind her as she sat eating her breakfast.

Rita Steiner looked up from the newspaper she was reading.

"*Hau*, Madam. I must be for one week off work."

She straightened, put down her paper, and swallowed her mouthful of toast.

"For a week!"

My chest tightened.

"What is it anyway? Another funeral?" she said, irritation lining her words.

"Oh no, Madam. I must take Miriam to her granny in the north. She cannot stay in Joburg no more. She must go back to the homeland like my other children, or police will make trouble for me."

The Madam shook her head. "No, Celia. Sorry, but *no*." The skin on her neck had risen into fat red blotches and her bosom was heaving up and down.

I did not understand. The Madam never showed strong emotion. Her white way was always so clipped and tidy, her face careful and controlled. Only once had I spied something different, something raw and unchecked—the day her baby died.

"I can't let you go. I'm sorry, Celia. It's a bad time; I'm just too busy at work."

My head felt light. I swayed unsteadily as I tried to understand what this answer would mean. I should have been pleased; I could keep Miriam for longer. Yet my happiness was a clumsy bird, unable to take off. I understood there could be no happy ending for a black person who turned her eyes from the law.

Maybe the Madam saw me dig my fingers into the back of my hand; perhaps she spotted the panic of a trapped animal in my eyes; because suddenly, as if a tight belt had been loosened, her expression changed and she pulled a smile across her face. "Later in the year, hey? You leave it with me. I'll try and make some inquiries about getting a special dispensation or something. I mean honestly, we can't send such a bright young button to a farm school, can we?"

She paused, waiting for me to answer, as if we were engaged in a real conversation. But what could I say?

"Now, today I want you to polish the brass," she said, picking up her newspaper again. "I've bought a new tin of Brasso. And remember to cover the table with a thick layer of newspaper. See how you've scratched the surface here with one of those heavy pots?"

I nodded and turned to go.

"Oh, another thing, Celia."

"Yes, Madam."

"I'm having guests on Saturday night so I'll need you to work late. Ask one of your friends to help, if you like. Maybe Mrs. Brink's maid, Sarah." She picked up her half-eaten piece of toast. Fig jam dripped onto the plate. "She must be here by six, and I'll need her until at least midnight."

So life continued, with Miriam shadowing me as I scrubbed toilets, peeled vegetables, polished floors, hung washing, and cleaned windows, her presence and cheerful chatter lending a welcome lightness to my day. Sometimes I sang to her as I worked, and, when not too busy, told her the stories my mother had once told me. These were the days we both loved best. She would listen wide-eyed as I explained how the leopard got his spots, why the giraffe's long neck once became knotted, and how people in the villages went blind if the smoke from burning tambuti wood got in their eyes. These tales carried us both beyond the concrete confines of Johannesburg to the red earth and simple life of my childhood—to a magical place where we trembled when the lion roared, laughed as the monkeys fooled, and basked in the glow of the sun as it set behind the old thorn tree.

At the end of each day, around five o'clock, Miriam would listen out for the sound of a car horn announcing the Madam's arrival, then she would race outside, beating me to the gate. There she would stand, out of breath and to attention, ready to help carry in parcels and bags from the car.

Sometimes the Madam arrived home with a special surprise for Miriam—a currant bun or packet of Marie biscuits—which she would be invited to share with the Madam in the sunroom.

Gradually Miriam grew less wary of my employer, and although she held on to the reserve every black child was brought up to have in the presence of a white person, I saw how much she looked forward to the Madam's homecoming—a welcome relief from the monotony of her days with only me for company.

One afternoon, as I dusted bookshelves and Miriam gulped down a long glass of lychee juice, the Madam reached into her big maroon bag and pulled out a book with bright orange letters scattered across the cover.

"Miriam, would you like to learn to read?"

I turned. My child was nodding excitedly. Fire and frost swept through me. I could not read. It would be good for her to learn . . . but I would not be the one to teach her. Up until that moment all Miriam's discoveries had been through my eyes; she had held my hand and I had led. Now that privilege was being pried from me.

"Ooh, yes, please, Madam, thank you!" she cried, her hungry excitement washing over the room.

And it wasn't long before her world, and so mine, burst its banks to embrace castles and crowns, Wonderland and Toad Hall.

# CHAPTER THREE

## March 1960

## Celia

The dead lay between lost shoes and scattered litter, their faces in the dirt, their limbs holding on to the shape of their last movement. Their blood showed up black in the newsprint.

I covered Miriam's eyes and took another look at the photograph that owned the front page of *The Star*.

"*Hau*, sixty-nine *dead*," Johanna whispered, her hands trembling like mine. "Too many wounded."

It was our lunch break and we were sitting in the generous shade of an old jacaranda tree. The day was hot and dry, but the mood dark.

Philemon, the gardener from number forty-three, kept reading.

I held Miriam tightly on my lap; danger felt close. But she squirmed and wriggled, unhappy to be restrained. There were crickets to be caught and ants to arrest.

"This is just the beginning," Philemon said, lowering the

newspaper. "There will be more violence. You will see. And not only in Sharpeville," he warned. "It is going to spread. The young people, they have had enough."

"So bad, so bad, so—" Johanna kept repeating.

"It was a peaceful protest," Philemon exclaimed, his voice rising above a safe whisper. "They were carrying no weapons. The crowd was well behaved. Yet the police, they gave no warning. Women and children shot in the back as they ran away!"

Was this the Philemon I knew? Philemon with the missing tooth and mischievous smile? The "yes-*baas*, no-*baas*" garden boy? The dependable Rhodesian worker? Anger distorted the calm lines of his face, and it scared me to see him this way.

I stood up. It was two o'clock. My lunch break was over.

"See you tomorrow, sister," I think they said. I barely heard them. The situation in the country was not right. I knew that. But to try to change it would only bring more suffering and bloodshed. It was easier to keep things the way they were; to dream was too dangerous.

That afternoon I worked on all fours outside the Madam's study, rubbing beeswax into the wooden floors with such force my arms ached. I was trying to scour the horror from my mind and erase the new and frightening uncertainty the day had imported.

The floor gleamed and I could see the shadow of my reflection in the golden strips of wood, my silhouette interrupted only where dark grooves divided each floorboard.

"*Yesterday thousands of black South Africans answered the call for protest against the pass laws. Peaceful demonstrations took place . . .*"

I stopped.

*"Early in the day, in Sharpeville, an unarmed crowd started to gather outside the local police station."*

The radio had been turned on in the Madam's study.

I shuffled closer and put my ear to the cool door.

*". . . policemen inside the station soon outnumbered . . . squadron of aircraft flew low over the crowd in an attempt to . . . reinforcements were called . . . conflicting reports . . . panic . . . no warning . . . opened fire . . . people turned . . . police continued to shoot . . . shot in the back. Women and children are among the dead. There has been international outrage. In a written statement, the Minister of Police—"*

Then without any warning, the study door swung open and I was staring at the Madam's green and gold sandals, her pale flesh spilling over the straps like rising bread dough.

"Celia!"

"Madam." I leaned back on my haunches, my head bowed, my heart beating out the long seconds that followed.

Finally she spoke. "Bring me a jug of cold water."

I jumped up and hurried to the kitchen, my breathing fast and loud in my ears. With shaking hands I grabbed a jug from the cupboard and opened the tap, water spraying over my face and uniform.

*"Hau!"* I cried, chiding myself for my clumsiness and more.

I twisted the ice tray, and frozen cubes dropped like hailstones into the pitcher, screeching and squealing as they hit the tepid water. Quickly I sliced a lemon, crushed the thick circles of fruit against the glass, then covered the jug with a crocheted cloth, before placing it on a tray.

"Put it down here," the Madam said evenly, pointing to the bamboo trolley beside her.

I moved into the room, my unease starting to settle. The Madam did not appear to be any different, despite her having discovered me eavesdropping.

I froze. Lying on top of the trolley was a copy of *The Star*. Time slowed.

The Madam followed my stare.

Her cheeks rippled.

She looked back at me.

I tried to look away, but I couldn't; the Madam had wound her gaze too tightly around mine. Then in two quick movements she'd folded the newspaper and slipped it into the wastepaper basket, her eyes never once leaving my face. I felt sick, as if I'd unwittingly uncovered some terrible secret, as if I had somehow found *her* out. Her eyes searched mine, looking for a way in. *I did not see anything. I know nothing. This day is no different from any other.*

After what seemed like forever, she leaned forward and picked up the jug. The sound of the ice cubes colliding with each other cracked open the silence.

I sucked in a stuttering breath.

That was when I noticed the Madam's fingers, which were gripping the jug handle; the newsprint had stained them black.

In the days following the Sharpeville Massacre, violence broke out in townships across the country. There was a boldness in the eyes of the black youths—an insolence I had not witnessed before—and it frightened me. These township kids had looked down the barrel of the future and seen little hope. They had nothing to lose.

Police vans were fuller and appeared from nowhere, more often than usual. Whites bought handguns and tiny tear-gas canisters, which could be slipped easily into handbags and blazer pockets; vicious dogs paced the perimeters of huge homes; and snatched snippets of dinner-party conversations were always about "getting out."

During our lunch breaks, the other maids and I pooled the crumbs of information we'd gathered from whispered rumors and stolen nibs of news. Slowly we pieced together a patchwork picture of what lay beyond the nervous calm of Saxonwold.

Riots were spreading. A man by the name of Nelson Mandela—a member of the African National Congress—had publicly burned his passbook and called for countrywide protest strikes. Black activists were being detained and tortured at Marshall Square, while some simply mysteriously disappeared, never to be seen again. Others were tossed from fast-moving vehicles, to lie like bloating sheep in the midday heat.

Unease hung over the country like a thick fog, dulling the gold from the mines, fading the rich crops of corn, and cooling the endless sunshine. And each day the knot in my stomach drew tighter. I didn't want trouble. This was the life I had been born into, the life I knew. Against a background of hardship, I had found a safe and comfortable corner. Change was frightening and promised nothing.

Then a state of emergency was declared, and just as if power and telephone lines had been brought tumbling down in a storm, all free communication ceased. Newspapers were muzzled, radio stations gagged, and public gatherings of more than three black people banned. Even our lunchtime get-togethers had to be cautiously pared. The police and the army were everywhere. The Madam seemed curter and the Master more distant. There was distrust in every shopkeeper's eye, even old Master Gupta's. I felt guilt and shame for all the trouble my people were causing.

Finally, an eerie calm spread over the country and hung there uncertainly.

After a time, rumors started to subside and worries, even mine, abated. One morning I awoke to find this pretend peace had become permanent. The white suburbs once more breathed with ease, and life as we had always known it began again.

## CHAPTER FOUR

### October 1960

## Celia

"Celia, the Master and I would like to talk with you after you've finished your dinner."

It was an unusually chilly October evening and the Madam had rung the bell, summoning me to clear the dinner dishes. The Madam, the Master, and Miriam had just finished their evening meal.

The first time Miriam was invited to join the Steiners for a meal had come as a shock to me, as if I'd chanced upon a burglar in my room. Yet when I looked back, there were many clues; my eyes had just been blind to them. For Miriam to join the Steiners for dinner was as natural as one foot following the other.

Miriam loved everything about these evenings—the heavy pieces of silver cutlery, the stiff white napkins I'd starched and ironed earlier in the day, the salt and pepper cellars in the shape of small dogs. Best of all were the tales Master Michael would tell her—he could stretch out a story like a beautiful sunset, painting it with color and magic and wonder. Twisting his lips, peaking his eyebrows, and making funny accents, he'd captivate Miriam so completely I'd have to bump the back of her chair to remind her to eat. Stories were a luxury, food a necessity. I knew the steak would have no gristle and there would be no pockets of green in the potatoes.

Miriam's favorite story was "The Gift of the Magi." I came to know it well. She never tired of hearing how the two poor lovers each gave up the one thing most precious to them in order to be able to buy a present for the other. Whenever Master Michael told the story, Miriam was always hopeful that, somehow, their predicament would be solved. But as Della's long hair inevitably fell to the ground, Miriam would be gripped by the calamity of it all, as if she were hearing the story for the very first time.

"*Hau*, Master!" she'd cry, devastated that Della had sold her hair to buy Jim a chain for his watch, only to discover he in turn had sold his watch to buy combs for her beautiful long hair.

And later, when the moon was high in the sky, she'd lie next to me, reliving the evening and retelling the well-worn tale over and over. "*Mme*, Della was too silly. When my hair grows long I will never cut it!"


I had been aware for some time of a change at the Saxonwold house. The mood had grown as light and easy as a butterfly in flight. Even the Madam seemed happy.

"Take Sunday off, Celia," she'd say. "Just set the breakfast table and that'll be fine." Or, "I've left out some pickled fish for you to have with your *mielie pap* today."

I noticed too that the bed in the spare room had often not been slept in, while most mornings the sheets on the big bed were in complete disarray.

The Master started playing records again, and his white man's music would travel out of the wide-open windows on an evening breeze to slip under my door and fill my room with gentle sound.

In the midst of everything, in the center of this new lightness, was my Miriam—her little brown body running, her infectious laughter ringing, and her wonderment spilling over into the airy, high-ceilinged rooms.

Then things started to *really* change.

Master Michael began coming home from work early to take Miriam fishing in the creek at the bottom of the garden, and one Saturday in late September, the Madam took her on an outing to the zoo. On another weekend the Master and Madam took her rowing on Zoo Lake, in one of the brightly colored boats I'd seen bobbing on the water's edge.

At first I was happy that my child had something to do other than follow me around on my mundane chores, but after a while, panic started to build inside me. Where would this end? Would Miriam grow up expecting a life that could never be hers? Would the police send me back to my homeland for ignoring the law?

But most of my misgivings would evaporate as soon as she rushed into my room panting like a puppy, her cheeks sticky with juice, her round eyes dancing. Then she would become the eager storyteller and I, her attentive audience.

This particular evening, however, the Steiners' request troubled me. Had something gone missing? Had a plate been chipped or a vase broken? Somehow I knew it would be more than this.

I was tired. My eyes were burning and my limbs ached. The long day and my monthly bleed had sucked the energy out of me. I dried the cutlery and set the breakfast table, then swallowed my dinner in the dim light of my room. The cornmeal porridge was stiff and the gravy cold, but I was too distracted to warm it.

My quarters came off the back of the house, my room opening onto a concrete yard and sagging washing line. Off to the right, down a steep flight of stairs, was the outside toilet I shared with Solomon, the gardener, and any other black, colored, or Indian tradesman who might visit.

My room was small and fitted little more than my bed, which balanced on four empty paraffin cans to keep Miriam and me safe from the *tokoloshe*—that mischievous evil spirit. Under the bed was stashed whatever I couldn't fit into the old wardrobe pushed hard up against the back wall.

The stale air of close living had dulled the white walls, leaving them sallow and grubby looking, even after I'd scrubbed them down.

Beside the door, on top of an empty tomato crate, was my Primus stove. When not in use, I covered it with a bright yellow tea towel the Madam had tossed out because of a rip in the hem. I had to be careful about taking things from the rubbish—once the Madam accused me of stealing a scarf she'd forgotten she had thrown out.

Across one wall of my room, hidden by a permanently drawn

frill of faded orange curtain, ran a long narrow window—the slit of an eye looking over a shaded courtyard where the Steiners ate their lunch most weekends. The Madam had planted a vigorous bougainvillea creeper to block my window from view, and, successful in this task, it prevented all but the faintest thread of light from reaching my room. A thick woody vine had even nudged its way inside, preventing me from shutting my window completely. In winter the gap ushered in an icy draft, and in summer served as a highway for a steady stream of insects.

I put a chattering Miriam to bed, then made my way back to the house, hovering outside the lounge until the Madam called to me.

"Come. Come in, Celia. Sit down," she said, gesturing to the couch.

Confused by this new familiarity, I balanced on the edge of the seat. It felt wrong to be sitting in the lounge I cleaned and dusted every day. Only once before, when the Steiners had been away on holiday, had I dared eat at their long dining room table—madam of their home for one day.

Master Michael stood behind his wife, his eyes avoiding me.

"The Master and I have been doing a lot of thinking lately," the Madam began. She spoke in a slow, deliberate voice, as if it was important for me to understand every word. "This country has a lot of problems, no?"

I nodded.

"Too many problems," she continued, sucking on one of her teeth. "It isn't a safe place for us anymore."

I waited for what was to follow, the Madam's words stirring up the thick layer of dread that lined the bottom of my days.

"The Master and I have decided we cannot stay here. We are moving to England at the end of the year."

My head started to spin, the security of the last nine years draining like water through a colander. I would need to find a new job. How would I send money to my mother? My children. Where would I live? Would I have to travel from the townships? When could—

"Celia."

I heard my name from beyond the chaos of my thoughts.

"Celia?"

Rita and Michael Steiner were staring at me.

"We would like to take Miriam with us," said the Master softly.

My mind landed back in the room with a thud.

"Celia, Master Steiner and I want to adopt Miriam."

The Madam's words drove through me like an assegai.

"She is a lovely child and very bright. Wasted, really," she said, shaking her head. "We'll be able to give her a good life in England, far better than she could ever hope to have here. She'll get to go to a good school, have whatever she needs, and, most importantly, be away from the difficulties of this cursed country."

I tried to speak, but my tongue felt fat and slow in my mouth, like a sun-drunk lizard.

The Madam went on, leaving me behind as I tried to grab hold of the words she was tossing into the room. "You have three other children, no?"

I opened my mouth.

"And what help is that husband of yours . . . Patrick, isn't it? How often does he send you money from the mines?"

I tried to swallow, but my throat was as dry as kindling.

"Too busy spending it on his girlfriends and Kaffir beer, hey."

Her words stung—the pain of confidences betrayed.

"Meanwhile, you are left to feed and clothe them. It can't be easy, I—"

Michael Steiner put a hand on his wife's arm, and when he spoke his voice was quiet and tender. For a moment it felt as if we were alone in the room, just the Master and me.

"Celia, your daughter is very precious to us. We will do everything we can, with your blessing of course, to give her a happy childhood and a good life."

*Your daughter, your daughter, your daughter.* The words were sucked into the whirlpool of my mind.

The Madam sat down beside me. "Of course we'll leave you some money to tide you over until you find another job. In fact, I know someone who might be looking for a char from January."

She turned to the Master. "The greengrocers. Their char's pregnant again."

I slumped back into the couch.

"I know it's a lot to think about," Rita Steiner said, motioning to me to stand. "But try to make up your mind as quickly as you can. There will be much to arrange."

I heaved myself up.

Master Michael moved toward me and rested a hand on my elbow, his white fingers cool against my hot black skin.

I cannot remember leaving the room, nor passing through the kitchen and out into the still night. I only became aware of my surroundings with the screech of the neighbor's cat as it darted in front of me. I stumbled, going down heavily onto the slate paving and splitting open my knee on the jagged footpath. Dazed, I lay there, sprawled across the pavers, until my limbs grew cold and stiff.

By the time I picked myself up, the thick trail of blood tracking onto the paving was dry. Climbing the three concrete stairs to my room, I stepped into the darkness and, without undressing, sank onto the mattress beside my Miriam. She didn't stir.

When sleep finally came, it was troubled and fitful, and when I awoke, my pillow was wet with tears. But unlike waking from a nightmare to the warm relief of reality, the events of the previous evening were lying in wait to suffocate my day.

I turned to face the child asleep beside me—her small chest rising and falling with each whispered breath. With my forefinger, I traced the slope of her eyelids and caressed her long black lashes as they curled away from carefree dreams. I cupped her tiny ears in my hands, stroked her untroubled brow, and kissed each of her little fingers. It was as if she were a newborn again and I was seeing her for the very first time.

Then she was awake—my cheeky jewel glistening in the morning sunshine.

# CHAPTER FIVE

## November 1960

## Miriam

The doors could not be closed properly, the church hall was so packed with people; I thought it would burst. Brown bodies were tossed in a salad of bright clothes and river-blue robes, faces glistened with sweat, and mouths were opened wide in song. I could see right to the back of one old *makhulu*'s mouth, to the two bits of pink skin dangling there. The granny was singing for all she was worth.

I was standing on a wonky chair, wedged between *Mme* and a wrinkly man who smelled of beer and beef bones. From my position I could see right over the bobbing heads and staffs swaying in unison, to the pastor conducting the choir. I loved singing in church, because my voice joined with all the other voices to make one loud voice that felt all mine.

Soon the service was over and we were tumbling out into

the golden afternoon to trestle tables laden with *mielie pap*, cream biscuits, and tins of sweet tea.

Church Sundays were my best. There were other children to play with, new hiding places to explore and trees to climb. And there was always lots to eat.

*Mme* was mostly happy too—talking and laughing and swinging her big bottom in time to the music. I liked *Mme* best on Sundays. When she untied her apron and removed the *doek* from her head, she shed her serious *don't-touch, put-that-down, don't-talk-too-loud, maybe-later* skin, like a molting snake.

My favorite church friend was Sipho. He lived in Orlando township and saw his mother only on Sundays. He was also six years old, but much cleverer than me. He could hop on one foot for an entire race without overbalancing and fold his tongue into a proper tunnel. My tongue just went out—never up and round like his.

After we'd drunk our tea and filled our pockets with biscuits, we ran off to play.

Sipho had made a car from bits of wire and scraps of wood. It had bottle-top wheels and a long, stiff handle, which meant he could steer it without having to bend down. It was a proper sports model—nothing like the old jalopies I sometimes made. We took turns driving it up and down the dirt track behind the hall, until one of the wheels came off. Then we had to look for a replacement. I searched everywhere for a suitable bottle top, but Sipho was very disparaging about the ones I found. He said there were much better ones to choose from in the township. I wished I lived there. It sounded like so much fun.

"Miriam." *Mme* was calling.

"Just a bit longer, pleeease."

"It's late, *Mbila*. After the bus, we still have a long walk home. I want to get back before dark."

I loved it when she called me *Mbila*. It meant "hand piano" in Tshivenḓa. *Mme* said I reminded her of the cheerful sound it made.

By the time we got off the bus the light was fading and *Mme* walked quickly. I had to run and hop every few steps just to keep up with her. After a while, though, she forgot about the time and slowed to her usual giraffe-ambling pace, stopping every now and then to chat with a passerby. Then I would skip on ahead, leading most of the way, except for when I'd run back to show her some prize I'd found. My best find was a rusty padlock with the key still in the lock. I also found a whole snail shell. I decided to keep both for a trade with Sipho, just in case he brought some of those special township bottle tops next time.

When I was really far ahead, I flung myself down on the spongy grass sidewalk and gazed up at the sky dotted with toothpaste-white clouds. I could make out several shapes—a rooster, a tortoise, and a man with three heads. As I was lying there, waiting for *Mme* to catch up, a dog began to bark from behind a very low fence. I shot back to *Mme*'s warm, solid legs and stayed by her side for the rest of the journey.

She'd decided to take the route past the old apricot tree on Griswold Road. The detour added a few extra blocks onto our trip, but this being the beginning of summer, we were sure to be rewarded with good pickings. Already from the top of the avenue I could make out some of the sweet orange treasure scattered across the pavement.

The tree was alive with wasps and we had to be careful not to get stung as we stuffed our pockets. *Mme* even picked a few unspoiled apricots from an overhanging branch, while I kept lookout.

With our pockets bulging and the sun slipping behind us in the sky, we set off again for Saxonwold, *Mme* promising to make stewed apricots and custard for pudding.

I had just jammed a whole fruit into my mouth when I heard footsteps coming from around the corner; someone was running. Then a dog began to bark. After this came the screeching of a car.

We stopped, then *Mme* yanked me back into a bed of dark green ivy just as a boy came tearing around the corner.

He was as tall as a man, but I could see from his eyes he was still a boy; they were stretched wide—dark brown disks sucking up all the white. His shirt was stuck to his skinny black body in round wet patches and his trousers looked too big for him. He'd looped a piece of string through the belt holds to keep them up. On one of his feet flopped a frayed *tackie*, without laces. His other foot was bare.

As he sprinted past, my Sunday happiness disappeared into his hungry brown eyes.

Then came the skidding of wheels. *Mme* and I pressed ourselves up against the wall as a police van hurtled around the corner. Police vans all looked the same—cream-colored cab in front, cage on the back, green canvas curtains on either side. If the curtains were down, you couldn't see inside. These ones weren't. They were rolled up like the curlers the Madam sometimes wore in her hair, and we could see inside. Packed into the darkness were the whites of many more eyes.

The running boy stopped for a moment—you could hear air whistling in and out of his mouth—then he was scrambling over the wall we were standing against. The ivy stole his only shoe. I reached out and freed it from the dark leaves, but *Mme* jerked me back, and I dropped it. I put my hand to my nose and breathed in the sour smell of the running boy.

We heard him drop to the other side. Then someone screamed. It was a white-madam scream—high and sharp like broken glass. More dogs started barking. The boy was now clambering back over the gate, the silver spears on top poking big red holes in his hands.

I squeezed *Mme*'s fingers. She was so still standing there beside me in the dark green ivy—I wished she would say something.

The van stopped in front of us and out jumped a policeman and his dog.

*Mme* put a finger to her lips.

"*Vang hom!* Catch him! Catch the *blerrie* Kaffir!" yelled another policeman from behind the wheel. He sped off, the door flying further open before slamming shut with the speed of the van. The dog was let off its leash and began gaining on the boy.

All of a sudden the string around the boy's pants snapped and his trousers started to slide down over his bottom. He wasn't wearing underpants. He was naked underneath.

I didn't laugh.

He kept on running, all the while trying to pull his trousers back up, but when he turned to look over his shoulder, they fell down around his ankles and he tripped.

Then the dog was on top of him.

*Mme* put her hand over my eyes. I tried to pull it away, but she held firm, so I only got to look through the thin gaps between her fingers.

"*Asseblief, baas!* Please, boss!" the boy begged.

*Mme* didn't have enough hands to cover my ears.

I started to hum one of the songs we'd sung in church that morning as the policeman's brown boot moved back and forward, thumping into the boy's bendy body. After a bit, the thumping changed to *whistle . . . thwack, whistle . . . thwack*. I opened my eyes for a quick look. It was the sound of a *sjambok*—the policeman's rhino-hide whip.

The policeman's face was like the side of a split watermelon—red and wet—and the boy's one-eyed snake was red too.

Tears spilled out of my eyes, but I held on to my voice so it couldn't escape.

After a while the street was quiet, except for the sound of a panting dog and a panting policeman.

The driver got out of the van and marched over to where the race had ended. He flipped the boy over, hiding his dust-dull face from the street's curious eyes. The other policeman put thick silver bracelets onto the boy's crooked wrists and both men dragged him along the road, his head bumping up and down on the gravel.

"*Een, twee, drie*," they counted, before swinging him into the back of the van.

I knew what *een, twee, drie* meant because *Mme* had been teaching me to count in Afrikaans. She said I'd have to speak Afrikaans at school.

The commotion had drawn quite a crowd, but *Mme*'s and

mine were the only black faces on the street. There were some shivering children—their bathing costumes still dripping— staring through the bars of a gate until a white madam hurried them inside. There was also a group of men dressed in white, leaning on their tennis rackets.

Luckily the day was already yawning and the sun so low that long afternoon shadows helped hide us in the ivy.

I looked at the boy's *tackie* poking out of the leaves. I was sure he'd want it, especially since he'd only had one to start with. But as I tried to reach for it, *Mme* yanked me back hard, hurting my arm. Suddenly I felt scared.

I was about to start crying again, when a master from the ivy-walled home walked out to speak with the policemen. "No, nobody harmed. Just saw this black leap over the wall and of course my wife got a terrible fright. I think her screams scared him off," he said with a chuckle.

"*Jirre!* Bloody Kaffirs," cursed the policeman. "Probably has no pass. She all right?"

"Thank you, yes. She's fine. Just a bit shaken."

They spoke as if they were good friends, as if they knew each other. White people were always friends with one another. They weren't really white, though, like *Mme* said, they were more a yellowy-pink color.

"Beda be going," said the policeman, straightening his safari suit.

My whole body was getting itchy in the ivy. Then my nose started to tickle. I scratched it. But the tickle grew . . . "Haichoo!"

The policemen swung around.

I heard *Mme*'s breathing go faster.

"Hey, you . . . Kaffir. *Kom hier!* Come here!"

*Mme* squeezed my hand. Sticky apricot juice had collected in heavy drops under my wrist. I crept behind her legs and quickly emptied my pockets, letting the apricots fall softly to the ground. Then we were moving toward the big khaki man.

"*Maak gou, ek het nie die heel dag tyd nie.* Hurry up, I don't have all day," he barked. "Where is your book? *Dompas?* Give it."

*Mme* looked so small standing beside him. His face was thick and wide, and his head had been stuck straight onto his body without a neck in between. The back of his hat was wedged into bulging folds of scalp and the front was pulled down so low I couldn't see his eyes. He was wearing the usual police uniform—green safari suit, leather strap over right shoulder, shiny brown belt, gun holster, truncheon. Droplets of sweat trickled down the thick strips of orange hair on his cheeks. He also had a box of brown bristles above his top lip. I ran my tongue over mine, trying to imagine what it would be like to have broom bristles there.

*Mme* fumbled with the top button on her dress and reached into her bra, pulling out a small worn book, the brown cover buckling at the corners. She always kept special things in her bra. I couldn't wait to have a bra so I could hide my treasures.

She handed the book to the policeman. I wondered what story was inside. I hoped it wasn't the one about Della and Jim, because the policeman didn't seem to be the kind of person who would like it.

His fat fingers flicked through the pages. The dog, now back on its leash, started to growl. Its teeth were all pointy and yellow, and it had ugly black gums.

"*Mme!*"

I couldn't help myself, even though I knew I was meant to keep quiet. But I'd seen how the dog had taken a big chunk out of the boy's skinny leg and I didn't want the same thing happening to me.

The policeman laughed and tugged on the leash.

As we were standing there, a white madam—I think it might have been the one who'd screamed—came out of her gate, carrying a tray. On it were two frosted glasses filled with guava juice and a plate of chocolate biscuits.

"Very kind of you," the policeman said, taking one glass and passing the other to his friend seated in the van.

The juice slopped everywhere and the open pages of *Mme*'s book sucked up the pink liquid, smudging the important black ink.

After a few gulps, the policeman shoved the book back into *Mme*'s trembling hands. "*Nou voetsek*—scat!"

"Yes, *baas*," she said, dipping her head.

We started walking straight away, and I looked back only once to check that the dog wasn't following us.

## Celia

Back at my room in Saxonwold, Miriam sat cross-legged in the deep dip of our bed, the bedclothes steepled high, her small body swallowed up by the mattress. She paged absently through her storybook, but even the charm of her favorite story now seemed to elude her.

It had been dark by the time we'd turned into the Steiners' driveway. We had run all the way, Miriam clutching my hand so tightly that pins and needles had blurred the ownership of our interlocking fingers.

As our feet hurried over familiar ground, I replayed the scene in my head, hoping for something, anything, to relieve me of the burden I now carried. But my load simply grew heavier, and my powerlessness more real. Nothing could change what had happened. I had been helpless to hide the horror. And in just a handful of minutes, my child's innocence had been stolen.

The window had misted up and the room felt airless. Even though the door stood ajar, the night was still and offered little relief.

"Miriam."

She looked up, her beetle-brown eyes meeting mine.

I paused, wrestling with what was waiting to be spoken, then I broke into Tshivenḓa, my native tongue, and the difficult words slipped more easily into the space between us.

"Miriam, would you like to go on a holiday?"

She tilted her head.

I focused on her shiny, rounded forehead, avoiding her questioning eyes. "To a special place over the sea."

I had never seen the sea, though I knew its taste; I knew its smell. On my request, the Steiners often brought me back a bottle of seawater from their travels. Just uncorking it would release the magic of nature's *muti*—the wind and salt and healing secrets.

Miriam picked up Tendani, the rag doll I'd made from old orange bags stuffed with newspaper. She pulled at a loose thread and the doll's face began to unravel.

"Why?"

I tried to silence the screaming inside my head. I had one chance to convince her. She was a willful child—more so than her brothers. Once she had made up her mind, there was no persuading Miriam otherwise.

I sucked in a deep breath. "The Master and Madam want to take you to England."

Her eyes grew wide. She knew about England from the Master's dinnertime stories.

"Where the queen lives?"

I nodded.

"The one with jewels?"

"The one with jewels," I said too loudly.

Miriam's face was still painted with the darkness of that afternoon.

"You'll have your own bedroom," I said quickly.

"I don't want my own—"

"And you'll be able to go to school with other children." I knew how much she longed for this. "One day, if you work hard, you might even become a teacher like *Mudedekadzi* Mafela."

She stood up. "I want to be a doctor like the Madam."

Little mountains crumbled inside me. "Or a doctor," I said quietly, taking her hand as she balanced on the edge of the bed. The light was seeping back into her eyes.

"Okay, *Mme*," she said and, without any warning, leapt into my arms.

I staggered backward, and we both tumbled onto the floor, laughing. As I lay there, her tiny body a wisp of cloud on top of me, I should have felt some relief. I had managed to persuade her to go. But I felt no such satisfaction.

She pushed my nose flat with her fingers.

"Will we still sleep in the same bed?"

My throat tightened.

"*Mbila*," I said, my voice faltering, "I must stay here. Who will look after my mother, your *makhulu*? Who will keep an eye on your brothers?"

"Oh," she said, pulling back to scrutinize me.

"But you will come back soon," I said, allowing the truth to lose its way. "Then we will stay up long after even the owls have gone to bed, and you will tell me all about your adventures."

"Yes! Yes! Yes!" she cried, bounding off my lap onto the bed again, the weary bedsprings creaking and groaning under her excitement. "*Mme*, does the queen have only one crown, or does she have lots?"

It was then, with that simple question, that I first glimpsed the enormous toll Africa was about to exact from me.

# CHAPTER SIX

## December 1960

## Celia

The Steiners had decided. The day before they were due to leave Africa, I would leave Saxonwold, telling Miriam I was going to visit her granny and brothers in the Northern Transvaal. I would return to Johannesburg, and my new job, after they had left for England.

As soon as this decision had been made, time hurried forward like a shepherd returning from the hills, and it wasn't long before the last Sunday was upon us.

For one final time Miriam and I made our way through the suburbs on our well-worn path to salvation. I shunned the company of others as we walked, Miriam's small hand in mine, her warmth pulsing against my fingers.

She did not run ahead to explore, nor chatter much at my side. And even before I had chided her for dragging her Sunday shoes in the dust, her bubbly exuberance seemed to have disappeared.

In church I did not take my eyes off her, chiseling her face into my memory and trying to imagine how it would grow and change. I breathed in the sweet smell of her young skin, bottling it like seawater in my mind, and only mouthed the hymns so I could hear her pure and cloudless voice more clearly in my head.

That night I could not eat, but I was hungry for every detail of my daughter—her every movement, her every breath. As she chewed and swallowed and prattled, I tried to hold on to it all.

She devoured the piece of steak I'd bought from the white man's butchery in Parkwood, then she took a chunk of bread, mopped up the gravy pooled in the corner of her dish, and stuffed the entire piece into her mouth in one go.

Seeing her little cheeks bulge around it reminded me of a picture I had once seen in her book *The Little Prince*. It was the drawing of a snake after it had eaten an elephant whole. I couldn't help smiling. Miriam had that way about her; she could bring light into the darkest of places.

Then our last night together had passed and I was standing on the steps outside my room watching the sun climb up over a charcoal dawn. Soon the sky was clothed in a pale, cloudless blue—a blue that would deepen over the day to match the kingfisher's bold coat. The dew would dry; the cool breath of morning would be stilled; an orchestra of insects would build to a parched crescendo. Bright blooms would open. A cricket would struggle on its back somewhere in the dirt, unable to right itself, and by evening would be dead. These things I knew as surely as I knew my name. There was nothing extraordinary about the day that lay ahead. It was just another day in Africa.

My taxi arrived early, the wide, turquoise Valiant sagging over an already shimmering road. I wondered where my luggage would fit, so laden was the car with cargo—cardboard cartons and enormous plastic holdalls secured to the roof with reams of fraying rope, and four laughing ladies packed into the back-seat as tightly as mangoes in a crate.

The driver was a cheerful fellow, with Malawi-black skin and an orange-segment grin boasting the occasional tooth. When he clambered out of the driver's seat, the car rose several feet.

With the help of the other passengers, I squeezed my bags into the already crammed boot—two rotund ladies using their combined weight to squash the past nine years of my life into the small space remaining.

With my belongings attended to, I turned toward my child. She was standing in front of the house, framed on either side by a Steiner.

I wanted to be alone with her. I wanted to push the two white people out of the picture, grab my daughter's small black hand, and run. I closed my arms around her, pressing her warm, wriggling body to mine.

"*Mme*, I can't breathe."

"*Ni sale zwavhudi,*" I whispered. "Go well, my child. God bless you, my last born, my shining star. May God watch over you on your big adventure." Then I let go.

"Now don't you go worrying about her," the Madam said, her face loosening. "She will be absolutely fine."

As I turned, the Master lunged forward and clumsily grabbed my hand.

"We will look after her, Celia. I promise."

I nodded and, as if under a *nganga*'s spell, moved toward the gate.

"Bye, *Mme*! Bye!"

Climbing into the front seat of the Valiant, I heaved the door closed. The car started with a growl and then we were moving.

I did not allow the tears to come until we had turned the corner and I could no longer see Miriam's small pink and black hand waving, waving, waving.

It was a long journey back to my homeland—ten hours squashed inside the hot, loud taxi. Yet I was glad for the discomfort and distraction; it kept my mind moving and stopped my thoughts from separating out and settling.

It should have been a six-hour ride, but the car was so overloaded we struggled to pick up speed. Then, just outside Potgietersrus, we got a flat tire.

Everyone had to pile out of the car and unpack the boot in order for the driver to get at the spare tire. While he struggled to jack up the car, I pulled out my Primus stove and boiled up a pot of tea with some of the water he kept for cooling the radiator. The hot, sweet drink helped smooth some of the creases in that awful day and helped our driver find his sense of humor again.

One of the other passengers, a boisterous woman called Grace, had brought a tin of bully beef and tub of cold *mielie pap* with her; I had two oranges and an opened can of condensed milk, which luckily the ants had not yet discovered; and the driver found a packet of Tennis biscuits stashed in his glove box. We pooled our provisions and had a picnic right there in the dry yellow grass on the edge of the highway north.

"Why are you traveling to Louis Trichardt, sister?" Grace asked as we drank our tea.

"I'm going to visit my chil—" I stopped. Children—the meaning of that word had changed. I could no longer pronounce it. It felt small and incomplete in my mouth.

"I am going to visit my mother."

I dozed for the rest of the journey, always glad to wake to the noisy chatter and unending stretch of road. We drove into Louis Trichardt just before midnight. An hour later I was making my way down the familiar dirt track to my mother's hut, buried deep in the dark blue night.

I pushed on the front door and it creaked open. The hut was in darkness.

A chirruping cricket and my mother's rumbling snores interrupted the blackness. I breathed in the smell of cow dung, bushveld, and family. Strangely, though, it did not satisfy. The peace that would always swathe me on my return to the tiny *rondavel* in the hills now eluded me. I had been returning home every year since the age of fifteen, yet this time it felt different.

Leaving my bags at the door, I crept through the room, past the shadows of my three boys—Christian, Nelson, and Alfred— their dark bodies longer and leaner than I remembered. Three pairs of feet poked out from under sheets that had once covered smaller boys' bodies. I ran my fingers lightly over their toes, but the reply of their skin was like nails driven into my hand.

I almost resented my sons for being there, their presence making Miriam's absence more real. At that moment nothing but Miriam mattered. God had given me a daughter and I had given her away. *I* had made the decision. Words had been easy to manipulate in my mind, but in real life . . .

I slipped onto the mattress I would share with my mother and lay there, looking out of the window at the navy sky clothed in stars. The ground was still swaying beneath me like the taxi chassis. Out of the corner of my eye I saw a moth snag its wing in the sweep of a spider's web. Dazed, the moth swung loosely in the moonlight, then began to flap its free wing, frantically trying to escape the spider's sticky silver trap, each jerk and shudder only entangling it further. I scanned the ceiling for the spider.

There it was, its swollen black body tucked into a corner.

Fear climbed up my throat and my heart began to flap about inside my chest like the trapped moth. I sat up, hungry for air, and whispered out loud the Steiners' last words to me.

*We will write often.* I had already asked Philemon if he would read to me the letters that would come. *We will send photographs. In about a year we'll bring Miriam home for a visit. She'll be fine, I promise.*

Like a punctured balloon, the certainty of these words shriveled and shrank. Could I wait for that first letter? Could I live through an entire summer and winter before seeing my child again? How would I fill the emptiness?

My mother stirred on the mattress beside me. I looked over at her aging body—her strong arms, her ridged fingernails, her collapsed breasts. For as long as I could remember she had lived in this valley, under this sky, never too far from my reach. Now Miriam lay somewhere under the same canopy of stars, but beyond my grasp.

Then, like a donkey's tail, my mind swung to the other side, and I was chiding myself for being weak. I had to be strong. I had done this for my daughter. My gift to her. The promise of a new and better life. There could be no room for selfishness.

Alfred cried out in his sleep and in an instant I was standing at his bedside ready to comfort him. He was my youngest son, yet I knew so little about him. What games did he like to play? Which songs made him giggle? Who was his best friend?

He'd been a colicky, clingy baby, and I'd had to send him home to my mother earlier than I had done with the others. He called me *Mme*, but I knew it was his *makhulu* he truly loved. She had been the one to cradle and caress him, to rub his small back when mischievous spirits toyed with his dreams.

I hurried from the room into the brisk black night and was sick, spewing my pain over the cracked red earth.

# CHAPTER SEVEN

## December 1960

## Miriam

The sheets on my new bed were as soft as tissues, and I slipped in and out of them a few times just to feel their coolness against my skin. But soon they became all warm and wrinkly. It was a very big bed and I had to hold on to the pillow to stop myself from disappearing down it, like Alice down that hole. I pulled the top sheet up under my nose. It smelled funny—different from the smoky blanket *Mme* and I lay under at night.

*Mme* had made the bed up for me in the spare room before she left. It hadn't been an easy job; there wasn't much space to spare with all the boxes of furniture for the holiday stored in it. I wondered why there was no furniture where the queen lived.

*Mme* had kept clicking her tongue and shaking her head as she'd wrestled with the sheets. Then big drops of water had trickled down her cheeks. I'd never seen her get so upset over a tricky job before.

The boxes made scary shadows on the walls and I was glad when the Master put his head around the door. He started laughing when he saw me. I giggled too, though I wasn't really sure what we were laughing about.

"How's my lucky bean?" he asked, sitting down beside me.

I liked lucky beans. A tree in the garden grew the skinny black pods. If you cracked one open you'd find a row of pumpkin-colored beans tucked into a long bed like well-behaved children. Every bean had a thin black saddle around its tummy. *Mme* said the beans brought good luck. I'd often collect them to trade with Sipho, because there were no lucky beans in Orlando.

"Would you like me to read you a story?" the Master asked.

"Yes, please, Master."

"How about you call me Michael, eh?"

"Yes, Master. I mean . . . Yes, Master Michael."

We both started to laugh again. This time I understood why. It was definitely hard trying to call the Master a new name, and I had to think very carefully about my words every time after that. "Master" just knew its way out of my mouth.

Then the Madam came into the room. At least she didn't ask me to call her something different. "It's half past eight, Miriam, and I think you should be getting off to sleep."

"I was just going to read to her a bit, Reet," said the Master quickly.

I was glad he'd remembered that.

"I think we should get into a routine right from the start," the Madam said, patting the side of my bed. "A well-slept child is a happy child."

I didn't know what a routine was, but it sounded bad, especially if it meant no stories.

"Just a little read, eh?" the Master said, winking at me.

I tried to wink back, but I couldn't without shutting both my eyes.

The Madam chuckled. "All right, then, just a quick one." She bent down to give me a kiss on the cheek. I didn't like the feel of her lips on my skin; they were floppy and wet and not at all like *Mme*'s soft, tickly kisses.

"Good night, Miriam," she said. "Sleep well. Tomorrow is a big, big day. Are you excited?"

"Ooh, yes, Madam. Very."

I *was* excited, but I was also a bit scared. Master said we were going to fly over the sea on a big bird. I hoped we weren't going to fall off.

"Michael, remember to put out the rubbish now Celia's gone," the Madam said, switching off the main light to leave us trapped in a small circle of light from the bedside lamp.

Hearing *Mme*'s name made me miss her. I wanted to snuggle up to her under our big blanket, just like we always did. But before I could say anything, Master Michael had opened *The Wind in the Willows*, and soon I was sliding toward sleep with Toad and Badger for company.


The shuttle bus shuddered and stopped, throwing me against a wall of legs and arms. The Madam caught me just in time. Then the glass doors were sliding open and all the shoes, skirts, trousers, and handbags were pushing to get out.

We waited for the bus to empty before stepping onto the tarmac. A hot wind was gusting, orange lights were flashing, and everywhere machines buzzed, whirred, and beeped. The air smelled just like the inside of Michael's workshop—of rubber, lawnmower fuel, grease, and ground metal.

I sucked in a big breath. "Look, Michael!"

Spread over us was the wing of a giant silver bird. The Madam had shown me a picture of one and I'd seen them flying overhead—tiny gray insects glinting in the sky. I could never understand how they went straight through clouds and not around them.

But this bird wasn't as small as an insect; it was as big as a Johannesburg building tipped on its side. Sipho would never believe me. The wings were straight and stiff, and I couldn't imagine how they were going to be able to flap properly. Before I could ask Michael about this, he took my hand and we followed the Madam up a steep, wobbly staircase.

At the very top, Michael stopped and turned. The wind had made his eyes water.

"Good-bye," he said, waving. I followed his gaze, though all I could see was a mango-orange sun melting in the sky and the long strip of road the bird was going to run along before taking flight.

Tears started trickling down Michael's cheeks, just like *Mme*'s when she'd made up the bed for me in the spare room. It seemed as if all the grown-ups were crying lately. Maybe a witch doctor had put a crying curse on all the big people.

"Michael, I want *mme anga*—my *mme*."

I don't think he heard me. Either the people pushing past us or the wind, or maybe the *tokoloshe*, had stolen my words.

Michael tugged at me gently, and we stepped inside the belly of the big, big bird.


"'Welcome to Norwich,'" Michael read aloud.

"And not a moment too soon," the Madam grumbled.

The windows of the car had steamed up and I was tracing pictures on the glass with my gloved fingers. I peered through the stripes of clear glass, my eyes searching for somewhere to stop. There were no edges or angles to land on, no color to catch me. My eyes just kept on going, sliding over the never-ending white. Someone had thrown a huge sheet over the world, covering everything in a soft, quiet whiteness.

Our car lights swung into an empty driveway. In the glare stood a little house with two droopy-eye windows, a red-nose door, and a thin gray balcony of mouth. I didn't like the look of this house. I don't think it liked me either.

"Here at last!" Michael said, pulling up the handbrake. "The rental agent's probably been and gone." He glanced at his wristwatch. "She said if we were delayed she'd leave the key under the mat."

"We're hardly late," muttered the Madam.

"At least she's left some lights on," Michael said, opening my door.

I was wearing a bright pink woolen scarf, a pair of gloves with red and black ladybirds on the fingers, a vest, *and* an itchy yellow jumper, but still I was cold. My body kept shaking without any instruction from me.

The three of us climbed the four concrete stairs to the front door. As Michael opened it, I peered down a cold blue runway of carpet into the narrow, gloomy passageway.

"Come on, then. Let's see what we have here," Michael said, stepping inside.

The Madam switched on some lamps, though they were shy to share their glow and cast stingy rounds of light on the walls.

Someone had been drawing on the walls—a brown swirly pattern. *Mme* would have been very angry. There were a few pictures hanging on the walls too, but I didn't recognize any of the people in them. There was also a dusty glass cabinet on my left, or maybe it was my right (the white mark on my left pinkie nail had disappeared, making it really hard to tell left from right), and imprisoned inside were lots of tiny figures: a lady with big blue hair playing the piano, a glass dove, a pink horse with a horn coming out of its nose . . .

"God, it's freezing in here," the Madam said, slapping her gloved hands together.

I copied her. This made her laugh, which was good, because she hadn't laughed very much since we'd left Saxonwold.

"Don't worry, I'll have it warm in no time," Michael said, dropping our bags and switching on a heater. Soon it started to creak and groan. Michael said the noise was just the oil heating up, but I didn't believe him. It sounded as if someone was locked inside and trying to get out.

After a while, the air in the house started to smell strong and bitter, the dust on the heater burning. There was so much dust in the house I knew for sure *Mme* hadn't been there.

I took some toilet paper from the bathroom and started to wipe down the furniture.

"Don't be doing that, Miriam," the Madam said, taking the paper from me. "Why don't you go and explore a bit?"

So I wandered through this strange holiday house with drawings on the walls, crazy creatures in the cabinets, and heaters that moaned and groaned. I was tired, my legs were slow and grumpy, and my head hurt. My tummy also felt funny—as if there were a hundred beetles buzzing around inside me.

Michael scurried back and forth, carrying in suitcases and supermarket bags from the car, while the Madam directed him this way and that, just as she always did with *Mme.* "Put it in here. God, I'm getting a migraine. Can you get my toiletries bag from the car? Don't forget the milk in the boot. We need to find the linen, Michael. What did the agent say about the linen?"

Someone had left the back door open, so I slipped out into the still, white garden. The air had no smell. Nothing. The section was steep and rose up from a small, bricked patio. I scrambled up the bank, leaving behind me a trail of crunchy, white footprints. At the fence I stopped. My throat was stinging. Then . . .

"Michael! Master Michael, fire!" I screamed, sliding back down the bank and sprinting toward the kitchen.

I collided with Michael coming out the back door.

"What is it, Miriam? Stop! Talk to me. Where's the fire?"

But I couldn't get any words out; the *tokoloshe* had tied up my tongue. So I just waved my arms and pointed at my mouth.

Michael lifted me up. "Miriam, speak to me. Slowly. Now, what is wrong?"

"In me," I managed. "The *tokoloshe* is here. Look, Master Michael." A cloud of smoke tumbled from my mouth. I was on fire.

The crumpled skin on Michael's forehead smoothed and his worried mouth turned into a wide, laughing smile. He laughed and laughed and all the while the *tokoloshe* kept stoking the coals inside me. Only when I began to cry did Michael finally stop.

"Dear child," he gasped, wiping his eyes. "It's not the *tokoloshe*. It's your warm breath meeting the cold air for the very first time. They've never met—and you've never been this cold before, have you?"

I shook my head, confused.

He blew a breath into the evening air and a ball of silver smoke rolled out of *his* pink mouth. "You won't have had a snowball fight either," he said, kissing me on the forehead. He put me down, gathered up a fistful of snow, and crushed it over me.

I squealed as the cold confetti fell into my hair.

"Well?" Michael said, already running away. "Aren't you going to get me back?"

I sank my hands into the freezing powder.

My first snowball hit him on the back of his head. Then lots of snowballs were flying. It was war!

"Enough, I beg of you," Michael finally pleaded. I was standing over him, threatening another bombardment.

I threw my last icy ball against a tree and lay down beside him on the frozen ground.

"Next thing we have to do," he said, pushing up on an elbow to look at me, "is make an angel."

"An angel?"

He started swooshing his arms and legs up and down in the snow as if doing star jumps on his back. He didn't look like an angel, but I didn't want to say so, because he was trying really hard. Then he stood up. Sunken into the snow was an imprint of a Christmas angel. It was beautiful. I made a whole family of angels before we finally went inside.

After I'd had a mug of warm Horlicks and two digestive biscuits, sleep started to slip its soft glove over me. I wasn't even in bed yet, but my eyes were already closing on their own.

"Go find Rita and get some pajamas on, then it's off to bed with you," Michael said. "It has been quite a day, young lady."

I wandered through the dark house in my cold, wet clothes, until I found the Madam unpacking her suitcase in the dim light of her new bedroom.

"Madam Rita."

"Yes, Miriam?" She glanced up, her tired eye smaller than the other.

"Thank you, but now I must go home," I said.

She stopped. "This *is* home, Miriam. Your *new* home."

"No. I must go to my *mme*."

She straightened, her lip curling to one side. "Come now. Your time with us has barely begun. Just you wait and see how much fun we're going to have." She patted the bed, beckoning me to sit down beside her open suitcase. "This house isn't very nice, I know, but we'll only be here for a short time until we find one to buy." She took my hand in hers. "What you need is a nice hot bath, then straight to bed. Michael shouldn't have let you play outside for so long. You're frozen, poor child."

I shook my head, my teeth chattering in my head. "I'm not cold, Madam Rita. Can I go home?"

She looked straight at me, her small eye growing bigger. "Now, I don't want to hear any more of that, Miriam." Then she went over to the door. "Where *has* Michael got to, anyway? Michael!"

She peeled off my damp clothes and wrapped me in a towel. I sat shivering on her bed while she drew me a bath. She called for Michael again, and when he didn't appear, she sat down beside me. That was when she said those awful words.

"Miriam, your mummy cannot look after you anymore. She has other children to care for, and your father gives her no help. Four children is too many for one mother. Michael and I, we have *no* children. Your mother has given you to us. We are your new parents. You're very lucky, you know, because—"

Her words crashed into each other inside my head like trapped grasshoppers. *Your mother has given you to us, given you to us, given you . . .*

"I want *Mme*," I cried, jumping up and running out of the room, past Michael, who was coming in through the door. He caught me in his long arms. I screamed, kicking and hitting out at him, but he held me tight.

"Miriam, settle down. What is it?"

"That's quite enough," Madam Rita said, grabbing my arm. I turned away. I didn't want to see her—ugly Madam Rita.

"Miriam," Michael said, his breath tickling my ear. "Miriam?"

I looked at him out of the corner of my eye. He looked worried and my anger went all floppy. "I want *Mme*," I whispered into his ear, so Madam Rita couldn't hear.

"Miriam, you get to have two mummies and two daddies.

Imagine that. Your mother loves you a lot. We love you too." He stroked my back.

My sobs fell into a pattern like the drawings on the wall, which Michael said were called wallpaper. *Sob, sob, breathe; sob, sob, breathe.* They filled my head with their loudness and, like big pieces of furniture, left no space for anything else.

"You're so light," Michael said, hoisting me up. "We'll have to feed you up so that when you see your mother again, she'll know we've been looking after you. We promised her."

*Sob, sob, breathe.*

Next door, he laid me down on the bed and took a scratchy blanket from the cupboard to cover me. I curled into a ball and turned my back on him.

Michael stayed there for a very long time, until I finally fell asleep.

Later that night I was woken by loud voices. At first I didn't know where I was, but the angry words soon reminded me.

"She's six years old. Just a child, Rita."

"Don't you think I know—"

"But there are ways of saying things. It's all so new for her."

"Well, you can't tiptoe around the truth forever, Michael. Better she understands now, and gets over it, than perpetuating half-truths."

"She's just lost her mother."

"She hasn't *lost* her mother, for goodness' sake! Not like *I* did. And I wasn't cute or pretty like her. No one wanted me after my mother died, I can tell you. Can you imagine what it was like being sent to boarding school at the age of eight? Eight! But I coped. I had to."

"Reet, this is not about you."

"I'm just saying, the child has no reason to be miserable when there are two people who very much want her."

"She's still going to miss Celia; it's only normal. It is going to take time to adjust. Have a bit more understanding."

"Just because I haven't given birth to the child doesn't mean I don't know how to care for her. I am not completely devoid of maternal instinct."

I stood in their doorway. Madam Rita's eyes were all dark and pointy. Michael's back was turned.

Madam Rita saw me first, then Michael. Both moved toward me.

Michael reached me first. He swept me into his arms. "Miriam, I'm sorry. Did we wake you? We're both just a bit tired and cranky. That's all."

"Yes, that's all," Madam Rita said, glaring at him and opening her arms to me.

He stepped back.

She moved forward and tried to pull me away from him.

"Rita," he said very slowly, then walked past her out of the room. He was holding me so tightly I couldn't breathe properly.

"She's mine too—" I heard her start to say, her voice as wobbly as jelly.

But Michael had already pulled the door shut behind us. It banged loudly, shaking the lamp in the hallway and making pockets of pale light bounce all over the walls.

It was my fault. All my fault. I felt sad for Madam Rita, but all I wanted was *mme anga*.

# CHAPTER EIGHT

## January 1961

## Miriam

The squirrel was standing so still it didn't look real. Michael and I waited. The animal's small black eyes flitted about, inspecting the treasure in my hand. My arm was aching. I couldn't hold it straight for much longer.

After the longest time, it finally moved, edging closer. I tried not to breathe, except every now and then, when I had to let out a burst of stored-up air.

Suddenly, without warning, the little guy darted forward, grabbed the piece of biscuit from my hand—his whiskers tickling like a feather duster—then shot back up the tree.

"Let's give it some more. Come on, Michael!"

"There'll be nothing left of your lunch," he said, rolling closed the top of the brown paper bag. "Anyway, we'd better be going. Don't want to be late for your first day at school, do we?"

School. It had taken forever for this day to come—but now I wasn't so sure I wanted it to be here.

We marched on through the park, three of my steps for every one of Michael's long strides. It was tricky walking fast in my new pinafore; my legs kept getting caught in the thick pleats of material. Madam Rita said the uniform had cost a lot of money— English money was much more expensive than African money— so she'd bought an extra-big size, hoping it would last a very long time. She took up a wide hem, but I was worried her wonky stitches would come undone, and then I'd be walking around school in a long dress that went all the way to the ground.

We arrived at the serious brick building just in time. I'd driven past with Michael once before, but now I was walking *through* the big, important gates.

"*Semper Verum,*" Michael said, reading the shiny words off one of the pillars. "'Always True.' Remember, Miriam, that—" I tried to concentrate on what he was saying, but my mind kept skipping ahead.

As we climbed the deep concrete stairs, a huge bell started to chime. With each peal, the ground shook. Michael cupped his warm hands over my ears, but still every clang hurt.

Then bodies, bags, shorts, and shoes were sweeping past us, separating me from Michael's safe arms. Before I knew what was happening, I'd been pushed hard up against the rough brick wall opposite.

I screwed up my eyes, trying to block out the hullabaloo.

It didn't last long. As quickly as the flood of children had started, so it dried up—a short burst of shouting and the banging of doors, and then silence.

I opened one eye, then the other. Michael and I were alone.

"You okay?" he asked, rescuing me.

I nodded.

"That's my girl," he said with a wink.

I winked back. Properly. I'd been practicing.

We continued with our journey, turning a corner into a snake-thin corridor with a shiny maroon floor. Rows of satchels hung lopsidedly off hooks—some spilling jumpers and books onto the floor—and frosted-glass doors revealed hazy silhouettes. My nose started to prickle. There was a smell of Domestos in the air. *Mme* always used Domestos to clean the toilets in Saxonwold.

"Seven . . . eight . . ." Michael counted aloud as we walked past the numbered doors. "Here we are!"

We were outside a door with a small brass number nine nailed lopsidedly to the frame. Inside, children were singing.

Michael tapped on the glass.

Nothing.

"They're busy," I said quickly. "Better we go home."

Michael knocked again, louder this time, and the singing stopped. Then a fuzzy figure was moving toward us. I closed my eyes and held my breath.

The door squeaked open.

"You must be Miriam," said a strange voice, smelling of bubble gum and air freshener.

I took a quick look. A madam with stiff yellow hair was standing in front of us.

"Welcome," she said, through a thin pink smile.

It was hard to understand her. Michael told me later that her words were wrapped in a thick Norfolk accent. We had to unwrap each word to understand what she was saying.

She looked just like the doll Madam Rita had bought me at the airport—small white hands, small white feet, and puffy yellow hair. I knew she'd have a small bottom too. You could just tell.

She wore a skirt the color of the sky—an African sky, not an English sky—and a jacket so tight it pushed her bosom right into her neck.

Her legs looked like two bendy spring branches and ended in the highest shoes I'd ever seen. They made a *click, clack, click, clack* sound when she walked. Later, when I tried on Madam Rita's only pair of high shoes, the chunky brown ones, they didn't make the same pointy sound.

The madam had a lot of powder on her face and pink paint on her lips. She smiled very carefully so her long teeth didn't smudge the color.

I looked at her nose. It was long too, with tiny slits at the end, which wouldn't easily let in a finger.

"You found us all right?" she asked, in a friendly Norfolk voice. Before we could reply, she went on. "My name is Mrs. Dee. I'll be your teacher this year, Miriam. So have you brought a bag with you?"

Michael tilted his body and the green canvas rucksack slid off his shoulder.

"Good. Find a free hook and then come on inside."

I peeked through the gap between her and the door. There were lots of *who's-she* eyes inside. I wished we could go home.

"Quiet, class!" the teacher shouted, swiveling around. Then

she was taking my hand. Her fingers felt like brittle twigs. "Now, Miriam, say good-bye to . . ." Mrs. Dee looked at Michael, then at me, then back at Michael. She swallowed, red washing up over her bosom, neck, and face and seeping into her hair. I thought she was going to explode, just like the plums *Mme* used to cook.

"Her father," Michael said, patting me on the shoulder. He smiled at me. I made my mouth smile back. "Pick you up at four."

Then the door had closed behind me and I was standing in a room filled with rows of wooden desks. Behind each desk sat two children. They all had white skin and a few had Milo-brown speckles on their faces.

At the front of the classroom was a dusty blackboard with yellow writing across it. Someone had written the letter *P* over and over again, from one end of the board to the other.

*P* for pin, *P* for pot, *P* for pan . . .

"Everyone, this is Miriam," said the teacher. "She's going to be joining us. Miriam has come all the way from Africa."

The class let out a whooping gasp, then the children started whispering and pointing. I felt like a hyena-lion—cowardly brave.

"Is that why you're so tanned?" a skinny boy with custard-colored hair and a speckled face blurted out.

Everyone laughed.

"That is quite enough, Kent Alsop! Now let's give Miriam our special new-pupil welcome."

"W-e-l-c-o-m-e, M-i-r-i-a-m," they sang, all their eyes stuck on me.

"You'll be sitting next to Emily," said the teacher, pointing toward a podgy girl with hair tied into two curly bunches beside her face, just like the ears of a spaniel dog. The girl quickly circled her arms around her pencil and eraser.

"Yes, Madam," I said, sitting down in the empty chair.

The whole class burst out laughing.

"Enough!" the teacher shouted, banging the blackboard duster on her desk and sending puffs of yellow chalk dust into the air.

"You can call me Mrs. Dee, Miriam."

It was getting very complicated trying to remember who to call what. In Africa it was much easier. A white person was either a master or a madam.

The morning passed quickly. I could do everything Mrs. Dee told us to do; Rita had taught it to me already. I kept waiting for the exciting things to happen, but they never did. School just wasn't as much fun as I'd thought it was going to be.

Once, when I'd traveled north with *Mme* to see my *makhulu*, I'd gone to my brothers' school for a day. It had been the best day ever.

"Three times two is six. Four times two is eight. Five times two is te-e-en," the schoolchildren had recited as the teacher, *Mudedekadzi* Mafela, tapped her ruler on the desk in time to the beat.

*Mudedekadzi* was very different from Mrs. Dee, her shiny black face hidden behind large spectacles held together with pieces of Elastoplast.

The day I visited, she was wearing a yellow blouse the color of frangipani, and a gray skirt clung to her thighs and bottom. *Mme* said *Mudedekadzi* had probably not used Sta-Soft in her wash.

She had a big bosom and an even bigger bottom, nothing like Mrs. Dee's. She wore high shoes too, but I think these were a necessity. She was the only teacher at the school *and* also the school principal, so the heels gave her the necessary height and importance. She didn't wear them easily, though, her feet leaking out of every weak point in the leather as she waddled from side to side.

"Veerry good, class! Now again. What is twooo times twooo?"

"Four!" we shouted in triumphant unison.

*Mudedekadzi*'s serious face broke into a wide grin, which showed off her white teeth. She tapped a broken cup on her desk with her pencil, announcing the end of morning lessons, and then the class was spilling out into the sunshine. I followed my brothers—Christian, Nelson, and Alfred—into the clearing. Nelson had a soccer ball tucked under his arm.

Despite their different ages, my brothers all took their lessons together in the same classroom. The school consisted of only one room. Master Davis had set it up for the children and grandchildren of the laborers on his farm, and because my *makhulu* worked for him, my brothers were allowed to attend. *Mme* said they were lucky they didn't have to walk all the way into town for their lessons, like some of the other black children. The journey was almost two hours on foot, and that was just one way.

*Mudedekadzi* and the children built the classroom themselves. Master Davis put up the money, and the children the muscles. The building stood in a forest clearing surrounded by sweet-smelling pines. The walls of the school were plastered with red clay, and the roof was made from sheets of rippled iron.

At break we lined up in front of *Mudedekadzi*, who stood guard over a tall urn the farmer's truck had delivered that morning. As I was a visitor, I was treated like a very important person and invited to stand at the front of the queue to receive the first mug of milk. It was warm and creamy and tasted much sweeter than the milk *Mme* would buy from the shop in Johannesburg. I had to drink it down quickly, though, because the child next in line was waiting for the mug.

When we'd all drunk our share, it was time to play. Everyone, from seven-year-old *piccanins* to fifteen-year-old boys with hair on their faces and girls with ripening bosoms, spread out over the grass. Even I was allowed on the pitch. Four boys hauled a pair of logs into goalpost positions while the rest of the class was divided into two teams—Leopards versus Lions. I was a Lion.

*Mudedekadzi* blew her whistle and the game began. Soon the ball was being headed and shuffled, dribbled and passed, and goals were shot to howls of delight.

At halftime the Lions were behind by one goal.

Then it was Christian taking control of the ball. He darted across the field, dodging his opponents, and just as the goalie rushed him, he kicked. What a kick! The ball shot past the keeper, through the posts, and into the surrounding trees. We screamed with delight—the score was even.

But just as he booted the ball, the seam of my brother's shorts split. Our cries of celebration turned to screeches of laughter as Christian stood in the middle of the clearing with a gaping hole in his gray school shorts. You could see right through to his red underpants. Even *Mudedekadzi* had to hold her sides to stop her bosom from bursting out of her blouse.

Then she was clanging her wedding ring against a tin mug to announce the end of break time. It was time to gather in the shade of the trees for a song.

I sat down on the pine-needle carpet with the others as *Mudedekadzi* taught us the latest song from the public health nurse.

*"Just one teaspoon of sugar, a pinch of salt, four cups of water, and see what you got. You got a re-hy-dration solution, a re-hy-dration solution. Yes, you got a re-hy-dration solution to keep you safe from the trots!"*

"Miriam?"

I looked up. It was Mrs. Dee, not *Mudedekadzi* Mafela . . . I was back in England.

After number skills, we had a lesson from the Bible, some handwriting practice, and then a story on the mat. Mrs. Dee was in the middle of reading us a story when the bell announcing "elevenses" rang. She stopped immediately, right in the middle of a sentence. I never got to find out what happened to the sailor on the sinking boat, because the door was flung open and everyone began pushing and shoving to get out. I followed. All the doors into the corridor were open, just like an Advent calendar on Christmas morning, and children were tumbling out. I was bumped down some stairs, along a passage, and across a courtyard. It was fun being part of this loud, bustling craziness.

Then we were outside and a cold wind was carving the long worm of children into smaller groups, until I was the only one left.

I looked around the playground. There were no trees, no grass, no goals—just a coal-colored fence, two benches, and an old purple jungle gym missing a crossbar at the back. At one end of the yard a group of boys knelt on the concrete, rolling marbles along a track. Beside the water fountain, three girls took turns hopping over a piece of taut elastic. Some other children sat in a circle eating their snacks. Nobody looked my way.

Spying a short flight of stairs hidden around the back of the school building, I ran over to it and sat down on the top step, tucking myself right up against the small trapdoor at the top. The concrete was cold and the chill crept quickly through my stockings and pinafore to start hollowing out my bones.

Two girls strolled past.

"Hello," I said, giving my best smile.

They giggled and walked on, one telling the other in a loud whisper that I'd called Mrs. Dee a madam.

Even though I wasn't hungry, I fumbled with the brown packet Michael had given me. I'd make myself eat like everyone else. I unwrapped the sandwich—two slices of white bread smeared with butter, peanut butter, and honey. I didn't understand why Michael always put butter *and* peanut butter on bread. Two butters just didn't make sense. I was about to take my first bite when the sandwich flew out of my hand and landed on the bottom step.

I looked up.

Three boys from my class, including the custard-haired boy, were standing at the bottom of the stairs, grinning. One had a catapult in his hand.

"What's the matter, Africa girl, got butterfingers?"

I edged down the steps and reached for my sandwich, but

the boy's shoe beat me to it. He dug his heel into the soft white bread and swiveled it from side to side, mushing it into a gluggy pulp. My eyes started to burn.

"Don't cry, nigger girl. Just go home." He turned to the other two boys. "My dad says blacks have smaller brains. He says they cause all the fuckin' problems in England."

One of the other boys made a gurgling sound and a blob of bubbly spit landed at my feet.

"Got any gobstoppers?"

I shook my head. I didn't know what gobstoppers were, but I wished I had some. Maybe then they'd want to be my friends.

"Too bad. See you 'round, gollywog."

I didn't cry; my tears were too scared to come out. But my stockings felt warm. I looked down. There was a wet patch spreading on the concrete beneath me.

# CHAPTER NINE

## April 1961

## Miriam

Over the term, I worked hard to make myself invisible. Sometimes I succeeded, managing to escape the taunts and teases for an entire day. But more often than not, I arrived home with a broken school bag, a bloodied shin, or maybe a ripped exercise book. With passing weeks, my uniform grew bigger, my shoulders pointier, and my days more wretched.

During school hours I was too busy dodging danger to think about anything else, but at night there was room in my head for my fears to grow. Like weeds, they spread over my mind, tangling up my thoughts and blocking out the light. And when I fell asleep, the badness simply followed, inviting scary shadows and monsters into my dreams.

I noticed Madam Rita and Michael had stopped mentioning *Mme*. Whenever I tried to remind them, they suddenly remembered something they had to do or somewhere they had to be.

Soon I started to forget what *Mme* sounded like, what she looked and smelled like. I used to be able to smell her on my rag doll, Tendani, and every night I'd go off to sleep breathing in her special *Mme* scent. But after a while I'd sucked it all off, and Tendani just smelled like everything else—of England.

This England was different from the place in Michael's stories. We didn't even get to visit the queen. I didn't want to see her anymore, anyway. Everything was different from how it used to be. The sun was always hiding, the buildings were old and crumbly, and church was very serious.

We moved house and left behind the dark, dusty one with drooping eyes and a thin, angry mouth, but after we moved, *Mme* felt even farther away. I began to wonder if she'd ever been real or whether she was just some pretend person in my head. Sometimes I'd see her shadow in my dreams, but I knew dreams weren't real.

The new house was much nicer than the old one. It had two levels, with windows that popped right out of the roof, like the headlights on a sports car, and a windy staircase with a balustrade you could slide down when no one was looking.

Because it was farther from school, Michael no longer walked to meet me each afternoon; I had to catch a bus home. I hated that—being locked into the small, smelly school bus for ten more minutes with just my tormentors for company.

At home, a note under the mat meant I had to go next door to Mrs. McKiddie's house until Michael came to collect me. I didn't like going next door. Mrs. McKiddie kept the curtains drawn, even during the day, and her house always smelled of haddock. She had a horrible cat called Queenie and a blue budgie called Mr. Churchill. Queenie would scratch me if I got too near her, and I wasn't allowed to take Mr. Churchill out of his cage, even though his wings had been clipped. So I was always happy when I didn't find a note under the mat; it meant Michael was home, probably bent over his desk, working. Then we'd share afternoon tea together, holed up in his cozy study.

Madam Rita usually arrived home after dark, the smell of dead people wound around her like a scarf. Her job was to cut up people who'd died, in order to find out what made them die. I didn't like knowing that. I didn't like the smell of dead people either. Madam Rita told me it was just the smell of the special bath the dead people had been put into to stop them from rotting. After she told me that, I didn't have any more baths; I showered instead.

Neither Michael nor Madam Rita could cook like *Mme* could. Most days they just warmed up something from Marks & Spencer. The trouble was that neither Mark nor Spencer was a good cook either—their pork pies had big bits of jelly in the middle and their peas were all mushy. I missed having slippery green balls to chase around my plate. In fact, I missed all of *Mme*'s cooking—the stiff chunks of *mielie pap* swimming in tomato gravy, the gem squash halves filled with pools of warm butter, the salty chuck stew. I missed apricot jam smeared thickly on wedges of soft white bread. I missed dollops of sweetened condensed milk stirred into my tea. I missed everything from Africa—especially the Saxonwold house. It had been so clean and tidy. I knew that if *Mme* ever visited us in England, she would be very disappointed. The house was such a mess. A lady called Louise did come on Tuesdays to clean, but she was not a proper cleaner like *Mme*. And she was always putting my suitcase back in the cupboard even though I wanted it out ready for when the England holiday came to an end. Louise smoked cigarettes too, and I could smell her even when she wasn't there.

One morning, I decided to give the kitchen a proper clean. I washed and dried the dirty dishes piled up in the sink, then packed them away in the cupboard—glasses on one side, cups and mugs on the other. I rearranged the fridge—vegetables and fruit in the bottom drawer, yogurt and cheese on the top shelf, meat in the middle. Then I took a bucket of warm water and, with a brush from the bathroom, scrubbed the kitchen floor till the water was brown and the tiles white again.

"What *are* you doing, child?" Madam Rita said when she came downstairs and found me.

"All tidy," I boasted, with a sweep of my hand.

Madam Rita was not pleased. She hauled me to my feet. "Miriam, I don't want you cleaning, do you understand? And certainly not with my nail brush!"

I didn't understand. It was all topsy-turvy, this new holiday life.

Madam Rita started coming home later and later from work. There were no more mealtime stories either. Any talk at dinner was either about work or about money. Though this was better than the long cold silences that could take hold of the house— Madam Rita and Michael sometimes not speaking to each other for a whole week. Talking, any talking, kept the *tokoloshe* away.

I hated England. It had changed everybody and everything.

All I wanted was my *mme*, but she had given me away.

# CHAPTER TEN

## 1962

## Celia

The noise drove nails through my dreams. I stirred, thick with sleep, then dozed again. The sound persisted, forcing open doors in my head until I was properly awake and staring into the blackness of 4:00 A.M. I slid a hand under my pillow and quickly silenced the old blue alarm clock. Someone coughed. Sleep-warm bodies restlessly rearranged themselves. I sat up. The air was thick and stale, breathed in and out all night by too many of us.

My surroundings came slowly into focus—seven sleeping shapes sharing the skew black space with a table, three chairs, a bucket, and a stove.

I rose and crept through the darkness. The floor was freezing; winter had fingered every inch of the shack. After washing in a bucket of icy water, I dressed and then lit the Primus stove, boiling up a tin of yesterday's tea. I sat alone at the table to eat my breakfast—two slices of buttered bread washed down with a mug of sweet tea—before stepping out into the gray light of dawn to join the silent river of figures wending its way down the dusty track to the nearest bus stop.

The small shack in Alexandra township had been my home for many months now. I had secured a new job, as promised by the Steiners, working four days a week for a Portuguese family—market gardeners who ran a greengrocer. There were servants' quarters on their premises, but I had not been allowed to use them.

"No, I know what you people is like. Next thing there is boyfriend coming in the night. The last girl is witch doctor. She kill chickens in the room and throw bones . . . No room!"

So I had been forced to find a place in the townships. After a long and futile search, an acquaintance finally offered me a place on the outskirts of Alex—a shack I'd share with seven others. In return, I looked after the woman's grandchildren two evenings a week while she worked at the local shebeen, serving home brew to drunken men and loud, loose women.

I cursed. The queue at the bus stop was already over twenty people long. There was no guarantee I'd get onto the five o'clock bus, and if I missed it, I'd miss the connection, which meant I'd get to work after seven. The last time this happened the Portuguese madam had docked my wages.

A youngster elbowed his way in front of me. "Sorry, Mama." His tone was mocking.

I straightened, my breathing picking up.

The kid turned. His eyes were dark, his black face rutted with dents and ditches. A thick scar tracked down one cheek to end in the sharp corner of his mouth. "Give us your money, Mama."

No one in the line moved. Even the breeze was still as the morning held its breath.

The boy brought his pockmarked face up to mine, his breath hot and sour. The whites of his eyes bulged. "*Tokoloshe* stolen your tongue?" he shouted, yanking at the brown paper bag I was carrying.

I let go.

He rifled through it like a dog rummaging through rubbish. My knitting hit the dirt, then my apple. My tub of talcum powder exploded in a cloud of white.

Five seventeen A.M. *Where is the bus? Where is it?*

The boy, finding no ticket or money in my bag, flung it aside. It trapped a pocket of air, hung suspended for a moment, then collapsed and sank slowly to the ground.

"Don't mess with me, Mama, or I'll cut off your titties."

I crossed my hands over my breasts.

"Now gimme your purse. Is it hiding in those big melons of yours?"

He lunged forward and forced a hand into my bra, his jagged fingernails snagging on one of my nipples. I kept only my passbook and a clean tissue there.

My pass landed at the feet of the woman behind me. She did not move. We lived in neighboring shacks and usually greeted each other every morning. Now she stood mute.

My nipple was stinging. I looked down. A bright ring of blood had seeped through the fabric to form an angry red button on my lilac uniform.

"Bitch! Give me money," he shouted, his heavy hand connecting with the side of my head.

I fell to the ground and landed with a thud in the dirt. Then I was being kicked over and over again, in the back, on my breasts, in my belly . . . I coughed and wheezed and tried to scramble away, but my movements were disjointed and the blows too many. Dazed, I swung there on all fours, bracing for more, the taste of my own blood strong in my mouth. I spat into the dirt. Something dropped into the frothy pool of pink saliva; it was one of my teeth.

Then I heard the sound of salvation, the screeching brakes of the Putco bus as it lurched around the corner. For a moment time stood still, then the *tsotsi* vanished into the suspended dust of dawn.

An old man bent down and helped me to my feet. Someone gathered up my unraveling knitting. My neighbor passed me my bruised apple. "*Hau*, Celia. I'm sorry for the *skelm*," she said as she wiped the dirt off my passbook.

The doors of the bus opened and the queue surged forward, as people clambered onto the already crowded vehicle. Trembling, I clutched my belongings to my chest and shuffled with the line. I did not think I would reach the door. When I did, I stopped at the foot of the stairs, expecting the driver to bellow that the bus was full and close the door in my face. He didn't. I bent down and slipped off my right shoe. In it, lying safely under the innersole, was a warm two-rand note and my bus ticket. My job was secure for today.

I had been with the Portuguese family for more than a year now. The job was no good—thirteen-hour days on wages barely enough to keep food on my table, let alone that of my three boys and their granny up north. But I could not leave. Jobs in the suburbs were scarce and those who had good ones guarded them fiercely. More importantly, though, the Parkhurst home was the only address the Steiners had for me. To leave would mean losing the one connection I had with my Miriam.

I'd heard nothing from the Steiners since the day I'd waved good-bye to them outside their big Saxonwold home. So many words and promises, yet the days had slipped into weeks, the weeks into months, and still no news.

I started to see my Miriam everywhere. The back of a little girl's head in the crowd was *her* head; the laughter tinkling across the park was *her* laugh. A lucky-bean pod lying on the path meant she would be just around the next corner, and the rustling in the night was her moving in bed beside me; but when I reached over, only the bedclothes met my caresses.

I chased people across streets, ran beside buses, and searched for the child I could hear crying. Every phone call was a trunk call; every envelope in the postbox, a letter from England. Every new day was *the* day I would hear from my Miriam.

I asked anyone who would stop and listen, what they knew of England. In my head it was just a shadow I couldn't pin down, a curtain I could not open. England was a word. There was no bus I could catch to take me there, no number to call. It was a shifting ghost, which haunted and taunted me and left me crazy with helplessness.

There were five in this Portuguese family I now worked for—the Master and Madam, their two teenage children, and the Master's mother. The only one I cared about was the old lady.

I found her now, her wheelchair parked beside a blaring radio, the music successfully drowning out her feeble moans. The rank smell of old urine filled the air.

"*Hau, Makhulu!* This would never happen with my people," I despaired. "Old person is very important and must be respected. Why you let them treat you like this?"

The old lady couldn't understand my English, but muttered something in her own tongue.

After switching off the radio and opening up the windows, I rescued her from her prison on wheels, easing her onto the bed. Then I began sponging down her crumpled body with warm water, gently cleaning under her shrunken breasts and between the wings of her sagging bottom. I loosened the crusts stacked high around her bedsores, and with a fresh cloth wiped away the food trapped between the purse-string creases of her wizened mouth. I cleared the sleep from her rheumy eyes and ran a comb through her baby-fine hair. Finally I powdered her neck with what was left of the talcum powder I had brought with me.

"Now, *Makhulu*, you look and smell beautiful!"

She smiled a lopsided grin, her false teeth grinding and clacking against each other.

I draped her thin arms around my neck and heaved her back into her wheelchair. "My daughter, she never to treat me so bad," I said, stroking her leathery cheek.

My own words lifted the scab of pain I worried at daily, and tears blurred my vision. I sank down beside the old lady. "Where is my daughter? Where is she?" I whispered.

Confusion and alarm swept across the old lady's face.

"My Miriam. I lose my Miriam," I moaned.

The granny leaned forward and grasped my hands in hers, her cold, thin fingers folding themselves around mine. Just for a moment I allowed myself to succumb to the comfort she offered, feeling her touch and accepting her caresses. Then I stood up and hurried on with my day.

The bathroom was next on my list of chores. The toilet stood unflushed and a bin of used sanitary pads overflowed in the corner. Dirty clothes lay piled around the laundry basket and a band of grime ringed the bath I'd scoured just days before.

As I knelt down to clean the lavatory, the eldest child of the house swung into the room. She brushed her teeth, pulled string through her teeth, and squeezed a pimple in the mirror. Then she left. I had been invisible.

My hands started to shake, panic climbing up my throat like a monkey. I stood up, gasping for air, and pushed open the small window above the cistern. But the cool breeze did little to ease my suffocation. I had to do something. I could not bear it any longer.

That night I sat in the quiet of the kitchen, waiting for the family to finish their dinner. My body was heavy with fatigue and my mind weighed down with worry. The breakfast table had been laid, but still I would have to wait to clear the dinner dishes before I could begin the long journey home to my room in the township.

I hoped the meal would finish soon, though I suspected a long night still stretched ahead. Many bottles of wine had been opened and there was much loud laughter coming from next door. On a night such as this I could expect a visit from the

Master—the only time I got to see the inside of the empty servants' quarters.

Suddenly, as though separated from reason, I found myself standing up. My hands untied the apron around my waist and unbuttoned the uniform I was wearing, before folding both and placing them neatly on the sideboard. I felt naked standing there in just my T-shirt and skirt. Then my hands were pushing open the back door.

I hesitated on the edge of the night, before stepping into the garden. God had switched on his torch and the moon's silver glow outed corners and crevices that on another night would have remained hidden.

The cool night air brought me to my senses. I was inside my body again, but I knew there was no going back. I crept across the lawn, hugging the stingy line of shadows until I had reached the open window on the far side of the house. Hooking my arms over the ledge, I hoisted myself onto the sill and teetered there for a moment, before scrambling headfirst through the gap and landing inside with a crash.

I heard the old granny gasp before I saw her, my eyes taking time to make sense of the shrouded surrounds. "Shhh, *Makhulu*," I whispered, holding a finger to my lips. "Is me, Celia."

The old lady's breathing was fast and tremulous, making the darkness shudder and shake. I crawled over to where she was slumped. "I am sorry, but I must to go, Granny."

The old lady frowned as she struggled to make some sense of my words.

I kissed her forehead. "Be safe. God must watch over you."

Then I unfastened the chain around my neck and pressed a small silver crucifix into her palm. "For you."

Tears spilled onto her wrinkled cheeks. "Celia," she whispered. "Celia."

"Zelia!"

I froze. Someone else was calling my name.

Now it was the old lady's turn to put a finger to her lips, then she was shooing me on my way. I squeezed back through the open window and landed softly in the plants below.

"Hey! What you do? Zelia, is you?" shrieked a high-pitched voice. "Where you go? Pedro quick! She go!"

For the briefest moment I faltered, then I was running—up the drive, onto the street, and down the road. I did not stop, fear winning over the pain in my side that threatened to sabotage my escape.

I reached the bus stop, my lungs clamoring for air.

The bus was pulling off.

"*Kha vha ime!* Stop!" I begged, knocking desperately on the moving door, but the driver stared straight ahead, and I was left standing in the middle of the road choking on black diesel fumes.

It was another hour till the next bus. An hour!

I looked quickly about me, then slunk into the shadows to wait.

# CHAPTER ELEVEN

## Miriam

Daffodils poked their yellow origami faces through the melting snow, birds built nests, and sunlight streamed through the library window, thinning the gloom and thawing the cold. It was spring in Norwich.

I was sitting in my usual corner, behind the books on religion—the quietest and safest spot in the school.

I had been living under England's gray roof for four years now—one thousand five hundred and seventy-nine days—and I'd become well versed in making myself invisible. I knew how to blend in, disappear; how to be no one.

Hiding in the library at lunchtime was one of my successes. The old stone building had become my refuge and my escape, the books carrying me beyond my lonely life to other worlds.

Spending so much time studying between the letters *R* and *S* also meant my grades were excellent, something Michael and

Rita found very reassuring, my report cards helping dispel some of the concerns they harbored about me.

"She's nothing more than four spare limbs and a pair of anxious eyes," I overheard Michael once say.

"Africans often are," Rita reassured him. "Look at the build of those Kenyan runners. It's a genetic thing. See how well she did in her English essay last week. Not the results of a troubled child, that's for certain. The thing about adoption is that you never really know what you're getting. I mean, there's no template to measure the kid against. Saying that, we do at least know what her—what Celia was like."

Now I sat poring over a colossal book on earthquakes, reading about fault lines and foci, seismic waves and Richter readings.

All of a sudden there was a *crash, thump* and then a scream. Instinctively, I threw myself under the table and curled up into a ball, the world I was reading about coming to life. Moments passed. No walls collapsed. No suffocating dust swirled. I felt no tremor or aftershock.

Hesitantly I opened one eye, then the other . . .

My gaze was met by that of an Indian girl. She was lying spread-eagled across the parquet floor. "Is that your bag?" she asked accusingly.

There had been no earthquake. The girl had tripped over my satchel.

I began to shake. "I'm . . . I'm sorry."

As she stood up to dust down her pinafore, I saw she was tall and leggy, with blue-black hair hanging in two solid braids down to her waist.

"Stupid me!" she said with a wide smile. "I never watch

where I'm going." Her voice rose and fell like a song. "I was caught in an earthquake in India," she went on, eyeing the book lying open on my desk. "It was sooo scary. I thought the sky was going to fall in." She waved her arms in the air theatrically. "You're meant to hide under the nearest table or something . . ."

Her voice trailed off as a look of understanding crept slowly across her face. Suddenly she collapsed in a fit of giggles. "You . . . You . . ." She clutched her belly. "Ah, my stomach hurts! You thought we were having an earthquake when I tripped over your bag!"

I stood there, humiliated, while the girl's melodrama continued.

Finally she stopped laughing. "Hey, I'm Zelda," she said, wiping away her tears on her shirtsleeve.

"Miriam," I mumbled.

"Cool name!" She perched on the edge of my table. "I hate mine. I'd love to be Colette or Ruth or *Miriam*. But no, my parents had to call me Zelda Sheetal Patel. What were they thinking?"

I found myself grinning, and for the first time in so long, the snake that lived inside of me loosened its grip.

"So who's your teacher?" she asked, lunging across the table in readiness for me to divulge top-secret information.

"Miss Sooty," I obliged in a thick whisper.

"You mean Miss Snooty!" she exclaimed, recklessly announcing the news to the rest of the library. "Poor you!"

"Shhh," hissed the library monitor.

Zelda rolled her eyes and gave me a knowing look.

The bell rang, announcing the start of afternoon classes.

I panicked. I didn't want this to end. I was entranced by the girl, who oozed happiness.

"Hey, wanna come over to my house later?" she asked.

It took a few moments for me to grasp what she'd so casually said. I was being invited over to play. "I . . . I . . . I have to let Michael know if I'm going to be late. I can't. I mean . . ." How could I not accept?

"Who's Michael?" she asked.

"Uh, he looks after me."

Her eyebrows peaked. "A guy nanny? Weird. Well, maybe tomorrow, then."

"Yes. Yes, please. I'd like that very much."

"Okay. Meet you under the crab apple tree after school."

And with that she was gone.

"Yes. Tomorrow," I said, my voice trailing after her.

I stood fixed to the floor, holding on to the sweetness for as long as it lingered. The swing door swished back and forth, back and forth, my mind swinging with it. Then the library was quiet and I was late for class.

The next day, school refused to end, stretching interminably over long division and health, religious education and French. I struggled to focus, and Miss Sooty told me off several times for daydreaming.

Finally the bell announcing the end of the school day started to ring. I shot out of class and into the weak afternoon light, arriving at the crab apple tree before any of my classmates had even reached the top of the stairs.

Throwing my bag down, I hopped onto the wall to scan the

faces of the kids emerging from the redbrick building. I was looking for long black plaits and gleaming white teeth. I was listening for laughter. With time, the stream of navy uniforms thinned to a trickle, and after about twenty minutes, it dried up altogether.

By 4:40 P.M. the last of the cars had pulled away from the school gates and the last of the kids on bikes were heading down the road. A small band of boys remained, kicking a soccer ball around on the hopscotch court, while a gangly girl with pink hair stood in an alcove practicing her violin.

I bent down to pick up my bag.

"Miriam!"

I swung around.

"Miriam, wait!"

Zelda was leaping down the stairs two steps at a time, her plaits swinging crazily from side to side, her pencil case threatening to topple out of her bag.

"Sorry, but that beastly Mr. Turnbull kept me in for talking during the French test. Silly old codger! I bet he looks like a constipated camel when he sits on the loo."

I giggled at the thought of Mr. Turnbull on the toilet.

"C'mon, let's get home for tea. I'm starving!"

She slipped her arm through mine. It was soft and warm. Then we were off, half running and half skipping down the street. My chest was burning by the time we stopped.

"Tada," Zelda said, blowing an imaginary trumpet. "My humble home."

We were standing at the top of a very long driveway. At the bottom crouched a scarred block of apartments—six blue doors opening onto six concrete pads, each with its own twist of washing line. The adjacent section stood vacant, the plot of frost-dead grass home to a couple of conked-out cars, an overflowing rubbish skip, and a dilapidated basketball hoop. I smiled. I felt so happy.

We ran down the drive and stopped outside the first apartment. The front door was open and I found myself peering into a bright white kitchen with blue windmill motifs ringing the room. Jangling music and a delicious aroma of seared meat and sweet spices wafted out.

"Hiya!" Zelda cried, pulling me in after her.

At the stove stood a tall Indian woman dressed in a flowing red dress. "At last," she said, swinging around. "Why so late?"

Her face was heavily made up and she wore dangly gold earrings, which sounded like wind chimes whenever she shook her head. Her black hair had been bundled into a thick roll and fixed with the stab of a shiny tortoiseshell pin to the top of her head. A radio with a bent coat hanger for an antenna was balancing on the edge of the shelf above her. Its volume had been turned right up.

"Mr. Turnbull gave me a detention."

Two teens—a slender, full-lipped girl and a boy with slicked-back hair and pimply skin—were seated at a table in the middle of the room. On hearing about Zelda's latest drama, the boy, who was slouching over a bowl of curry, sniggered. The girl opposite rolled her eyes—eyes as startlingly green as glow-worms in the night. I'd never seen anyone so beautiful before.

"Detention!" Zelda's mother exclaimed, taking her apron off as though readying for a fight. "Why? What did you do this time, Zelda?"

Ignoring the question, Zelda stood aside, blowing my cover. "Mum, this is my friend Miriam."

*My friend.* The words were as sweet as jam.

Her mother's face softened. "Mir-iam. What a lovely name." She flicked the boy across the back of the head. "Get off the chair, Naresh. Let Miriam sit down."

He ducked before she could wreak any more damage to his Brylcreemed waves, and reluctantly gave up his seat.

"You look as if you could do with a bit of fattening up!" Mrs. Patel said, looking me up and down.

"Muuumm," Zelda groaned.

"Shush, Zelda. Now what would you like, Miriam? A samosa? Some chicken curry? I have this lovely almond cake."

"A piece of almond cake, please . . . Thank you," I stuttered, though I'd never tasted anything almond before.

"Me too, Mum. And can we have a hot chocolate?" Zelda said, flinging her bag into the corner and pulling up a chair. "With marshmallows."

Zelda's sister paused from brushing her long mane and eyed her sister menacingly from under her gleaming sheet of black hair. "Don't throw your bag down like that. How many times do I have to tell you? And did you borrow my gold bangles? I can't find them anywhere."

"I put them back," Zelda blurted out defensively.

"You did not."

"Did."

"Zelda! Mum . . . can you talk to Zelda?"

The phone rang, abruptly stalling the dispute. Zelda's mother picked up the receiver. "Patels, hello!"

A sound of whimpering came from the sofa and I turned to see a chubby baby lying tucked between two cushions.

"Come here, babs," Zelda's sister said, sweeping the infant into her arms and signaling for Zelda to turn down the radio.

The inviting aroma that had greeted us on our arrival started to take on a burned note. I was wondering whether to say something when Mrs. Patel interrupted her phone conversation to remove the pot from the stove.

As I stood wallowing in this wonderful chaos, the back door burst open. There was a rush of cool air and the musky scent of cologne, then a short Indian man waddled in. He placed his briefcase on the table, loosened his tie, and headed over to Zelda's mother, planting a quick kiss on her cheek. I could tell right away who he was. He had Zelda's eyes.

Mr. Patel had a round baby face, with shiny brown skin. Across the bridge of his nose was a splatter of small black spots, which looked like fly droppings, and on his chin sat a large knobbly mole. He was balding, but had trained and plastered some long strands of hair over the bare bit.

Mrs. Patel placed her hand over the receiver, muttered something about burned curry and school detentions, then resumed her telephone conversation.

Mr. Patel still hadn't acknowledged anyone else in the room when he poured himself a cup of chai from the teapot on the stove, added one . . . two . . . three spoonfuls of sugar, before sinking down onto the sofa. Only then did he seem to notice the rest of us in the room.

Zelda piped up. "Dad, this is my new friend, Miriam."

"Oh ho! Good afternoon," he said, heaving himself off the sofa.

He stretched out his hand and shook mine vigorously. "Delighted to meet you, Miriam." His voice was as deep and smooth as my hot chocolate.

"And how is my little Jewel of India?" he said, turning to Zelda and pulling her in to him.

Zelda's mother broke off her telephone conversation. "She got a detention from Mr. Turnbull, Sanjit."

"Just because I asked Sophia if her tadpoles had turned into frogs yet," Zelda said, pouting. "During a French test," she added, quietly.

Sanjit raised his eyebrows, showing just enough disapproval to satisfy Zelda's mother.

"And my baby, Navin?" he asked, clicking his tongue against his teeth.

The baby on Zelda's sister's hip stopped whimpering and started to gurgle with excitement as his father reached for him.

Seeing Mrs. Patel was still on the phone, Zelda sorted out the rest of our afternoon tea. The almond cake was the best—buttery, crumbly, and drizzled with a sharp lemon icing, which made the insides of my cheeks tingle. I had two slices. It was now officially my favorite treat.

After tea we escaped outside. There was already a group of kids playing basketball in the adjacent lot.

Zelda headed toward them. I didn't follow.

She turned. "You coming?"

"No, you go, I'll just watch from here."

"C'mon, don't be a stick in the mud!"

I couldn't move. I was trapped between a strangling fear of the other kids and the dread of losing my new and only friend.

"Hey, Zel," someone cried. "Coming to play?" The others had spotted us. "We *so* need you. Zane is grinding us into the ground!"

Zelda grabbed my hand and hauled me after her. "Sure thing. There are two of us and we mean business!"

Next thing we were in among the others, so close I could feel their heat. There were dark faces and light, brown bodies and white—and no one I recognized from school.

"Hey, everyone, this is Miriam."

"Hiya!" "Hi there." "Hello." Grins and smiles and friendly faces.

Blood started thumping in my ears. The ball was tossed to me. My hands opened like a robot's and I caught it. It was heavier than I'd imagined, and warm from someone else's touch. I ran my fingers along the dents of dark brown stitching and over the soft bulges of leather. Then I threw. Where, or to whom, I don't know, but that first throw was as exhilarating as rolling down a hillside curled up in the rim of an old car tire. I remembered doing that once, somewhere . . . or perhaps it was in a dream.

Instantly the game was back on, with kids running and hurling, catching and slam-dunking, and I was a part of it. I was so happy, I didn't want the afternoon to end, but it did. As evening wrapped itself around us, and mothers called their children indoors, Zelda walked with me to the end of her road.

"See ya tomorrow," she sang, as we parted ways.

"Yes, tomorrow."

I walked backward, waving, until I had to turn the next corner.

Michael and Rita were both home by the time I got back—

Michael in his study on a business call and Rita in the lounge sipping a sherry and reading a medical journal.

"Hi, Rita," I said, bouncing into the room.

She glanced up. "How was school?"

"It was so much fun. I—"

"Good," she said absently.

I hovered, bursting to talk. I wanted to let the happiness of the afternoon pour out. I wanted to tell Rita about my new friends, about my best friend. I wanted to tell her about basketball and sweet almond cake, Mrs. Patel's kitchen and—

"I'm tired tonight," she said. "I think we'll just heat a tin of soup for supper, hey?"

I nodded, the fullness of the afternoon quickly collapsing.

"Why don't you hop in the shower before dinner."

And with that, darkness folded itself over my day.

# CHAPTER TWELVE

## 1967

## Miriam

"Make a wish, Miriam," Mrs. Patel said, handing me a knife.

I held it over the tall pink cake, a number thirteen marked out in red glacé cherries and silver balls.

"Hurry up, slowcoach," Zelda teased. "How long is that wish of yours? It'll double as a Christmas cake if you take much longer!"

I laughed and sank the knife into the sponge. Almond cream bulged from the sides.

"Thank you for making my favorite cake, Mrs. Patel," I said, handing her the first piece.

She dipped her head in acknowledgment, then passed the plate on to Mr. Patel. "Too much for me."

We ate cake, sipped copious cups of iced tea, and shared riddles long into the afternoon. It was the best birthday ever.

Zelda and I were at different schools now—her parents

choosing an all-girls senior school in a somewhat futile bid to limit the distractions. As a result Zelda and I didn't see as much of each other as we once did, though I still visited frequently. And even if Zelda wasn't home, I often ended up chatting to Mrs. Patel for hours on end. She was a remarkable woman—a lighthouse in the fog that always seemed to surround me. All my insecurities magically evaporated whenever I was around her. Zelda was so lucky to have her as her mum.

"Miriam, I think it's time to officially make you an honorary member of our family," Mrs. Patel said, sweeping cake crumbs into her hand. "Remember the first time you visited? So shy and quiet."

"And look at her now," teased Mr. Patel. "Thirteen years old and nearly as cheeky as our Zelda."

I giggled.

"Doing something special tonight with the family?" he asked cautiously.

I looked down. "Rita and Michael might be taking me out for dinner. I'm not sure."

He flashed a brief smile, cut himself another slice of cake, then opened out the classifieds section of the newspaper.

I'd seen Mr. Patel do this so many times before, scanning the pages and circling advertisements with a red pen.

"Mr. Patel," I pried, "every afternoon you page through the classifieds. What are you looking for?"

"Well may you ask," Mrs. Patel interjected, skewing her eyebrows.

"May *I* answer?" he protested. "Women!" He shook his

head, then hoisted Navin onto his lap just in time to stop the wee boy from picking another cherry off the cake.

"Since your brother Naresh is no longer living at home, I'm relying on your support, young man." He tapped his small son's chest with his forefinger. "This house is steeped in estrogen. We have to stick together."

The little boy struggled to get off his father's lap.

"Now, if I can answer Miriam's question," Mr. Patel said slowly, throwing a mock scowl at his wife in anticipation of another interruption. "I trained as a mechanical engineer in India, and Rahini as a midwife. We came to this country eleven years ago, looking for a better life and greater opportunities for our children. We hoped to find jobs in our respective professions." His face darkened. "Sadly, this was not to be."

He moved over to his wife. "Out of necessity I became a taxi driver and my dearest Rahini . . . Well, you've done everything from being a janitor to working in a Launderette, haven't you?"

She shrugged in resignation.

"Just so long as you could be home by the time the kids got out of school." He held out a hand to her.

"But . . ." I was perplexed. "But why can't—"

"Sanjit still applies for jobs eleven years later," Mrs. Patel interrupted, her voice tremulous. "And with each rejection, another little piece of him dies."

"It's so unfair, Dad." Zelda sulked. "Just because you're—"

"What are you complaining about, young lady?" Mr. Patel said, swinging around. "Do you have a roof over your head? Go to the very best of schools? Is this home always filled with friends *and* the ever-comforting aroma of your mother's cooking? Hm?"

Mrs. Patel smiled.

"No guest visits without receiving a good dose of your mother's hospitality and a dash of Indian philosophy too. Am I right?"

"Okay, okay, Dad! Don't get carried away," Zelda protested. "This is Miriam's birthday. Remember? Time to get out of here," she cried, grabbing my arm.

I excused myself and we set off on our bikes for Curls department store.

There, Zelda treated me to my first ever manicure. She couldn't have one, though, because she'd chewed all her fingernails right down to the quick, and the manicurist said there was nothing she could do about that. My hands didn't look as if they belonged to me by the time the woman with mauve hair was done. I felt like a proper English lady. And afterward, even though I was still full from afternoon tea, we shared a double-thick lime milk shake, before heading our separate ways home.

I was about halfway home when the resistance in my pedals gave way and my feet started to spin furiously. My bike chain had slipped off its cogs. Not wanting to ruin my new nails by fiddling with a greasy chain, I decided to push my bike the rest of the way.

I'd had the best time ever, yet as I struggled uphill the warmth of afternoon started to leak out of my day. For some time now I'd been feeling a vague sense of disquiet. It was nothing I could articulate or define, but rather a peculiar, haunting awareness of something—a restlessness without clear shape or definition. And it seemed to plague me the most whenever I was alone and had time to ponder things.

As I pushed my bike up the street, a familiar circuit of dark thoughts slipped into my mind. *Thirteen years ago a woman gave birth to me. My mother. But she gave me away. Was I not good enough? Why didn't she want me?*

For almost seven years I'd forced these thoughts down, depriving them of oxygen and light. It had taken all my energy to keep them buried this way—existing only as a dull gnawing grayness. But then, as my body started to grow and change, and womanhood knocked at my door, questions—relentless questions—forced their way into my head. I tried to ignore them, tried to plug the holes, but they were insistent and soon became the backdrop of my every day.

I pushed my bike up the gravel path of our house. The place was in darkness; no one was home. I'd hoped Rita and Michael would have come back from work early on my birthday.

I was unlatching the back gate when, without warning, my morose thoughts and questions morphed into something more. I sucked in a stuttering breath. An image, which had been hiding in the dark room of my mind, was finally developed. And it didn't fit with what I'd always been told.

*She stands in front of the stove, her black frame erect and proud, wooden spoon poised over a battered preserving pan. She is completely still, seemingly mesmerized by the rise and fall of the sugary sea. It is a hot African morning and the air is thick with the sweet smell of fig jam.*

*Just when I think she'll never move again, she scoops up a spoonful of the scalding liquid and drops it onto a saucer, then, tilting and rotating the blob of gold, she checks for fine creases in the sample.*

*I cross my fingers, hopeful for one more saucer to lick before the golden sweetness is locked away in squat glass jars with shiny brass lids—treasure that will belong to someone else.*

*I can almost smell her—a comforting cocktail of Sunlight soap and wood smoke—and touch the beads of perspiration hiding in the creases behind her knees. Her laughter bursts into my head. Then I hear her call me—my name full and round in her mouth. Frustratingly, though, her face blurs under the pressure of my focus.*

I was confused. Had this picture simply grown out of longing? Out of a desperate wish to be wanted? Had I painted it to fulfill a fantasy?

But there was more. The corners of this beautiful snapshot were curling in and a darkness appeared to be growing like mold over the color.

I wheeled my bike around to the back of the house. The light was on in the shed. I could hear voices.

"How can you live with yourself? You *promised* to give it to her. She was the child's mother, for God's sake!"

"Don't lecture me with your high-and-mighty morals, Michael Steiner. And don't pretend you weren't in on it too. If you go giving it to her now, it'll just be more difficult. A nightmare, in fact. It's been no picnic to this point, I can tell you. Had I only known how hard it would be, I don't think I—"

"But *why* keep it hidden all these years?"

"How is it any different from everything else we've kept from her? You tell me! You didn't want to share her either."

"Is there nothing we can agree on, Rita?"

"How about you trying, just for once, to see it from my side. It's no wonder the kid doesn't like me, with you forever critical of what I do. I've never been good enough, have I?"

"Reet—"

"Anyway, next time don't go prying under my bed."

"I *wasn't* prying. I told you. I was looking for somewhere to hide her present. I can't live with myself, Rita. I promised Celia—"

"You promised *Celia*, did you? *Of course* you did!"

My bike fell to the ground with a clatter.

Michael flung open the shed door, outing me in a white shaft of light.

"Miriam!"

Behind him stood Rita, her face flushed, her eyes glistening with tears.

No one said anything.

Rita cleared her throat. "Miriam, Michael is taking you to dinner tonight. Sorry, but I have a talk to prepare."

"But, Reet, it's Miriam's birthday." His eyes implored her. "Your presentation isn't due till next week. Don't do this."

She pushed past him, past me, and headed for the house.

"Don't ignore your duty, Rita," he shouted after her. "Your responsibility to our child!"

She turned, her eyes ablaze. "*Our* child? Don't you dare talk to me about responsibility, Michael Steiner. You . . . you . . . *Her* bloody mother gave her away," she shouted, pointing a shaking finger at me.

Michael lunged at her, trying to put a hand over her mouth. I covered my ears and ran blindly into the night.


Several hours later, Michael and I sat opposite each other in a dimly lit Chinese restaurant. We were the only patrons in the forlorn room with red and orange lanterns drooping from the ceiling.

I looked down at the flat banana fritter in front of me. The fizzing sparkler in the middle of my melting ball of ice cream was listing to one side, silver sparks leaping from it like fleas into the night.

I turned and saw my reflection in the window—a skinny black girl illuminated intermittently by a flashing neon light— *The Golden Wok, The Golden Wok, The . . .* And as if hypnotized, I fell into a soothing state of numbness.

# CHAPTER THIRTEEN

## 1967

## Celia

At 10:40 A.M. an orange light flashed above the vacated counter. "Next!" A small voice, made bold by the microphone, boomed across the room. I hurried toward the light and the square black letters I knew by heart read *Bantu*.

Behind the glass division sat a tiny madam. She could have been no more than twenty years old, but her pale face was empty and her blue-ice eyes flat.

"*Ja?*"

"Thank you, Madam. I come for this."

I slid a hand into my bra and pulled out two yellowed sheets of paper, unfolding them carefully on the counter.

The white madam became impatient. "Here. Pass it under the glass."

I let go.

Her eyes moved quickly over Miriam's birth certificate and the letter the Madam had written with me seven years earlier.

"Mm-hm. Uh-huh. Yes. And?"

"I want to speak with my daughter. On this paper, you see, Madam, Miriam, she is my daughter."

"Not anymore," the madam said. "This says you gave her to a Mr. and Mrs. Steiner, who were going to live in England. She's theirs now."

That was not right. I had to explain. "*Hau*, no, Madam. They say to me they will bring her back and she will write me letters, but nothing."

"Look here . . . uh, Celia. According to this letter, you've signed away your rights to the child. It says you agreed to them adopting her in England. Is this your name? You put this cross here?"

I couldn't keep up with the madam's fast words as they spilled out of her thin, pink mouth.

"Is—this—your—name?" she repeated. "Celia Mphephu?"

"Yes." I smiled. We were getting somewhere. "Yes, this is my name."

"Then you have agreed. There is nothing more I can do."

*Nothing more I can do.* I understood those words.

"*Hau*, Madam. I am trying for so long. Six years. Please, you must help me—"

A loud buzzing noise rang out, interrupting us. I spun around, ready to run. It was either a bomb scare or a fire alarm. But no one was trying to escape the room. I turned back to the madam just in time to see her pushing my papers back through the small gap between us, then she pulled down the sliding glass partition with a loud clunk.

*"Koffie?"* I heard her say to the white master in the next booth, as she rolled her chair away from me and tottered toward a door at the back of the office. It was her coffee break.

My swollen feet throbbed and my tummy growled as I stood waiting for the pretty one to return. I had been up since four that morning and had caught three different buses to get to Pretoria, where all official matters were dealt with. My boss had agreed to give me the day off, so long as I worked Sunday instead. I was hungry, and the thought of coffee made my stomach call out, but I dared not leave the queue I'd been waiting in since before sunup.

At 11:00 A.M. the madam lifted the glass wall and sat down.

*"Ja?"* There was no recognition in her eyes.

I pushed Miriam's birth certificate back under the counter, uninvited.

"You? Still here! I thought I told you there's nothing I can do."

*"Asseblief, miessies.* Please. I love my daughter so bad. She needs her mummy."

"You should have thought about that before you gave her away," she said, refusing to pick up the document. Her blue eyes met mine. My heart looped inside my chest. For a moment we were just two women together in this world. Then she looked away.

"Please, Madam."

She sighed a sigh that said, *I'm not going to get rid of this girl so easily.*

The master in the next booth looked up, and she rolled her
pretty eyes at him. He laughed, commiserating with her over
their frustrating job. "Whites *adopting* a native," she said, lifting up the limp sheet of paper. The master's smile disappeared
and his top lip rolled back over his square white teeth.

"Look," she said, turning back to me. "Leave your details.
I'll see what I can find out. I doubt this is even a legal document.
What's your address?"

"Thank you. Thank you, Madam!"

Before I could give the answers she wanted, she realized it
was going to be quicker to get the information herself than wait
on my broken sentences. *"Dompas."* She stretched her arm under
the glass, opening and shutting her hand like a duck's mouth.

I fumbled for my passbook.

The madam scanned the pages. "You're working as an office
cleaner in Joburg?"

"Yes, Madam. Office cleaner. You can write me at my boss—
Master Nicholson. Nicholson Commercial Cleaners, P.O. Box
196, Johannesburg."

The woman scribbled the address down. "And your full
name and date of birth?"

"Celia Dembe Mphephu," I said, feeling important.

The white one continued to page through my passbook, preferring to trust the official print. Suddenly she stopped. "What's
this?"

I craned my neck. All I could make out was a meaningless
blur of print, stamps, and pen marks.

"You've been in jail?" she said, her small voice growing loud.

The big hall went quiet. People in other queues turned to see what the commotion was about.

My mouth felt dry. "Yes, Madam. But it is mistake. Big mistake."

The pretty one's cheeks had turned pink and her blue eyes were now almost all white, as if finally frozen over. She wasn't listening to my words.

I kept trying. "Six year ago I leave very bad job. The madam—a Portuguese madam—*hau*, she get too angry. She tell police I am a thief. But it is wrong. It is not true."

"Go! Don't waste my time."

I wanted to say more, but I couldn't; her words had winded me.

"See how long the queue is behind you? We have no time for *tsotsis*. Your daughter is better off without you. Now leave!"

Her words kept coming, exploding like bullets as they hit.

In a daze, I turned to walk away. My mind was tired and my desperation finally robbed of its power. Then I remembered Miriam's birth certificate. I swung around just in time to see the flimsy sheet shimmying off the counter and floating to the floor. The Bantu queue parted as I dived between bags and black legs and scrambled on all fours to retrieve the document. People looked on, my story distracting them from their own. Clutching the crumpled prize to my breast, I climbed slowly to my feet and, putting one foot in front of the other, crossed the wide-open space. The piece of paper in my hand was the only proof I had that thirteen years ago I had given birth to a baby girl. It was the only piece of Miriam I had left—all that stood between me and madness.

Above the hush of the room, I heard the master ask the one

with empty blue eyes out for a drink that evening. *"Drink vanaand?"*

I looked back.

The madam, her cheeks still an angry pink, smiled coyly. *"Ja, goed,"* she said, crumpling up the paper with my details.

I stumbled out of the building into the white afternoon light.

# CHAPTER FOURTEEN

## 1969

## Miriam

One Tuesday morning as I finished my breakfast and contemplated the prospect of double algebra, I became aware of a strange, warm sensation between my legs. Thinking I'd spilled some porridge, I looked down and saw a bright red stain on my seat. I was bleeding.

"Reet!" I called out, dashing into the hallway. Rita was just leaving for work. "Reet, something's wrong! I'm bleeding."

Already wrapped in her coat and scarf, she dropped her bag and, with a bemused expression, retraced her steps. I'd come to understand Rita didn't like surprises. Anything unexpected challenged the order and routine for which she perpetually strove. To Rita, life was either black *or* white; she detested the gray messiness of real living. Feelings frightened her. It was no wonder she and Michael clashed constantly. Dear, disheveled Michael. He embodied the very muddle of existence—the capriciousness of emotion, the color of chaos. Michael was all heart and humanity; Rita, all reason and logic, her career at least offering a comfortable corner on the edge of the bedlam. The labeled laboratory slides, obedient corpses, and microscope magnifications were predictable, manageable, nonjudgmental.

"Must be *the curse*," she said with a barking laugh. "No need for an ambulance, then."

I swallowed. "The curse?"

"You know . . . a woman's curse. Your monthly."

I knew a little about monthly periods, gleaned mostly from discarded snippets of schoolyard talk divulged in whispers and giggles. You could bleed to death if your period was heavy. If you kissed a boy while you were bleeding, you could have a baby. You could also get off PE if you brought a note from home.

"Hang on," Rita said, ducking into her bedroom and reemerging moments later with an opened packet in her hand. "There you go," she said, shoving it at me. "Now I'd better be on my way, or I'll be late. See you tonight."

"Okay."

I inspected the bulky parcel of maxi-sized sanitary pads. Inside were five rectangular wads of cotton wool with a loop at either end. A rip in the packet had obscured the diagram, but it appeared the pad attached to some sort of belt worn around the waist. I looked inside the packet. No belt.

The front door opened and Michael walked in with the newspaper. I shot into the bathroom and locked the door.

"Miriam, I'm just off now," he called out, his bright voice pushing into my loneliness. "See you tonight."

"See you," I said, trying to sound normal.

I'm not sure how long I sat there in the long, narrow room, leaning against the cold green tiles. My bottom was numb and my legs clumsy with pins and needles by the time I finally got up and headed for the Patels', where Mrs Patel demystified menstruation for me over chapatis, sweet tea and tears, and a loaned sanitary belt.

"Wait," she said after our long chat, disappearing into her bedroom. I half expected to see her emerge bearing a pack of pads. Instead, she was holding a small velvet box, which she put down on the table in front of me.

"This is for you, my dear, to celebrate your entrance into womanhood."

I didn't know what to say. This whole womanhood thing didn't seem like something I wanted to celebrate.

"Open it," she said encouragingly, pushing it closer. "It's a present."

I picked it up. The box felt so light I thought it was empty, but as I turned it over, something inside clinked. I fingered the corners where the smooth navy velvet had been worn away to expose gray card, then I lifted the lid. Inside, lying within a nest of coils, was a rose-gold locket.

"Mrs Patel, it's beautiful!"

"It was my mother's," she said, touching my arm. "She was a fine woman, just like you."

It was the most beautiful thing anyone had ever given me.

"But—but it's yours," I stuttered. "Your mother's. I can't keep it."

Mrs Patel dispensed with my protestations with a wave of her hand.

I opened the locket. It unfolded into two perfect ovals.

"Maybe someday you'll put a photo inside of someone special," she said, choking up with tears. Everything blurred. "Come now, aren't we a right pair!" she said, passing me a tissue. "No more tears. I want to see it around your lovely young neck." She shot a dissatisfied glance in the mirror. "Not my old, crepey one."

The locket was still warm from her touch as it settled in the gap between my collarbones.

"Thank you, Mrs Patel."

"And, while we're immersed in women's business," she said, "I think it's time we bought you your own bra, young lady. Definitely overdue." And with that, we headed into town.

I didn't go to school after our shopping expedition. Instead, self-consciously wearing my first bra, I wandered down to the local library. It was still my favorite haunt whenever the real world came at me too fast. This time, though, instead of losing myself in the world of fiction, I sought out something different.

As I skimmed over the myriad titles, a brightly colored spine caught my eye. I eased the big book off the shelf and sat down with it at one of the desks. On the dust jacket was a striking photograph of a lone African hut, its clay walls painted in bold geometrical designs. Inside were many more photographs.

I flicked through the pages, bewitched by the landscape of wide-open spaces, vibrant color, and a rust-red earth. Toward the end of the book I came upon a chapter entitled "Initiation." It was then I began to read. And soon I was standing on an open plain—a young African girl who had just begun to menstruate.

*Her tribal initiation must occur before she has her first sexual encounter or she risks being shunned forever.*

*It is full moon. Under the watchful eye of her mother, the young girl's clothes are removed and all her body hair shaved— even her eyebrows. Only women surround her, all contact with men and boys forbidden. She and the other initiates and their mentors dance around a fire. Then the girl is led down to a stream to be cleansed, after which she is taken to a hut built especially for her. There she will spend up to three months isolated from the outside world. Her only contact will be with her mother and other senior women, who will instruct her in tribal tradition and the skills required to become a proficient homemaker.*

*At the end of this time the mother gives her daughter a beautiful beaded apron she has made and a feast is held to celebrate the initiate's transition from girl to woman. During the festivities she is introduced to eligible young men sanctioned by the tribe. The clothes she has worn during the long period of guidance are now cast aside and burned, for she is leaving behind her childhood to embrace a new life as a woman.*

I closed the book, my hands trembling, and carefully replaced it on the shelf, hiding it behind another big book; I needed to be able to find it again. Then I wandered out into the dreary English afternoon.

The next morning I spent in the school sick bay with period cramps. After lunch I managed to persuade the nurse to let me walk home. She wanted to ring my parents, but I was adamant it wasn't necessary; I was fifteen. Anyway, Michael was in Cambridge for the day and Rita didn't take kindly to being interrupted at work.

The day was a cheerless gray, the promise of winter seeping in around the edges. I stopped at Boots to buy some aspirin, then meandered on home, taking a shortcut through the park. The playground was deserted except for an empty crisp packet that the wind was toying with, sweeping it up and then dragging it down. The seesaw, jungle gym, and patches of worn grass looked all the more wretched for the absence of children.

At home, I put my key in the lock, but it refused to turn. I fiddled with it, wriggled it, tried to force it . . . Still it wouldn't budge. Finally, in frustration I banged my fist against the door and, to my astonishment, the front door swung open. It had been unlocked all this time.

I had been the last one to leave home that morning. I knew Rita would be furious if she found out I'd left the house unlocked, especially since there'd been a recent spate of burglaries in the area. I looked around. Everything seemed in order, so I dropped my bags at the foot of the stairs and headed for the kitchen to make myself a warm drink.

As I grabbed the kettle to fill it up, scalding water splashed out of the spout onto my hand. I ran to the sink and shoved my smarting fingers under the tap, the cold water quickly soothing the pain. However, something was bothering me more than the discomfort I still felt. The kettle. It was hot.

I turned off the tap. That was when I heard voices, upstairs.

Tiptoeing to the phone, I lifted the receiver, then put it down again. If the police came, Rita would find out I'd been the one to leave the house open. Perhaps if I scared the intruders away . . .

Arming myself with a broom from the laundry cupboard, I crept cautiously up the stairs. The light was on in Rita's bedroom and the door ajar. From inside came the sound of groans.

"Reet? Reet, is that you?" I whispered.

Silence.

"Rita?"

I pushed tentatively on the door, my broomstick positioned like a javelin.

Rita was lying on the bed naked. A kaleidoscope of images flashed before me—purple disks of nipple, a mound of fuzzy pubic hair, a man's balding head, sagging buttocks astride . . .

Two heads turned, Rita's face red, and another—not Michael's.

"Get out!" Rita's words charged through my surprise.

I couldn't move, my limbs unhinged from my body.

"Now!" she shouted.

I strained to free myself. Then, like a robot suddenly switched on, I turned and broke into a shambling run. I careered into the corridor, down the stairs, and out the front door, running and running until my lungs threatened to explode. And by the time I burst into the Patels' kitchen, my legs, my chest, my heart—all were screaming in pain.

# CHAPTER FIFTEEN

## 1971

## Miriam

"Come on, babe. If you love me you'll do it."

It was almost two years since my body had ushered me into womanhood; yet as I sat hunched up in the front seat of the dilapidated orange Ford Escort, I still felt very much a child. It was black outside and raining. The boy sitting next to me, in the driver's seat, was a pale and gangly guy with a bad case of acne and lank, brassy-yellow hair, which fell limply to his shoulders. One of his hands clasped my leg; the other stroked my neck with some urgency.

*If you love me* . . . Love. So appealing. So elusive.

He'd left the engine running to keep the heater on, and the windscreen wipers swooshed from side to side, erasing the fine web of raindrops on the glass and lulling me into a sort of stupor. The car was parked absently across the entrance to a dark alleyway at the back of Woolworths, and a security light flicked on and off in the unsettled weather, intermittently lighting up the inside of the car with unforgiving white light. At least it bleached my brown skin.

"Come on, sweetie," he urged with more than a hint of impatience. "I'll love you even more. It's not good to keep a guy waiting . . ."

His hand pushed uninvited under my denim skirt, his skin dry and rough, his fingers hot against my coldness. There was a gap between my thin, boyish legs, making it easy for him to reach between my thighs.

I'd show them. I'd find my own love.

Right, left, right, left. The wipers continued, hypnotically.

The boy's fingers were forging a groove in my underwear. I started at his boldness, but made no protest as they slipped under the elastic of my panties and started probing, tentatively at first, then more brazenly. Black girl. White boy. See, I *was* somebody.

"You're one seriously hot chick," he huffed, his breath hot and rancid. He pulled at my knickers.

Right, left, right, left. A leaf was trapped in the wipers' clutches.

His hands squeezed my breasts, then he was unhooking my bra. The smell of stale beer filled my nostrils. I couldn't make out the letters on the delivery truck parked in front.

"Let's get in the back. More room," he gasped.

So we tumbled into the backseat, buttons tearing away, seat squealing, the boy grunting. My head was wedged up against the armrest as he clambered on top of me. I couldn't see the wipers any longer, just the torn mustard upholstery of the seat in front and the stained ceiling.

He pushed open my legs and shoved himself inside. The pain was like a razor blade tunneling its way to my throat. I cried out, but I was drowned out by the boy's moans. By now the windscreen wipers were screaming. It had stopped raining and the screen was dry, no longer lubricated by falling water.

"Shit, doll, you're one hot chocolate—and a virgin. Far out!"

He lay on top of me, heavy as a sack of coal. I thought I was going to suffocate. At last he slipped out of me and sat up. A strange smell of body, intermingled with beer and pie, filled the car. As he stumbled out to have a pee, cold wet air rushed in, diluting the musty baseness of what had just happened. I sat up and inhaled, hungry for its freshness.

We drove home in silence, the boy taking a long way around through his housing estate, past rows of rigid chimneys poking through semidetached brick boxes, past car wrecks and graffiti, burglar bars and vandalized bus stops, past a pack of kids slinking through the shadows. The boy was already looking for his next thrill; the night was still young.

It was wet and sticky between my legs.

He switched on the radio and "In the Summertime" crackled in the background. He fiddled with the dials as he tried unsuccessfully to get better reception, but even the static was better than the awkward silence.

The scenery changed abruptly as we pulled into my suburb, the battered orange Escort jarring with its new surrounds— stately chestnut trees and manicured hedgerows, bay windows and brass knockers, Volvos, Triumphs, and Rovers. This had been my haunt for so long, yet the familiar served only to heighten the alienation I now felt. Somehow the grunge of council housing was more real, more honest. This affluence was a pretense of perfection. Hidden behind the plastered walls and sandstone pavers were pockets of rot and decay.

As we drew up outside my house, I looked up at Rita's window. Her light was still on.

"I'd better be going," I said, my limbs suddenly heavy.

"Yeah. Hey, thanks, doll. You were great. I'll call ya."

"Yeah."

As I hurried up the path I turned to wave, but the orange Escort was already halfway up the road, disappearing into the wet night.

I slipped inside, closed the front door quietly behind me, and stood for a moment in the silence of the entrance hall, beside the cowhide drums grouped incongruously beneath Monet and Degas prints. The walls started to close in on me. Faces grimaced, beadwork distorted, and masks moved. The absurd mix of African and European art was mocking me, shouting out my own confusion.

I crept upstairs.

"Miriam, is that you?"

It was almost a relief to hear Rita's voice split the silence.

"Yes."

"Come here," she commanded.

I moved down the dark corridor toward the bright rectangle of light skewed across the passage wall. Rita was sitting up in bed surrounded by a pile of textbooks and hospital reports.

As I walked in, she peered over her half-moon glasses.

"Did we or did we not agree nine o'clock was your curfew during the week?"

I stared blankly ahead. "Forgot the time."

"Well, that's not good enough." Her voice started to rise. "I'm sick and tired of your disobedience. Your surly manner, your ingratitude, and your flagrant disregard for the rules of this house! Sometimes I—" She stopped in midsentence.

"Say it, then. Why don't you say it?" I shouted. "You wish you'd never adopted me! Well, I wish you hadn't either! I wish you'd left me in Africa where I belong, you cheating, unfaithful—"

Rita's eyes widened and her mouth opened.

I felt a hand on my shoulder and swung around. Michael's eyes and mine collided—his, sad and weary. "Come now, my girl. It's late and you have school in the morning. Off to bed." And he ushered me from the room.

Later, in the empty hours of dawn, I stood under the shower as the warm water mixed with my tears. I scrubbed and scrubbed my thin, brown body, but I couldn't wash away my color, or the awful smell of the boy.

The waiting room was crowded and stuffy, and the windows had fogged up, clouding my view of the bleak afternoon outside. Despite the bright yellow No Smoking sign pinned to the door, the air was laced with old cigarette smoke, which had hitched a ride inside on coats, jumpers, and tepid breath.

The low background chatter was intermittently punctuated by the receptionist's efficient voice. "Family Planning. How may I help?"

My innards tensed, threatening to hurl what could only be bile; I hadn't eaten all day. I lowered my head between my knees, pretending to look at something on the sole of my shoe.

"Helen James?" A stocky, red-faced nurse with a warm voice put her head around the door and scanned the room.

A girl across from me stood up. She had Swedish-blond hair, which fell to a blunt end halfway down her back. Even in my bilious state I managed to envy her long, fair hair.

She was wearing faded black stovepipes, which accentuated her anorexic frame, and a loose black jumper with the words *Dream On* stitched across the front. Rings of kohl encircled her eyes and a row of silver studs marched up her right earlobe. Another girl with a nose piercing stood up too.

"Come through," the nurse said, leading them both down a corridor.

I grabbed a crumpled magazine from the pile beside me and paged absently through it. It was out of date, with pages ripped out. The print started to flicker. I opened my eyes wider, trying to halt the swarm of black dots invading the page. Then the room started to list. I was going to be sick. I had to get out. I stood up, grabbing at the chair next to me. It wobbled and . . .

"Catch her," I heard someone shout.

Then blackness.

"Ms. Steiner. Ms. Steiner?"

I struggled to focus, my mind searching for a mooring. There was a pendulum swinging in front of me—a red stethoscope dangling from a woman's pale, puffy neck.

Her face came into view, receded, then reappeared. Large maroon glasses dominated her face, which, aside from a smudge of bronze lipstick, was devoid of makeup.

"Where am I?" I asked, trying to sit up.

"Slowly, Ms. Steiner. You've just fainted."

The mature face was reassuring.

"Rest there a while. You've got a lump the size of a golf ball on the back of your head."

Immediately my head ached. I still couldn't work out where I was. Panic started to take hold as I floated outside any recognizable reality.

"You're at Family Planning. Remember?"

Oh.

Oh yes.

I preferred the oblivion.

"Here, sit up slowly and have a sip of sugar water." It was the stocky nurse.

I swallowed a mouthful, my teeth aching at the icy shock.

She wrapped a cuff around my arm and inflated it. My fingers began to tingle, but just before real discomfort set in, she opened a valve and the air rushed out again. "Ninety-eight over fifty-six."

"Thanks, Joan. I think we'll be fine from here."

A different voice. I'd forgotten about the woman with glasses and a red stethoscope. She passed me an ice pack. "Hold this on that bump for as long as you can tolerate. It'll reduce the swelling," she said, helping me to my feet and sitting me down beside a cluttered desk.

The room was vast and airy, with a generous bay window overlooking a small, treed courtyard. My throbbing thoughts seeped into this pleasant space.

"I'm Dr. Pepall." The woman's voice was steady and kind. "You gave us quite a fright, collapsing like that. How are you feeling?"

I nodded sluggishly. "My head hurts."

"Yes, you've got an impressive lump. Do you still feel up to a consultation today, or would you prefer to reschedule?"

"No, no, I'm fine."

"Well, let's *take two*, then," she said, settling back in her large leather armchair.

I shifted in my seat, looked out of the window, stared up at the ceiling, then down at my feet.

"How can I be of help, Ms. Steiner?" the doctor said, gently persistent.

Where would I begin? The fainting had only delayed things. A temporary escape. Now I was supposed to divulge my secret to a stranger. Tell her about the thing that consumed my every waking hour and fractured my long, sweat-drenched nights? This first meeting had begun on the floor. How could I regain my composure and say what I had to in the way I'd practiced in the mirror over and over again? I could feel tears gathering, my emotions enlisting the troops.

Then it all burst out. Everything. Rita cheating on Michael. She wasn't even my biological mother. My real mother had given me away. I couldn't really remember her. Not her face. The boy in the orange Escort said he loved me, but never called again. He was white. A *white* boy had asked *me* out on a date. White boy, black girl. Woohoo! I hated being black. I hated it. Black. Black. Black.

It all poured out . . . but only in tears. There were no words.

"What is it? Try to tell me, Ms. Steiner."

That question again. Finally three words broke through and the whisper of them was more frightening than the noise they made inside my head.

"I'm pregnant."

She nodded.

Had she heard what I'd just said?

"I'm pregnant," I said, louder, "and I can't keep the baby."

It was 4:30 P.M. and already dark by the time I emerged from the consulting room with the bay window and cluttered desk. In my hand were several forms.

Dr. Pepall rested a warm hand on my arm. "I'll see you back at the clinic on Friday after the scan."

I didn't want to leave this room and walk out into the cold, blustery world. I wanted more of the doctor's warmth. I wanted this kindly woman to tuck me up in bed, stroke my head, and read me a story. I wanted her to turn out the light.

"Susan Parker. Come through, please."

The next patient was already making her way down the corridor.

I had owned my secret for eleven weeks when the doctors at the clinic relieved me of the burden of motherhood and scraped a baby from my womb.

## Celia

"Ma! It's me! Open the door."

I was awake, my heart running, my breath jumping. My eyes were open, but I could see nothing. Then shadows started to own their shapes and sounds of the night identify themselves—the traffic that never slept, my clock counting out the hours, a barking dog, the drill of a mosquito . . .

Peering at the luminous red numbers, I saw it was 2:17 A.M. and thought I must have been woken by *that* dream again—the one in which Miriam was calling for me. I hadn't dreamed it in such a long time. I turned over, pulling the blanket with me.

"Ma! Wake up, Ma!"

In an instant I had thrown back the bedclothes and was standing beside my bed, swinging somewhere between sleep and wakefulness. Miriam was at my door! I stumbled over and grasped the key in my cold, stiff fingers. I'd been renting this room for just a few weeks. How had she found me? The rusty hinges screamed and I peered into the darkness.

"Christian!"

My eldest son glanced over his shoulder, then slipped quickly past me into my room.

I shut the door behind him and turned on the light, wincing at its neon brightness.

"Lock it," he said, peeling off his jacket. He was wearing a faded yellow T-shirt with a clenched black fist driving out of it. My skin prickled. He was wearing the clothes of a revolutionary.

Ripped from my dreams, I felt disorientated, confused. I had heard Miriam calling for me, but now Christian was standing there, defiance on his chest, fear in his eyes.

"What's wrong? Why are you here?"

In the few months since I'd last seen him, his face had lost its boyishness, hardening into fixed angles and hungry hollows. The rest of his body had changed too, his skin stretching over the peaks of bone and troughs of absent flesh.

"Are you in trouble?"

His face broke into a wide grin, those dimples I'd always loved creasing his sunken cheeks and melting his seriousness. He pulled me into a bony hug. For an instant I resisted. If I brushed against his shirt would I be infected by its insolence? I sank my face into his neck and inhaled the smell of my son, now all man. As I held on to him, I could feel his heartbeat through his shirt and it told a different tale to his casual grin.

"Can we have some tea?" he asked, pulling closed a gap in my curtains.

Minutes later Christian sat stooped over his steaming mug,

greedy for its warmth. I wasn't sure if it was just the cold making his hands tremble. "Put your jacket on if you're cold. Are you sick?"

He stared into his mug, as if reading his future.

Dear Christian. He had always been my earnest one, shouldering the responsibility that came with being firstborn and catapulted to the head of the family when his father abandoned us. I had tried not to lean too heavily on him, but after my own mother became ill, I had been forced to rely on him more and more. At the age of fourteen he'd had to leapfrog over the remainder of his childhood to raise his younger siblings and keep house. He had not let me down.

However, he had always harbored greater dreams. For as long as I could remember, Christian had wanted to be a doctor. My mother would tell me how he used to follow the rural nurse around on her visits, helping clean stinking wounds, immunize crying children, and teach proper hygiene to his people. Over time the village children started calling him "Dok Dok," and the elders often sought his advice before traveling the long road to see the proper *dokotela*.

Neither my mother nor I could discourage him from this path, even though we both tried. I knew the disappointment that would one day be his, when he grew to understand the implications of his color.

But Christian was like an iron rod that would not bend, and despite the many demands I placed on him to collect water, repair the house, tend to his ailing *makhulu*, feed his brothers, sow the seeds, and harvest the *mielies*, he continued to work hard at school and study long into every night.

Finally, with *Mudedekadzi* Mafela's help, and without my knowledge, he'd sent an application to the University of Natal in Durban—the only place where as a black man he could study to be a doctor. When I found out my son had been allowed entry into this important school of learning, I was giddy with pride and fear. Christian was traveling far beyond where my own journey had ended, and I could offer him little advice.

"Ma, I have to go away for a while," he said, his teeth chattering in his head.

"What do you mean? What about your lessons? What is it, boy?"

His face contorted. "Ma, the police are after me."

The police. Those two words never traveled alone, terror and dread their constant companions. Christian had always tried to protect me from worry, but this night he offered little to ease my mind. "Is it your pass?" I asked, although I already knew the picture on his T-shirt held the answer to my question.

His eyes shifted nervously about the room. "The security police," he whispered.

The words landed like a dead body in the middle of the room. I froze.

He grabbed my hand. "Ma, don't worry. I'll be all right. I've just got to—"

"You haven't done anything wrong, have you?"

He looked at me, my young son, his face strong and still. His eyes, however, were not as successful at hiding what was in his heart. I saw fear and I saw something else—pride. Pride in himself and his people, shooting like new growth from a sleeping tree. It scared me.

"Ma, I must do this for you, for me, for every black man. What about Biko? Hector Pieterson? Should their deaths mean nothing?"

"Do what, son? What have you been doing?"

He did not answer.

My begging became more desperate. "Christian, I cannot lose you, my boy. I have lost one child already. What about your studies? You are going to become a doctor."

He pulled away. "What good is the qualification if I am considered inferior by white patients? If I am not permitted to attend the delivery of a white woman's baby because I will see her genitals?"

My earnest and obedient boy had changed since he had gone to university. New and dangerous thoughts filled his head. He took a mouthful of tea.

I slumped back in my chair and covered my mouth with my hands. I was about to lose a second child. Like Miriam, Christian had simply been lent to me.

"Ma, I don't have much time." He stood up and put on his jacket. "If they come looking for me, you know *nothing*."

My mind was searching for a solution. I could hide him under the bed; I could disguise him; I—

"You have not seen me for many months, do you understand?"

"But . . ." It was pointless. "Where will you go?"

Tears tracked across his large brown eyes. "The less I tell you, the better."

His tears brought mine—furious and silent.

"I'm sorry, Ma." He kissed my forehead. "*Ndi a ni funa.* I love you."

I grabbed his big, cold hands and kissed them over and over again, clinging on to him for as long as I could. Then he was gently pulling away.

The key turned in the lock, the door screamed open, and he was gone, melting into the darkness.

# CHAPTER SEVENTEEN

### 1977

## Miriam

"That'll be seven pounds and five pence. Would you like the cold items wrapped?"

The woman shook her head and handed me a ten-pound note. "Not to worry. I'm headed straight home."

A queue was gathering behind her. Juliet, the other checkout operator, was still on morning tea and my till was the only operational one. I hated the pressure of a queue.

"Darn, I've forgotten the coriander!" It was the Indian guy next in line.

I handed the woman her change and flicked the conveyer belt switch, bringing forward the next mound of groceries.

"Mind if I grab some?" he asked. "If I go home without coriander my mum will freak out. She's making a special meal. A celebration." He flashed a broad smile. "Coriander is the vital—" He stopped in midsentence. "Miriam? Miriam Steiner, is that you? My god, it is!"

I looked at the customer's face properly for the first time. It was Naresh, Zelda's brother.

"Hi," I said, wishing it wasn't him.

"Long time no see!"

I flashed a quick smile.

Naresh's eyes were wide with excitement. "I think the last time I saw you was at Zelda's eighteenth birthday. That's almost five years ago."

I started to ring up his groceries.

"So how you been? What's going down in your neck of the woods?"

I shrugged. "Oh, you know."

The queue behind Naresh was growing. I didn't need this. I just wanted the day to remain uneventful, generic—a steady, uninterrupted march toward five o'clock.

"Are you at uni?"

I shook my head. "Nah. I'm working here full-time."

"Full-time?" he repeated, clearly surprised. "Hey listen, Zelda's up from Bedford for the long weekend. Come around. Mum and Dad would love to see you."

*No. Leave me be.*

"Um, I'm not sure. I'm working late tonight and—"

"Zelda will have my guts for garters if she finds out I've seen you and didn't get all the goss! What time's your lunch break?" he persisted, undeterred.

I shot a glance at the clock on the back wall. "In about an hour. Around midday."

"Let's grab a beer across the road then."

My boss put his head out of his glass booth where he sat most of the day reading girlie magazines. He hated it when staff spent time talking to friends.

"Okay." Anything to get rid of Naresh. "Better find that coriander," I said, tilting my head at the lengthening line of people behind him.

When I next saw him, Naresh was sitting at a table in the blue winter sunshine, amber pint in hand. I crossed the road and wandered over. He leapt up, greeted me with a kiss on each cheek, and enveloped me in a hug. I pulled away.

"What can I get you? An ale? A cider?"

"I'm not allowed to drink during work hours," I said. "But an orange juice would be good."

Naresh cast around, hoping to catch a waitress's eye, but instead found himself face-to-face with a broad-shouldered, bearded guy dressed in a chunky Aran-knit jumper and baggy khaki trousers.

"Blast from the past! If it isn't Dave Bloomfield," Naresh exclaimed, laughing the same throaty laugh I'd known so well from years of his tricks and teases. "Today is definitely a day for bumping into old friends."

Dave Bloomfield had an open face, long wheaten-colored hair bunched loosely into an elastic band, and a dark brown beard. Around his wrists hung a jangle of copper and twisted twine. He slapped Naresh on the back, then spotted me and peaked his wild eyebrows by way of greeting.

"Naresh Patel, good to see you, mate. You on midterm break?"

"That I am. Why don't you join us? This is Miriam, an old friend of my sister's whom I also haven't seen in ages."

The guy put out his hand. His grip was strong and determined, his warmth spilling onto me. "Hey!"

My mind went blank.

The arrival of a waitress lanced an awkward pause. She took Dave's order, then turned to me. "And you?" she said dismissively.

I retreated into my chair. "Orange, please."

"Juice? Cordial? Irn-Bru? Big, small? What?"

"Jui—"

"Excuse me." Dave stood up. "I'm not thirsty anymore."

Naresh took the cue and slapped the coins for his beer on the table.

My mind started to spin. Naresh and David were already standing. Clumsily I pushed back my chair and made to leave. The waitress shrugged and walked off.

As the three of us made to cross the road to the park opposite, I struggled to understand what had just happened. Had Naresh and his friend taken a stand against the waitress's rudeness toward me? Surely I'd got it wrong. Discourtesy was so commonplace, I barely noticed it anymore. I'd come to accept being treated differently. After all, I *was* different. I was black.

Dave stepped off the curb. "Jeez, sorry about that, Miriam." He'd remembered my name.

So, it *was* true. No one had ever stood up for me in public before. It was a heady feeling. I floated over the road.

Naresh bought us each a cool drink at the corner store, then we found a shady spot under a giant poplar and sat down on the grass. Naresh and his friend did most of the talking, which I was grateful for, and nothing more was said of the incident at the pub—also a relief.

I was captivated by Dave Bloomfield—this guy with big hands and gray-green eyes. He was quietly self-assured, interesting and interested . . . He'd awakened something inside of me.

It felt as though the end of my lunch break arrived before it had even begun, and I reluctantly took my leave, but not before Naresh had extracted a promise from me to visit his family the following day.

Zelda sat cross-legged on her bed. Her hair had been cut into a short bob and her lanky body had filled out, but otherwise she was still the same ebullient Zelda I remembered. The difference was that now her spark and cheeriness, which had first drawn me to her, irritated me.

I perched on the edge of her desk in a room as familiar as my own. Snoopy and Scooby-Doo still slouched in the corner, and the same lime-green bedspread covered her bed. The pine desk was there too—pushed up against the wall—equations and doodles etched into the wood, and the blackened bunch of roses from her school dance was still suspended from the ceiling.

The physical familiarity remained, yet everything else about our friendship felt different. Once we'd been as close as sisters, but now our conversation stumbled along the edges of a rift that had opened up between us.

I knew exactly the day the decay had set in—the day I'd

discovered I was pregnant. I'd shut everyone out, including Zelda. Our relationship did manage to hobble along for a time after that, but eventually petered out.

"Cigarette?" She held up a packet of Peter Stuyvesants, her eyes glinting like a naughty schoolgirl's. I'd never seen her smoke before.

"It's okay," she reassured me, flinging open a window. "Mum's out all afternoon. Just need to keep the air circulating."

I took a cigarette and leaned forward, letting her light it for me. This was as close as we'd come in five years. It felt good—holding the cigarette. Something to do with my hands. I inhaled and soon the nicotine was working its calming ways, thawing my unease.

"Working full-time at a grocery store?" she said incredulously. "I just don't understand. You were the one who was going to be a psychologist. *I* was the one just wanting to fool around till I landed some gorgeous hunk, got married, and had hundreds of kids."

"Well, at least you filled your end of the bargain," I flashed. "Training to be a teacher—you'll be surrounded by kids all day."

"But don't you want more?" she persisted. "I mean, you can't work as a cashier all your life, not with that brain on your shoulders."

"I need the money. I'm not living at home."

"Oh. I didn't know." She looked hurt, perhaps by my tone and the fact that she was no longer privy to what went on in my life.

"Yeah, I left at the end of last year. I'm staying in a studio on Beaconsfield Road."

She nodded. "So won't Rita and Michael pay for you to go to university?"

"I don't want their money," I said, spitting out the words. I could hear the hardness in my voice, as if it didn't belong to me. "I'm a failed experiment. They thought I'd study at some prestigious college and do them proud." I tossed back my head. "Maybe even give them a few grandchildren—a few little brown babies to continue the Steiner lineage."

Zelda leaned forward and touched my arm. "Hey, where's my old friend gone? You were never so cynical."

I pulled away.

She grabbed my hand back. "Don't shut me out, Miriam. Remember me, your crazy friend?"

I stood up. It was time to leave.

As I turned, something on Zelda's bookshelf caught my eye. Propped against a yellow vase was a photograph of a little girl with a mass of tightly wound auburn curls and deep, delicious dimples. She looked about six years old. *You ar the best teecha in the hole werld, mis patel* was scrawled in crayon at the bottom of the picture.

I picked it up.

"One of the kids from my first teaching prac," she said, coming up behind me.

I put the photograph down and quickly wiped away a tear.

Feeling Zelda's hand on my shoulder I tensed, trying to shrug it off, but she swung me around to face her. I was so close I could see the tiny pores in her flawless complexion and smell her cigarette breath. Then the scaffolding I'd so carefully constructed around me began to collapse.

We spoke late into the day, leaving a bin full of used tissues and an empty pack of cigarettes in our wake. I told Zelda my story and she listened as I filled in the gaps that had almost toppled our friendship.

"When I was seventeen I had an abortion."

"What?"

"The weeks leading up to it were terrible. I couldn't tell anyone, not even you or your mum. She would have been so disappointed in me." I cleared my throat. "I was terrified someone would find out. If the school discovered, I'd have been expelled." I felt the twisting knot of apprehension all over again. "Anyway, after it was all dealt with, it was good for a while. Just an incredible relief to have it sorted." I picked up the picture of Zelda's little pupil again and fingered the edges of the frame. "But then they started haunting me—nightmares, about the baby." I closed my eyes, the darkness behind my lids offering no reprieve.

"I saw her eyes everywhere—my daughter's eyes. In every kid's face I saw my own child interrogating me. *Why, Mama? Why?*"

"God, Miriam, I wish you'd told me," Zelda said, running a hand through her hair.

"She'd be six by now," I went on. "I know it was a girl. I just do. Now I can't get her out of my mind. My unborn daughter is everywhere. I see her in every child and wonder if that's what she would have looked like, been like, smelled like . . ."

I tried to laugh, but it came out sounding false and bitter. "Maybe that's why my own mother didn't abort me. To avoid the *what-if* curse. Not that she knows anything about me. I may as well have been the spirit of an aborted kid surfing the underworld for all she cared."

Zelda listened, and although she said nothing, I could feel her lifting off the load I'd carried around for so long.

"Sometimes it gets so black, Zel, I just want to end it all. Join my baby. Tell her I love her. Because I do. I did." I was rambling, my words spilling out in a dizzy jumble. "What's the point of going to university and training to help other people when my own life is so stuffed up? What a joke! What do I know anyway? I threw away my only chance at love."

Outside, the wind was toying with the washing on the line, punching pregnant bulges in the sheets, then sucking them flat.

"Rita had an affair. And poor pathetic Michael, he knew . . . yet still he hangs on. I don't know why. It's tragic. She treats him like dirt, as if he's black or something. Shit, I hate being black. I hate it, Zelda. I hate it!"

She put a slim finger to her lips. "Shhh, I'm going to get you help. I promise."

Bizarrely, it was the sight of her gnawed fingernail that finally triggered my tears. Perhaps it was the wonderful familiarity and constancy of it—Zelda had been chewing her nails for as long as I could remember. Some things never changed.

"I'm glad you came today," she said. "I thought I'd lost you forever."

Later, as I wandered down the Patels' driveway, I heard someone call my name. I looked around.

"Hi again." It was the Aran jumper guy—Naresh's friend. The one from the pub.

He touched my elbow in greeting. My whole body tingled.

"We must stop meeting like this," he said with a deep, playful laugh. "Been visiting the Patels?"

I nodded.

"You headed back into town?"

I nodded again.

"Hang fire a minute," he said. "Just got to drop off a fiver Naresh lent me yesterday, then I can walk with you."

"Okay."

I stood in the purple dusk waiting for Dave Bloomfield to return. A breeze blew across my face and I breathed it in, savoring its cool embrace.

# CHAPTER EIGHTEEN

## January 1978

## Celia

I could not make out the faces in front of me. They had melted like butter against the glare of the naked light bulb. Even the shouting voices had grown indistinct and muffled. I let my head fall onto my bare chest, and my eyes closed. I could not keep them open any longer. I wanted to sleep. Nothing else mattered. The scalding pain in my vagina had dulled to a throbbing ache; the boiling water they'd forced inside me had long since trickled out. Even the blood from my left ear had dried to a crusty black ribbon.

I slumped there, no longer ashamed of my nakedness. My bruised breasts did not belong to me. I had no tears left to cry, nor words to speak. Sleep was taking over—the blissful blanket of darkness, which had been kept from me for so long.

The heavy metal cell door slammed shut.

I hauled up my head and scanned the room through the slit

of my right eye. So there was still some residue of fear inside me after all, still a speck of will to survive.

I braced for more blows.

None came. The square of room was empty.

I lapped it again with my good eye.

No one. They had left. With nothing.

*I am not knowing where Christian is or who his friends are, Master. No, I never know he is part of the ANC. Yes, baas, I understand it is banned. Communist. Bad. Very bad. Yes. I have not seen my son for many month. I believe he is at the medical university studying to be a doctor. Aikona, baas! I am knowing nothing more. Please, baas. It is true. You must believe it.*

I slid off the chair onto the concrete floor and into a pool of my own filth, and there I fell into a sleep that took me closer to death than life. In this darkness I dreamed a dream, a happy dream that took me, Miriam, her brothers, and even Patrick, my husband, back to the beginning.

*We are holding hands in a field of golden grass beneath an endless blue sky. Michael Steiner is there too, in the shade of an old thorn tree. And though he stands apart from us, his brow is smooth and his eyes are smiling.*

Some hours later I was awakened, feverish and shaking, and flung out into the day like a discarded piece of rubbish. I was of no use to anyone, least of all the big men at John Vorster Square—the notorious security police headquarters.

With not enough money in my purse to pay for a taxi fare, I stumbled down the dirty Johannesburg streets. People stared. Others rushed on—high-heeled shoes, business suits, and shopping bags giving me a wide berth. It was busy day in the city of gold.

"Hello? Hello? Can you hear me?"

I opened one eye; the other remained shut, pressed closed by a ball of bruised flesh. I was lying on the pavement, my body shaking, hot and cold quarreling over me. I looked up and saw nothing but sky. Then a face was leaning over me—a white madam's face.

One moment she was kneeling down beside me; the next she had jumped up and was stepping off the curb into the traffic and waving her arms wildly. I did not understand. I was confused until I saw an ambulance driving down the narrow street. It pulled over.

"What a stroke of luck," the madam cried, as the driver rolled down his window. "Quick! I need your help. There's an injured woman on the pavement. We've got to get her to hospital. I think she's been mugged."

My body slackened. I could relinquish control. Someone was going to take care of me. Two ambulance officers jumped out of the vehicle and broke through the small crowd that was gathering. I saw surprise register on their faces when I came into view.

"I found her collapsed here," the white woman said, speaking very fast.

The two men stood over me, their uniformed bodies blocking out the sun and casting a welcome shadow. Yet somewhere in my scrambled mind I knew men in uniform never brought relief.

"Lady, we cannot transport this patient in our vehicle."

"What do you mean?" she said, squinting into the sun. "She needs urgent medical attention."

"Yes, but this is a *whites-only* ambulance," one said. "You need to call the service for blacks. Anyway, *is* she black? She looks more colored to me—got quite a light complexion." He peered closely at me. "She must be taken to Hillbrow Hospital if she's black and Coronation if colored. Hard to tell, hey?" He stuck a finger in his ear. "She's definitely got a Bantu's nose. You could always pull a comb through her hair. If it sticks, she's probably black," he said, rolling a piece of earwax between his fingers.

Even through the thick fog in my head I could see and feel the white madam's anger. With electricity crackling all around her, it was like being too close to a power pylon. I think the ambulance men felt it too.

"She's probably drunk and been beaten up by her husband," one said quickly. "You know what they're like."

I lay on my back in the midday heat, a broken insect, life leaking slowly out of me. At that moment I would have been happy to slip from this world. I felt ashamed for wanting to give back God's precious gift, but even my shame was tired and did little to frighten me.

"You've got to be joking!" the madam screamed. "What about the Hippocratic oath? What about helping your fellow man? This is appalling!" She was throwing her hands about as if directing traffic. "Help me get this woman to hospital before she dies here on the pavement."

"Look, lady, we don't make the laws."

The crowd was growing—a concern of mostly black faces. The ambulance officers shifted uneasily, then, after a quick nod to each other, they turned and jumped back into their vehicle.

"You've not heard the end of this!" the madam yelled, as the ambulance lurched away down the road. The madam turned back to the crowd. "Someone. You. Yes, you! Come on. Help me put this woman in my car."

Strong black arms were lifting me, carrying me, laying me across the scorching backseat of a car that smelled of wet dog, sweating leather, and ripe pineapples. A horn blared and we were moving.

I recall only pieces of that wild journey as I drifted in and out of consciousness. I do remember hearing the madam say she was taking me to Hillbrow Hospital, and thinking that at least she had got my classification correct.

When I awoke, the smell of the car had been replaced by the strong stench of disinfectant. I was surrounded by a sea of white—white sheets, white coats, white faces, white voices.

"Overwhelming sepsis, ruptured eardrum, renal contusion, second-degree vaginal burns, and burns to both breasts—probably cigarette inflicted. Speculum, Sister." A fat white man with an unshaven face and caramel-colored skin stepped forward. His doctor's coat was spattered with old blood. A cigarette hung loosely from his mouth.

A black nursing sister appeared. At first I was relieved to see her, but then I saw what she was carrying—a stainless-steel instrument surely only the security police would use. She drew a green curtain around the bed, shutting me in with the fat doctor and five others. The cigarette still hung from his mouth as he spread my legs and pushed the cold steel inside me. The pain was terrible, but I could not cry out. Not in front of this important white audience.

One by one, the serious white faces peered up the metal tunnel into my vagina.

"IV antibiotics for another forty-eight hours, then we'll review," were the doctor's last words as he trotted away, the others hurrying after him like suckling puppies chasing a bitch.


One week later I was discharged.

I had never missed one single day of work cleaning offices in the city for Master Nicholson, nor had I ever been late for a single shift. Yet on the day of my discharge from the hospital, I lost my job.

I tried to explain to my boss I had not been able to contact him to let him know I was in the hospital. I even offered to work a week for no pay. But he would not listen. He just said I was like all the rest. Anyway, he had already replaced me; some other black person from the pool of people in the townships had filled my position.

I sat down on a bench in a park. I had just six rand and twenty-five cents in my post office book. Not even enough for taxi fare to Louis Trichardt. And hardly enough to live on for more than a few days in Johannesburg.

I was tired. My back was stiff and my joints ached; my body had lost the elasticity of youth. The tool that had always guaranteed me work was wearing out.

"Be strong, Celia," I said out loud. Self-pity would not earn me a wage.

Two children playing on a seesaw near me stopped and stared at the crazy black woman talking to herself.

I fingered the few loose coins in my purse, trying to plan my next move. And that was when I felt it . . . I pulled out the crumpled gray card and turned it over. It was covered in red scribble. How had it come to be in my purse?

*"Ndi khou humbela u vhudzisa!"* I called out, flagging down a passing black man.

The well-dressed man looked at me suspiciously, my face still a swell of cuts and fading bruises.

"Sorry, brother. Can you read for me, please?" I asked, holding up my find.

He stopped, but refused to come closer.

"Please," I begged.

Relenting, he stepped forward and squinted quickly at the card. "Sylvia Eloff," he read and rattled off an address in Parktown North. Then he turned and hurried on.

"God bless you," I called after him. "God bless you, brother."

"Sylvia Eloff. Sylvia Eloff," I repeated. It did not make any sense.

Then I remembered something. When I had been lying in

the emergency department of the hospital, slipping between this world and the next, the kind one who had driven me to the hospital had pressed something into my hand. I couldn't keep a hold of it and it had floated to the floor. Perhaps she had picked it up and put it in my purse.

It was early afternoon when I climbed off the bus. I hadn't wanted the journey to end. The rumble and shudder of the old vehicle had sieved out my thoughts and left me in an easy state of numbness. Yet now, as I stepped onto the pavement at the top of Chester Road, my life stood waiting to demand more of me. My legs felt heavy and reluctant to move. Not only because of the injuries I'd received at John Vorster Square—the uncertainty of what lay ahead also slowed my progress.

I turned into Second Avenue. A cool lane lined with plane trees stretched out in front of me, yellow light spearing the dense canopy of green to break up the tarmac with splinters of warmth. The scene reminded me of another life I had once lived, and I realized how much I'd missed the soothing stillness of the sub-urbs. For such a long time now the dust and dirt of the town-ships and the anger and screech of the city had been eating away at my soul.

I breathed in the sweet, shade-cooled air and started to walk with difficulty, but less reluctance. Then I was standing outside the house. Doubt and fear circled like buzzards. I had never before asked anyone for charity. However, hunger was gnawing at my insides, hollowing out my final shame.

I unlatched the small wrought-iron gate coming off the main

entrance and pushed on it tentatively. The jarring sound of metal grinding against metal startled me and I felt instantly guilty, as if I'd just stolen something, even though I had only opened a gate. I made my way up a winding brick pathway overhung with lush vegetation. The bricks were wet and the dark green leaves heavy with beads of water. A hosepipe lay coiled beneath a garden tap like a snake asleep in the sun, and a wind chime jangled in the breeze. I stood in front of the glass front door for several minutes before finally lifting my hand and rapping against the glass.

Two small dogs appeared, yapping excitedly and steaming up the glass with their hot breath. Then a white madam was making her way down the passage toward me. My whole body started to shake—my hands, my legs, my heart.

As she came closer I saw her face was different from the picture I had held in my head. My hope plunged down a shaft. The card in my purse had *not* been from the madam who had rescued me. I had got it all wrong. I wanted to turn and run, but it was too late; this madam with bark-brown hair and sloping eyes hidden beneath soft hoods of skin was already standing on the other side of the glass.

She opened the door and her dogs shot out. "Fleabag, Piglet, down! Down! Don't worry, they won't bite."

I was relieved by the sound of her voice; it was the voice of the kind one.

"May I help you?"

I lifted the card made limp by my clammy hands. "Madam is very good to me last week when I am in trouble. You take me to hospital. Thank you."

Her face softened. "Of course! Goodness, how are you? I didn't recognize you."

When she touched my arm I tensed. Her fingers were soft.

"You look a lot better than you did a week ago. Come. Come inside, please."

Her polite words were like a *nganga*'s spell. Parts of me simply fell away, the Celia I'd lived for so long—the maid, the char, the black—all dropping off me like ill-fitting clothes. I hesitated, then stepped into this madam's sweet-smelling house a woman.

She led me into a room filled with sunlight. On the floor lay a huge Basotho rug, its knotted wool woven into mountains, a river, red earth, and a blue sky. The scene felt instantly familiar, like a distant cousin. A tall vase of lilies filled the air with a soothing freshness, and a clay pot in front of the fireplace, though cracked and old, leaked the faint aroma of my childhood. Not thinking, I steadied myself against a leather chair, then quickly lifted my hand off the polished hide.

"Can I get you a cup of tea?" the madam asked. "I was just about to have one."

A white madam offering to make me a cup of tea! My head—a room of rules—screamed *no* . . . but my mouth was dry. I had not drunk anything all day. "Thank you too much, please, Madam," I said, lowering my eyes, ashamed at my impertinence.

I would soon learn that this madam, Sylvia Eloff, was different from the other white madams I had known. She worked for the Black Sash—a group of white women who fought the laws of the land from their position of privilege.

As I sat in her beautiful home drinking tea from a cup and saucer, a thunderstorm blew up as so often happened on a hot and humid African afternoon. For ten minutes we talked over the sound of the rain clattering on the tin roof above us, both of us forced to raise our voices above the giant rattle God was shaking in the sky. I'd never spoken so loudly, nor so boldly, to a white madam before; nor had one listened so intently to me.

Then the rain stopped. The day had been washed clean and the dust dampened. Black thunderclouds peeled back on a baby blue sky, and from where I was sitting, I glimpsed the faint outline of a rainbow.

## CHAPTER NINETEEN

### June 1978

## Miriam

"Hope you find everything you're after," Rita said. "We've been using your bedroom as a storage den."

By aligning herself with Michael and using "we" instead of "I," Rita was lending her actions some legitimacy. I knew her too well.

"I see what you mean," I said, tripping over a box angled across the doorway.

"Well, you couldn't expect us to keep it vacant on the off chance you'd be back."

Dust particles rose and hung there, momentarily suspended in a matrix of light. My old room—now cluttered with cardboard boxes, trunks, and a broken record player—had been robbed of its former identity.

I'd always kept it immaculate—the only space in my life over which I'd had any measure of control, especially during the early years. I'd been determined to keep my room as neat and tidy as my mother would have and had often lain awake worrying about what she would have said were she to arrive in England unannounced and discover the chaos we lived in. At least if my room looked respectable and the bath rim had been cleaned, she wouldn't be too disappointed in me.

I looked about. A corner of my bed—a lone fixture of former days—was just visible under the boxes, but my photographs, certificates, and school memorabilia were all gone.

While I didn't really have any right to be angry—after all, I'd been the one to leave—I was. How quickly and easily Rita and Michael had erased all reminders of me.

Rita hovered. "So what exactly are you after?"

"I'm moving into an apartment and could use some of the things that didn't fit into the studio. You know—my books, my guitar . . . things like that. You haven't thrown them out, have you?"

"New place, huh? Pay can't be too bad for cashiers these days." Her tone was biting. I knew where this would lead. I didn't feel like another altercation. I just wanted to be left alone to sift through the wreckage.

"Actually, I'm moving in with someone," I said. Talking about it made it real—but as soon as the words escaped my lips, I regretted them. It was never wise to let Rita in on a confidence. My relationship with her had been dysfunctional at best, and the year since I'd moved out had seen a succession of infrequent and mostly dissatisfying meetings. I'd grown resigned to this, even though a small part of me had never stopped hoping that somehow it could be different. This aspiration sometimes tricked me into an intimacy, which I later always regretted.

For Rita, my adoption had been a failure, a blot on her copy-book. I understood that now. I was a constant and harsh reminder of her inadequacies as a woman, a wife, a mother. Out of this festering disappointment in herself had grown a strong dislike of me, my existence only serving to highlight her failures. That I had uncovered her extramarital affair hadn't helped.

"Aha! So that's what this little spring clean is all about," she said. "Finally you're doing what the rest of us have been doing for ages. What's his name?"

I was trapped. "Uh . . ."

"Oh, God, Miriam, tell me it's a man and not a woman!"

"His name is David Bloomfield. He's a sociology student at Cambridge."

There, it was out, and already spoiled by her knowledge of it. I began to shift the furniture and boxes with greater urgency, anxious to get away.

Rita loitered.

I hauled my old guitar case out from under the bed. As I did so, a shoe box with a moth-eaten lid fell off and toppled over, spilling its contents onto the floor—a small wooden figure, a photo frame, and a wad of pale blue air letters. The glass in the photo frame tinkled as it broke.

"Sorr—" I stopped in midapology. The uppermost letter was addressed in large childlike handwriting to a *Miriam Mphephu*.

I picked up the whole blue bundle and sank back on my haunches.

The noise of Rita moving closer startled me. For an instant I'd forgotten about her.

I put out a hand to steady myself, but as I pressed down on my palm, a sharp pain sliced through my hand. Blood dripped onto my jeans, the rug, the floor . . . I'd cut myself on the broken glass of the photo frame.

Undeterred, I reached for the now naked photograph, but as I did so a fine mist of my blood sprayed across it, obscuring the details of a black woman. I tried to wipe the photo clean, but only smudged it further.

"You've cut yourself!" Rita said, snatching the photo off me and lifting my arm sharply. "Let's have a look."

"It's nothing. I'm fine," I said, trying to wrestle free my wrist.

Without letting go, she hauled me up and led me to the bathroom. Strangely, despite all that had transpired, her touch felt good. It was the first physical contact we'd had in such a long time.

She sat me down on the closed toilet seat lid and examined my hand. "Luckily you've missed the tendon," she said, retracting the flap of skin with a tissue.

I looked away and found myself staring at our reflection in the mirror. Rita bent over me in a pose of concern. My mind started to wander, pretending this woman whom I was supposed to call mother loved me.

She straightened. "Looks like you're going to need a couple of stitches," she said, her voice softening. "I'll get you a bandage, then take you down to the emergency department."

"Just tape it," I urged her. "I'll pop down later. I'd like to finish collecting my things."

"No." Rita's voice reverberated around the hollow room.

"You can come back another day for your stuff. You've waited this long, a few more days won't make a difference." Her tone was unrelenting. Then she disappeared down the corridor, to reappear with a roll of bandage.

She was finishing binding my hand when the telephone rang.

"Hold that a second," she said, passing me the free end of strapping. "Back in a tick."

So I sat there on the toilet seat holding up my half-strapped hand and waiting for Rita to return.

Five minutes passed. Then ten. I could still hear Rita's voice down the hall.

I stood up, steadying myself against the basin as a wave of dizziness washed over me, then lurched woozily into the corridor.

Back at my bedroom door I stopped. It was shut. I placed my swaddled hand on the knob and turned. My palm slid against resistance. I tried to get a better grip, wincing under the pressure, but still the knob would not budge. The door had been locked.

"Just can't keep away, hey?"

I swung around to find myself dwarfed by Rita's solid frame.

"Why . . . why have you locked it, Reet?"

She looked away. "Safer. Work things, you know. Confidential patient reports—that sort of thing."

Minutes later we were driving to the hospital.

"Rita, who is Miriam Mphephu?"

She screeched to a halt, seeing the red traffic light only at the last moment. Staring straight ahead, she gripped the steering wheel so tightly her knuckles blanched.

"What?"

"The name on those air letters. They were addressed to Miriam Mphephu. Is that . . . Were they for me?"

"Miriam, I really don't know what you're on about." Rita's voice was strained and her tone final. She was warning me off. "I'll drop you outside the entrance and then find parking, okay?"

The light changed to green and once again the sound of the engine filled the car.

I returned to the house a week later, timing my visit carefully to ensure Rita was at her weekly morbidity and mortality meeting. I had to get those letters; I'd been unable to think of anything else.

Michael opened the front door.

"Miriam, what a lovely surprise!" he cried, his drawn face plumping into a smile. He pulled me into an eager hug. "And to what do I owe this pleasure?"

"I'm sorry, Michael," I said, gently extricating myself, "but I can't stay for long. I'm in a bit of a hurry. I just popped by to collect some of my things."

"Right, of course. You youngsters lead such busy lives."

I could feel his disappointment.

"We miss you, Miriam," he blurted out suddenly. "The house is positively empty without you."

I shrugged awkwardly.

"What have you done to yourself?" he said, suddenly noticing my bandaged hand. So Rita hadn't told him of my visit.

"Oh, it's nothing. I managed to cut myself on a piece of broken glass. Just a few stitches, but they come out tomorrow."

He reached for my hand, but I eased past him. "I'll just shoot upstairs."

"Of course."

At the foot of the stairs I stopped. "Michael, what was my name before I became a Steiner?"

His eyes widened. "Your name?"

"You know, before I got your surname."

"Oh. Right. Uh. It was— Gosh now, my memory," he said, flicking his thumbnail against his forefinger.

"Was it something like Mpepu?"

Color rushed into his face and he gripped the handrail. "Mphephu. Yes, Miriam Mphephu."

M-phe-phu. M-phe-phu. I smiled. It sounded so appealing the way he pronounced it.

"*P-h* is pronounced *f* in Africa," he said, putting his free hand, which was trembling, behind his back.

"What's Africa like?"

"Africa?" he said too loudly. "So many questions, young lady. I thought you were in a hurry."

I glanced over my shoulder. Rita would be returning soon. "Yup. Better grab my stuff." I scaled the stairs two at a time.

I heard Michael say something.

"What?" I said, looking down from the landing.

"I just said that Africa is beautiful and that one day you should go back and visit."

My heart whooped in my chest. "Yes. Yes, I'd like that very much."

He started to walk toward his office, then stopped. "What are you after, anyway?" he said. "Only last weekend Rita gave your room a thorough clean-out. She took loads of stuff down to the Salvation Army."

My gums prickled.

I ran down the corridor. The door to my room was open.

I burst in . . . into a perfectly ordered, foreign space—bed, lamp, desk, curtains. Nothing else. Nothing. She'd removed it all.

# CHAPTER TWENTY

## December 1978

## Celia

I was ironing in Missus Sylvia's kitchen when I heard the crash. The house shuddered, birds took flight, and Fleabag shot under the table, his tail tucked between his legs.

I rushed into the living room. The soft salmon drapes were billowing around a ragged hole in the window. Loose shards of glass swinging from invisible threads clinked and chimed in the breeze. Missus Sylvia was sitting at her desk in the corner, as pale and still as a dead person.

I ran over to her, tripping on a rock the size of my fist lying in the middle of the lounge floor. "Missus S?"

As if she'd been suddenly brought back to life, she jumped up and ran toward the door. "Quick, Celia. Hurry!"

"No, Missus," I called after her, "they are *skelms, tsotsis!*"

But she was faster than me, and I only caught up with her at the top of the drive, my chest hungry for breath and my calves burning. A battered brown Toyota was careening off down the road.

"TJ64 . . . Darn! I didn't get it all!" Missus Sylvia cursed as the car and its number plate disappeared out of sight. "Not that it would have been much use."

I stared down the tree-lined avenue. All of a sudden the shade felt menacing.

"Come on," Missus Sylvia said to me, patting me on the back.

We turned together, and that was when we saw it—red paint dripping down the plastered white wall like fingers of fresh blood.

"*Hau*, Missus S! What does it say?" I asked, frightened to hear the answer.

"*Kaffirboetie.* You know—a Kaffir's friend."

"This is terrible!"

But my boss was already headed inside to call a man to repair the glass, and after that to retrieve the tin of white paint that lived in the shed. I was not yet used to these sorts of attacks, despite their increasing frequency. Every unexpected noise, phone call, or ring of the doorbell made my heart jump and my breath run. Missus Sylvia and Mister Jo seemed more accepting, as if they were just an unavoidable part of the life they lived.

Master Jo Eloff was a man of the law, and much of his day was spent helping those who had been held in detention without trial and tortured by the security police. Missus Sylvia was a teacher. She'd set up a school for children in Soweto where the pupils could take lessons in their own language and not the prescribed Afrikaans. However, when the Department of Bantu Education found out, the school was closed down for "inciting revolt." Undeterred, she simply moved the small school to a secret location.

I had never met white people like them before. They were risking their lives for us—black people. I did not properly understand why. Living under their roof brought both good and bad things to me. I was paid a very good wage, ate good food, and could again sleep in the suburbs. There was laughter in this house, and kindness too, and I was sheltered from many of the hardships my friends endured.

But being a part of the Eloffs' household also meant I was shot to the front of the struggle and knitted, like an extra stitch, into "the resistance."

Tension stretched across our days like a taut elastic band. I had to be constantly on the lookout for danger, and the threat of arrest circled like a pack of hungry hyenas. Master Jo told me a tiny policeman's ear lived inside our telephone, so I had to always say the opposite of what I really meant, when I used it.

Letters and parcels coming to the house also had to be checked before being opened. One time the master opened a small parcel bomb, which luckily had lost its boom.

But there was much to be content with. Missus Sylvia taught me to read and write. And with her encouragement, I discovered things about myself that had been hidden for all my lifetime. I came to believe I was a good person. I could be trusted. I had a talent for drawing and a head for numbers. I had the right to get angry and the right to be heard. At fifty-three years of age I was discovering a different Celia Mphephu, and I liked her.

One hot December morning I was hanging up the washing outside when Piglet started to growl.

"What is it, Piglet?" I asked, as I pegged my colossal bra beside Missus Sylvia's very small one. Hers could barely hold two plums, while mine had space for two fat pawpaws. The sun was not long out of bed and its gentle warmth had doused me in lazy contentment.

Piglet growled again. The little brown terrier often argued with the billowing sheets, but this day they hung without life. There was not even the murmur of a breeze. Then his growl turned into a bark, and he shot up the driveway. I looked around the wall of white linen. A black boy was peering through the bars of the gate.

My heart jumped in my chest.

Dropping my pegs on the ground, I moved cautiously toward him. As I got closer I saw he had a blotchy face with patches of pale skin where skin-lightening cream had left its cruel mark. His eyes were hard, and he looked as if he had seen more than his youth would suggest. I stopped well back from the gate.

"Celia?" He spoke with a rough, urgent tone.

I was surprised; he knew my name. I did not know his. I nodded. By now both Piglet and Fleabag were barking furiously.

The boy flung something over the gate, then turned and was gone.

I jumped back, away from the letter.

It did not explode.

After a few seconds, I stepped cautiously forward. The crumpled envelope was too thin to hold anything more than a single sheet of paper, so I bent down to pick it up. My name and the Eloffs' address were written on the envelope. I tore it open. Inside was a piece of toilet paper with one line scrawled across it in biro. Immediately I recognized the rise and fall of the script. It was from Christian.

It had been over fourteen months since I'd been woken in the middle of the night by his agitated knocking. I had heard nothing from him since, except for when the security police arrested me, and they seemed to know as little as I of his whereabouts.

After many sleepless nights I had finally managed to convince myself that no news from my boy was in fact a good thing, especially when Missus Sylvia suggested Christian could possibly be living over the border in Angola.

I'd held on to this one thought and never allowed myself to think beyond it. It offered me a calm place in my mind where I could see my eldest son safe and out of harm's way.

Now I was swiftly robbed of that peace.

### 28 October

*Ma, I have been arrested. Please try to get help.*

C

I struggled to understand the note—my hands were trembling and my reading was still slow and clumsy. I checked the date. The letter was already five weeks old. I'd been lent an empty peace for five whole weeks—a peace that, all this time, had been a foolish lie.

Fumbling with the gate, I opened it and raced onto the avenue after the mysterious messenger, but the street was empty. I scoured gardens and driveways, parked cars and bus shelters, but with no success. The blotchy brown face had vanished.

It took many weeks before Master Jo managed to find where Christian was being held; however, his discovery did little to lessen my pain.

"Celia, I'm afraid Christian is being held incommunicado, which means he is not allowed to talk with us. He will be in solitary confinement and have no access to a lawyer. His detention is even beyond the jurisdiction of the courts."

Master Jo's lawyer words were difficult to understand. They only confused and frightened me. But when Missus Sylvia explained them, I realized they carried bad news.

"There is not much we can do from this end," he went on. "I will try to reach him, but I don't want to get your hopes up. I can't promise anything."

Master Jo was a kind man, but this time his kindness would not be enough. And on 17 January 1979, on a clear and cloudless morning, he was notified by the security police that my eldest child, Christian Mulalo Mphephu, had slipped on a bar of soap in the shower, hit his head, and died.

Only after much work by Master Jo and many phone calls was a doctor whom he had chosen allowed to examine Christian's body.

*Brain hemorrhage. Ruptured spleen. Genital contusion. Contusion of the trunk and chest consistent with sustained beatings. Aspiration pneumonia.*

Christian had been tortured to death.

Finally, after too many days, I was allowed to be alone with my boy in an ice-green room with frosted-glass windows. He was lying on a stainless-steel trolley, his long body stiff with death.

The skin of a dead person follows familiar lines, yet feels like a stranger's to the touch. Robbed of the fullness that comes from breath and blood and life, Christian's skin felt as thick as rubber and achingly cold.

I stroked my eldest son's face, now a collapsed mask, and cradled his broken body in my arms—a body twice dishonored, first by the police and then by the doctor's scalpel. I wept savage, raging tears. I wept for the cheeky *piccanin* running along the red dust road to welcome me. I wept for the schoolboy carrying his satchel and seriousness with such a proud, straight back. I wept for the pain and fear he had suffered alone in a comfortless cell, and I wept for a life that had been so full of promise, so brutally put out.

With two children taken from me, I sank into a life stripped of hope. It was a lonely place to be, but more real than the life the Eloffs had led me to believe was possible. I continued to work for them, but I drew away from their cause. The rainbow I had once briefly glimpsed had faded.

# CHAPTER TWENTY-ONE

## 1984

## Miriam

It was Christmas Eve and snowing. Dave and I had been invited to a party hosted by one of his squash mates. Stooping under a bower of fairy lights, we made our way up the freshly shoveled path.

Dave clasped my gloved hand firmly in his as he knocked on the half-open door. He knew how much I hated these first moments.

Voices and funky Christmas music emanated from within.

"Hellooo," he called out.

A guy with greasy brown hair appeared from a side door, balancing three full glasses in his hands. "Dave, mate! Season's greetings and all that jazz. Follow me, the action's this way."

"Nick, this is Miriam . . ."

I smiled, but our host was already heading toward the din, sloshing Christmas punch out of the glasses with inebriated carelessness. Dave winked at me as we eased past a couple snogging in the hallway.

Soon we were standing on the edge of a room packed with florid faces, raucous laughter, and gyrating bodies. A wave of marijuana, beer, pizza, and cheap perfume smells hit us. Nick disappeared into the maze of bodies and party people quickly resealed the hole. We'd just lost our introduction. My pulse picked up. I always felt our separateness so acutely. Dave slung his arm around me and gave me a kiss on the ear. Heads turned, then more, until, like a Mexican wave spreading through the room, all eyes were on us. "I Saw Mommy Kissing Santa Claus" competed with the awkward hush.

"Right, now what'll you guys have? Beer, glass of wine, some punch?" It was the Nick guy, miraculously returned.

Chatter clumsily restarted, the uncomfortable silence lifted, and we—the conspicuous mixed-race couple—began to mingle.


It was after midnight by the time Dave unlocked the door to our inner-city apartment and we stepped in out of the minus-four-degree night. He left the lights off, allowing the moon to steep us in its silver shadow. One of the sash windows in the lounge was partially open, the gap channeling in an icy draft and the discordant sounds of revelers on the street below.

Dave pulled it shut, sealing us into a space where the only sounds were those we made—a chair leg scraping across the floor, the squeak of Dave's sneakers, the jangle of my bracelets. The familiarity of these surrounds began to debrief us and soon we were making love—slowly and deeply, but as always, tinged with sadness. Outside our walls the world balked at the very notion of our bond and tested it at every turn. We could only play at being free inside this cocoon.

Seven years had passed since the evening Dave had accompanied me home from the Patels'—seven years since our surreal love affair had begun. Yet *still* it felt illusory—me and Dave Bloomfield. Kind, white Dave. He had persuaded me to leave my job at the grocery store and pursue my dream of becoming a psychologist. A scholarship from Cambridge saw that goal eventually realized and, equipped with Dave's unconditional love and Zelda's unwavering friendship, I'd risen to the challenge. I was now in my final year, on clinical attachment.

"Dave, you awake?"

He grunted, on the brink of the weightless sleep that follows lovemaking.

"Sorry, must have been dozing," he said, sitting up on the sofa, his hair all tousled. "God, it's freezing. Let's hop into bed."

"Dave, I've been thinking. I need to go back."

He rubbed his eyes. "What do you mean? Did you leave something at the party?"

"Africa. I've got to go back to Africa."

He pulled on his boxer shorts, as though his nakedness was inappropriate for the words he knew would surely follow. This day had been threatening forever. For years it had been hanging in the wings, and now I was about to confirm what we'd both always known—that our relationship was transient and our happiness borrowed.

He nodded, as if any protestation would be selfish and point-less. Dear, gentle Dave. He'd understood the conditions of our partnership. He knew the limitations the world imposed on us.

"I sit in sessions listening to my patients—troubled individu-als trying to find themselves. They hang on my every word, but really I have no more of an identity than they do. I don't know who I am."

He closed his eyes.

"Don't block me," I said, even though he'd offered no verbal resistance. "Tonight I listened to all those Christmas songs and felt *nothing*. I ate plum pudding as though eating some strange foreign delicacy. I looked out on the snowy landscape and I felt like a *visitor*. These things are not a part of me. Not my heritage. Not my custom. I'm an observer, looking on at life from behind a screen. I can't feel it. I can't believe it. It eludes me. I don't belong here!"

He turned, the moonlight silvering his silent tears.

"I'm tired of trying," I went on. "Trying to fit in. I want to be accepted. I can't swim against this tide anymore. I just can't."

He picked up my hands and kissed them tenderly.

But there was more. I couldn't stop. "I feel dead inside. Are there smells somewhere that will wake me up? Landscapes that will move my soul? You delight in Handel's *Messiah*, in Mozart and Brahms, yet I still haven't heard music that moves me."

He was sitting so still it frightened me.

"I love you more than you will ever know, and the thought of us splitting up is unbearable, but I can't keep offering you only half of myself. I have to go back. I have to see what I've left behind so I can navigate the road ahead."

After a long silence he spoke. "What about us?"

I looked at him.

"What about marriage, kids, everything?"

I sat, silent. I couldn't say the words he wanted to hear. I'd always been able to use the demands of my degree to delay this discussion. Now my studies were nearing completion.

He dropped my hands.

I stood up and started pacing the room. "I know how much you want kids, but how can I have a child when I flushed the last one down the toilet? How can I be a mother when I don't know my own?"

He bent over and held his head in his hands. It tore at my heart to see him like that. I sat down again beside him, but his body was stiff and held me off.

"Could we really bring a colored child into this world," I whispered, "when we know what sort of reception it'll receive, what sort of existence it'll have? We live the difficulties every day and we're adults."

The moon had slipped behind a cloud and darkness enveloped us. We sat there camouflaged by the blue-black night—our love, our sorrow, and our color momentarily hidden.

Silver cutlery clanged on the fine bone china.

"It was such a nice surprise to get your call the other day," Michael said, rescuing another long pause. "We don't seem to have seen much of you two this year."

Rita, Michael, Dave, and I were spaced out around the large mahogany dining table that could have comfortably seated twelve.

It was Dave who had helped me salvage my relationship with my parents, the one who'd insisted I maintain regular contact. He didn't like Rita, but he understood how fragile my emotional well-being could be and recognized that the good Michael brought into my life outweighed the cost Rita exacted.

"How's that thesis of yours coming along then, David?" Michael asked with overanxious zeal. "Must have been quite a strain being a student again. I bet you'll be glad to be soon earning a proper wage again."

"More potatoes, anyone?" Rita interrupted, spearing one with her fork.

"Not for me, thanks," I said.

"Anyway, it must be time for a toast," she said, pushing the dish of spuds aside. "Get the champagne, Michael."

On cue, he stood up and disappeared into the kitchen.

"There's a bottle of sparkling grape juice in the door of the fridge for Miriam," she called after him, then turned back to the table. "*So*, tell us all about it, then."

Dave hesitated. "Uh, Rita, the thesis has yet to be marked. Maybe a toast is a bit premature."

"All in good time, David," she said with a dismissive wave of her hand. "We'll toast your success soon, I'm sure. But today we have something even more important to celebrate, don't we?" She gave me a vaudeville wink.

Had I missed something?

David cast me a questioning glance. I shrugged.

"I must admit, Michael and I *were* beginning to lose hope—perpetual students that you are. We'd almost resigned ourselves to an end to the Steiner lineage."

"Reet!" Michael tried to silence her.

"How many weeks, then? You're barely showing," she said, eyeing my midriff. "Mind you, careful you don't go eating for two now. So many do and later regret it."

I looked across at Dave, his mouth agape as Rita's words swept with careless ease into the room.

"I'm not pregnant," I blurted out. "Whatever gave you that idea?"

Rita's face collapsed. She looked across to Dave for help. "You phoned us yesterday, David. Said you had something important to discuss with us and—"

Comprehension dawned. Dave pushed back his chair. "Rita, Miriam is *not* pregnant. That is not what we came here to discuss."

"Not pregnant?" Rita repeated. "You can't be getting married? I know how antiestablishment you both are."

Ignoring the melodrama, Dave carried on. He was good at that sort of thing—defusing and placating. "Miriam is going back to South Africa to try to track down her birth mother. We just wanted to let you know and enlist your help. We need to gather as much information as we can before she leaves."

Michael righted the listing tray of champagne glasses just in time.

"Put the tray down, for God's sake!" Rita flashed.

I sat back in my chair and watched the scene unfold before me. I felt strangely detached. Even the words "Africa" and "birth mother" sounded one-dimensional and unreal. I watched Dave with his big doe eyes and strong hands. He was so caring and loved me so much. I didn't deserve him. What I offered in return was muted—merely an outline of the real thing. I felt like a ghost, a guest, a visitor. Always a visitor.

Michael retreated to the kitchen and started making a lot of noise at the sink.

Rita sat sulking.

Dave continued. "Miriam's past is integral to who she is. For her to move forward she needs to explore her past. It's her history, her connectedness."

"Bravo! Very eloquently put," Rita retorted, quickly recovering. "What noble intentions! Pity they're the product of two completely out-of-touch kids espousing purist notions from the safety of their university towers. Let me tell you about the real world."

Michael hadn't resurfaced. He was hiding, and I was angry with him for his cowardice.

"Have you thought through how it will be for Miriam, returning to a country where apartheid rules? Where she'll be treated according to the color of her *brown* skin? Have you?" Rita leaned forward on both elbows. She was on the attack. "By all accounts it's not safe for anyone." Her voice trembled. "Not with the recent unrest. Sally Wilkinson's sister was shot at point-blank range, for ten rand. Life there is cheap, Miriam!"

I stared into Rita's angry pink mouth, at her large tombstonelike teeth. She was desperate, pulling out whatever she had in her armory to dissuade me. But why was she so against my going? It didn't make sense. Why did she even care?

"We've given you—given you *everything*, and this—this is— this is how you repay us!" she said, her sentences splintering.

"So you want to meet your birth mother. And where do you hope to find her?"

"Stop!" Michael boomed. "Stop, right now. I'll have no more of it, you hear?" He was standing in the doorway.

No one moved. Rita closed her eyes. Then Michael slammed the kitchen door behind him.

# Miriam

I edged through the sliding doors and squeezed onto the tube. It was rush hour and the train was packed.

The doors closed, sealing me into the overcrowded compartment. Then we were moving—a bullet of fluorescent light shooting through the blackness.

Usually I enjoyed people watching, but today bodies were crammed too closely to gaze freely. I didn't know where to rest my eyes and kept diverting them from the hungry stare of a man two people away from me.

A bright orange advertisement on the ceiling caught my attention. It was for a recruitment agency. *Do you know where you are going?* in bold black letters.

I smiled to myself. *No, I don't.*

*Bayswater. Bayswater. Bayswater* flicked by like the start of an old cine movie. Metal screeched, the tube slowed, and we came to a standstill. All motion was momentarily suspended—people frozen facing their closest door. Even the haunting moans of the tunnel drafts were for a second silenced. Then the doors slid open and the train gave birth to a monster of jostling arms, stiletto heels, and striding purpose.

A rough hand squeezed my crotch. I swung around. There was just a wall of faces. Everyone looked like a pervert.

"Swine," I cursed, feeling tainted and grubby. But before I could gather myself, the crowd was sweeping me toward the escalator and I was moving up, to be finally flung out onto the street with the rest of the human flotsam.

Aboveground, the chaos and color were immediately calmed. It was snowing, and rooftops, chimneys, fire hydrants, and cars had all been given a magical dusting—one centimeter of white transforming London.

I stopped to buy a bag of roasted chestnuts from a nearby vendor and stood against a shop window savoring them, their heat percolating through the brown paper bag to warm my frozen hands. Then I was continuing on my way.

Eventually I spotted the sign—*The Ploughman*—swinging from a bracket above a large wooden door pockmarked by staples and Borer. I peered through the small square of bars set into the door, then heaved it open and was met with a wall of heat and noise.

I stepped inside and self-consciously scanned the heaving room, my eyes snagging on the absent glances of patrons purveying "the newcomer."

Finally I spotted Michael at a far table, beside an open hearth. He must have been there for some time to secure such a prime position. He waved and, like a lost child claimed at a fair, I felt the knot in my stomach loosen.

I removed my scarf and coat and made my way across the room, dodging trestle tables, rowdy men, and miniskirted waitresses balancing jugs of amber ale.

"Sorry I'm late." I leaned forward and gave him a kiss, the tip of my nose thawing against his cheek. "I was delayed at work and then the Underground was so busy . . ." I was out of breath.

"Sit, child." He always had such a calming manner. "What can I get you to drink?"

"I'd kill for a glass of white wine. Sweet, please. But I'll get it."

"No, you won't," he said, and before I could protest, he was swallowed up by the crowd.

I sank into a chair beside the fire. Archaic farming implements decorated the hearth, lending the place a rustic, earthy feel. It felt homely—an honest sort of place—except for the suspender-belted waitresses.

Soon the heat had melted the chill inside my bones, and the flickering orange flames were seducing me. The stresses of my day, my week, the past month, began to dissipate.

After a while, Michael returned, glass of wine and tankard of stout in hand.

"What an obstacle course!" he shouted above the din, sipping off some of the froth on his stout. "But not a drop spilled."

I tapped the side of my mouth.

He chuckled and wiped away the white mustache with the back of his hand.

Over the next hour we chatted about this and that—inconsequential things happening on the surface of our lives—until I began to wonder whether there had been anything more to our arranged meeting than one of our intermittent catch-ups coinciding with us both being in London for the day. When he'd phoned I'd assumed he'd wanted to clear the air after the recent altercation. But judging by the ways things were going, either my assumption had been wrong or he'd lost his nerve.

As if reading my thoughts, Michael's face suddenly collapsed and his posture wilted. "Miriam," he said, focusing on my forehead.

"Yes, Michael?"

He seemed to be having trouble getting the words out.

I waited as I'd been taught to do—"patient-centered listening." Clearly he was wrestling with something. He finally began—clumsily, as if the speech had already started in his head.

"I have to tell you. I've wanted to for so long. I . . ." He was fidgeting with his watch clasp. Open, shut. Open, shut.

"What is it?" I was growing alarmed by his behavior. "Are you unwell?"

"No, no," he said, carving a groove in the soft wooden table with his thumbnail. His eyes filled with tears.

I didn't put a hand out to comfort him. Something held me back.

He pulled out a bulky brown envelope from under the table and slid it across to me. "You'll need this if you're planning to go back."

I stared at the package. "What is it?"

"Your adoption papers, and the address of the people Celia went to work for after we left South Africa. They may be able to help you find her."

"Celia," I repeated. "My mother?"

He nodded.

"Oh, thank you, Michael!" I felt instantly alive and excited. "This means such a lot to me. I can't tell you . . ." I planted a loud kiss on his head.

But Michael held on to a more earnest expression, his lips as tightly pursed as his clasped hands. He looked away, avoiding my questioning gaze.

"Is something the—"

"Open it," he interrupted, pointing to the envelope.

I unpeeled the seal and put my hand inside, momentarily fingering the mysterious contents as if playing the game we used to play at school where we tried to identify objects in a velvet pouch by touch. I pulled them out. A sheet of paper with a pharmaceutical firm's letterhead. Rita's hallmark. She was always getting freebies from the drug reps—pens, writing pads, once even a trip to Sweden. Several names and addresses had been scribbled down. Another sheet of paper—limp and yellowed and almost split in two along a well-worn fold. *The adoption of Miriam Lufuno Mphephu.* Miriam Mphephu. That name again. My name? My hands trembled as they clasped the old document. Also a wad of pale blue air letters bound with fraying twine. *Those* letters. Impatiently I pulled at the knot, the string disintegrating in my fingers.

"Miriam, I've wanted to tell you for years," Michael said, his voice strangled. "But Rita . . . Then you and David visiting the other night . . . I couldn't keep it from you any longer. I just couldn't."

I barely heard his words as I rifled hungrily through the letters. Something slipped out from between them. A photograph. I'd seen it before—the picture of a black woman, her face obscured by a dark speckled stain.

"Your mother," Michael whispered.

I drew the photograph up close, straining to see what lay beneath the smudge of my own blood. She looked beautiful. My mother looked so beautiful.

Then, as if there had been some delay in a long-distance telephone conversation, words Michael had uttered moments earlier now reached me.

"What? Kept *what* from me?" My voice was shaking.

"Your mother loved you. She never wanted to give you up."

I felt as if I was falling down a steep ravine and the air was being sucked from my lungs in one silent scream.

Michael looked instantly different, as if relieved of some great burden.

I tried to speak, but nothing intelligible came out.

"Celia—your mother—loved you."

My skin rose into a thousand goose bumps.

"She only gave you away because she thought you'd have a better life out of South Africa and away from the cruelties of apartheid." He swallowed loudly.

I downed the rest of my wine.

"We desperately wanted a child of our own. You filled that void. Rita had suffered two miscarriages and then a stillbirth. She was devastated. Broken. We both were."

He was staring into the distance, the painful scene once again unfolding before him.

"You brought warmth back into our home, a purpose, something that had been missing for so long. You gave our relationship a second chance. Rita seemed almost happy when you were around. I thought it would change everything—a child we could call our own." He shook his head despairingly.

I couldn't move. My joints had been set in concrete, my lungs squeezed thin.

"When your mother agreed to the adoption, Rita was so excited and made promises. Promises she couldn't keep. She promised we'd visit at least once a year. She promised we'd write often."

"Couldn't keep?"

"Rita had a change of heart once we were here. I think she was scared she'd lose you, just as she'd lost her other babies. Sharing came at a price she wasn't prepared to pay. So she, or rather *we*, made a decision to cease contact with your mother."

I held my hand over my mouth, stifling the strange sounds coming from it. A kaleidoscope of emotion was twisting through me—disbelief, elation, horror, anger. My mind could find no starting point, nor any end. I started gasping as my heart and lungs escaped their straitjacket.

"Are you okay?" Michael put out a hand.

I pulled away.

"We kept the letters your mother sent when we first came to England, until Rita started returning them."

Panicked, I looked down at the pile of letters. Some were

missing? Some sent back? I'd had nothing for so long, yet now I was mourning the few I would never have.

"We wanted the best for you. Your mother. Rita. We all had a common goal, just different ideas on how to achieve it. We all loved you."

"That's a lie," I hissed. "Rita *never* loved me."

Michael straightened. "That's not true. She just doesn't have the tools to express it. Growing up she was never shown much affection. Do you know that once, as a child, she spent an entire midterm break at boarding school, because no one came to collect her."

"I don't care!"

Michael opened his mouth. Nothing more came out. At least he'd stopped talking. I couldn't bear it any longer. I was addicted to his words, but repelled by them too.

I saw the envelope on the table was distorted by something else. I tipped it upside down and a small wooden figure rolled out. Michael caught it before it fell off the table and passed it to me.

"And this? What's this?" I shouted, holding up the doll with large owl eyes and a beaked nose.

People at the next table turned.

"I think it's a mythological character," Michael whispered. "Meant to watch over you and keep you safe from harm. Your mother sent it."

In a daze I put the doll back into the envelope, then the letters and the adoption papers. I stood up. My chair toppled over, but I left it lying on its side as I made my way blindly out of the pub, bumping into people and furniture as I went.

Michael didn't follow.

I don't remember how I got home, but I remember Dave's warm neck and his comforting smell. I remember that.

*24 January 1961*

*My dear Miriam,*

*I am lucky because as I speak this letter, Philemon writes it. He is knowing of all the rules to write a proper letter. He has standard eight in qualifications. You see it is very important to be at school.*

*You must be in England now and I am asking to myself if you see the queen yet and what she looks like from close. I hope she is wearing her crown when you meet. Everyone here is very jealous for you.*

*I am hoping you are happy with the photograph of me. To make it I must sit in a funny box with a curtain at my shoulder. When I put a coin in the machine, there is a bright light and the sound of a hungry lion. Then my picture pops out. It is magic for sure. Please ask the Master to send me a picture of you. You must grow taller every day.*

*Philemon's hand is now tired so I will end. I love you and miss you too much, but I am excited for your adventure. I wait for the Master and Madam to write soon.*

*Your Mme*
*One Celia Mphephu*

*13 March 1961*

Dear Child,

*I hope the Master holds this letter and reads for you. Soon you will be able to read it on your own. I am not yet getting your letter. Please it must be soon. Philemon waits to read to me.*

*Now I am living in Alexandra location, but the Master can write me at my work in Parkhurst. He is knowing the address.*

*How is England? Do you eat all your food? It is important to grow strong. I hope Tendani is liking her new house? Remember to cuddle her even if you are getting new toys. Philemon says it is very cold in England so I knit you a warm hat of many colors.*

*Yours honorably*
*Mme*
*(Celia Mphephu)*


*27 May 1961*

Dear Mbila,

*I could not find Philemon this week, so I must to pay one student where I am sleeping to write you. I am very anxious for your news. Please ask the Master or Madam to write straight away. I must to know my precious child is*

*safe. I see Sipho at church on Sunday and he is very much
missing his friend. Have you made new friends? What is
their name? I am to be very excited when you visit which
I hope comes soon.*

*Dearest child,*

*I am too worried . . .*
    *I am loving you.*

1 February 1962

*Master Michael and Madam Rita,*

*When do you visit? You make promise . . .*
    *I must to change my address for letters.*

I snatched at pieces from the blue pile of words like a starving animal scavenging meat from a carcass. But instead of satisfying, they only tantalized and teased and made me hungry for more. I wanted to scream out my frustration, my desperation, my all-consuming guilt. I had allowed Rita to paint over the memories of my mother with lies.

I had to go back to Africa. I had to find her. But there was something I had to do first, before I left Britain. I had to cut myself loose from the Steiner name. I would change my name back to Miriam Mphephu by deed poll.

# CHAPTER TWENTY-THREE

## January 1985

## Miriam

"International Directory Enquiries, how may I help?" A friendly Glaswegian accent was on the end of the line.

"Yes. Uh . . ." My voice quivered. "I'd like to trace a number in South Africa."

"Certainly, madam. What city?"

"Johannesburg."

"Name and address?"

"P. and M. Rodrigues. Sixth Street, Parkhurst."

"Please hold the line while I connect to the South African exchange."

The line crackled, then there was ringing.

A strong Afrikaans accent. "*Goeie môre*, good morning. Directory Assistance."

"Good morning, South Africa." The Scottish voice again.

"This is the United Kingdom. I'm trying to trace the telephone number for a P. and M. Rodrigues in Sixth Street, Parkhurst."

"Is that *M* for maple?"

"It is."

"In Second Street, Parkhurst," repeated the slow, thick voice.

"No, not *Second*!" I interjected, unable to be a silent member of this triangle.

"That is Sixth Street, sir," the Scottish lady corrected.

"Juz hold the line, please."

The leisurely pace of the call was killing me. Even a two-minute delay seemed intolerable.

Dave was balanced on the arm of my chair, caressing my back. He raised his eyebrows questioningly. I didn't respond.

"We have no listing for a P. and M. Rodrigues in Parkhurst—"

I should have known it wouldn't be as easy as a simple phone call.

"—but we do have one listing for that name with those initials in Orange Grove."

"Please hold, sir, while I speak with the caller. Caller, there is only one listing for a Rodrigues, and it's in Orange Grove. Do you wish to try that number?"

"Yes! Yes, please."

Silence, two beeps, then ringing.

A woman's voice.

"Go ahead, caller."

My mind went blank. "Uh . . . Hello . . . I'm calling from England. I'm not sure if I have the right number. Do Maria and Pedro Rodrigues live there?"

My hesitant voice echoed back at me. "Live there, live there, live there."

"This is Madam Morela house," said a native African voice.

"Oh. Oh, I'm sorry. I must have the wrong number."

A click and the line went dead.

Slowly I replaced the receiver.

"No luck?" David said, squeezing the back of my neck.

"I should have known it wouldn't be easy," I said, pulling away. "How stupid of me to think I'd get to speak to her today I mean, even if I had found the right people, it's been twenty-five years. My mother will be long gone. What's the likelihood of her working for them after all this time?"

I sank back into the chair, defeated.

Dave crouched down on his haunches and took my hands in his. "It just proves what we've known all along. You can't do this from thousands of miles away. You need to go back. You need to *be* there."

I almost resented his compliance and understanding. It would have been easier to make the decision to leave had he fought with me.

"I was speaking to a colleague at uni today," he went on, "who has a friend in Johannesburg—a newspaper reporter for *The Star*. He's offered to contact the guy and see if he'd be interested in following your story. Act as a sort of a guide. You can't do this on your own." He caressed my inner thigh. I shut my legs. "Miriam, Africa is waiting for you."

"I've done the maths," I said, standing up. "It's not going to be possible. I can't afford the fare. We're both living on my student loan."

His face broke into a broad grin. "You're forgetting the lecturing post."

I was annoyed. What was there to smile about? He hadn't even started the job yet. He slid a hand into a pocket in his jeans and pulled out a crumpled, peach-colored envelope. "Michael came to the university today."

I winced at the mention of Michael's name, the pain of our meeting still raw.

"He dropped this off for you."

I'd had enough of Michael's surprises.

"It's a check for two thousand pounds."

*Do you know where you are going?*

The orange poster on the tube door hadn't given up on me as I caught the Underground the following morning. This time, though, I smiled.

*Yes. Yes, I do.*

# PART TWO

# CHAPTER TWENTY-FOUR

## February 1985

"Please fasten your seat belt, do up your tray table, and place your chair in the upright position." The air hostess moved on through the cabin.

I rubbed my eyes. My neck ached, my mouth was dry, and my skin felt stale and itchy.

"You were out for some time," said the old lady next to me, as she touched up her foundation.

The plane's wheels hit the runway, the cabin shuddered, then came the screeching of brakes and we were thrust back into our seats. As we taxied toward the terminal, I pulled up the oval of blind covering my window and in an instant was doused in a shower of warm, yellow light.

The queue of passengers filed slowly out of the aircraft. Too slowly! I was impatient to get out.

The cabin attendant, her lipstick freshly applied, smiled

politely as I stepped out of the plane. "Thank you for flying British Airways."

Above me stretched an endless blue sky. A warm breeze carried smells to me, at once both foreign and strangely familiar. I inhaled deeply, feeling this new air seep into my body and filter to the ends of my fingers and toes. I hurried down the steep staircase, the moldy dampness of an English winter rising like steam as a dry, baking heat enveloped me. I stopped on the bottom step and teetered there for a moment before lowering first one foot, and then the other, to the ground.

Terra firma pushed back. This was the same soil I had walked on twenty-five years ago. It was overwhelming—the permanence of it. Humans were the transient ones—mere incidentals on this, nature's grand stage.

I climbed aboard the shuttle bus and with a jolt we were headed for the terminal building. Once inside, I joined the queue in front of the sign that said *Foreign Passports*.

Eventually I found myself in front of a heavyset man with lines of perspiration tracking across his greasy brow. Two dark patches of dampness ballooned out from under the arms of his khaki shirt. A lone table fan had lost its battle and was simply stirring up the rancid smell of sweat. I peeled off my cardigan.

The man eyed me suspiciously. "What is the nature of your business?" he barked, his rough voice matching his dented and pockmarked complexion.

"I . . . I'm here to . . ." I was caught off guard by his guttural hostility. I handed him my permit to visit, which Dave, after numerous letters and phone calls, had finally managed to secure for me.

"Born in Elim Hospital, hey?" he said with a snigger, his thick, nicotine-stained fingers paging through my British passport.

"Yes."

He gave me a long, contemptuous stare. "Where will you be residing?"

"With someone in Soweto," I said nervously. I couldn't bear the thought of anyone or anything sabotaging my journey at this late stage.

"Fill in the details," he said, shoving a sherbet-green form at me, then he stamped my passport with a thud. "Remember," he said, rolling his *r*'s and wagging a stubby finger at me, "it is a punishable offense to enter any public place reserved for whites or use any whites-only amenities."

I nodded obediently and scuttled through the turnstile.

My bags were already circuiting on the carousel when I reached the baggage collection hall. A bent black man with graying hair was heaving suitcases off the conveyor belt as passengers pointed to their moving luggage. A traveler half his age slipped him a coin.

"Sank you, *baas*," said the old man, his shiny black face lighting up, his hands clasped together in a ritual of gratitude.

I collected my own luggage and followed a white family down the green corridor—*Nothing to Declare*.

A woman dressed in khaki intercepted me. "This way," she directed me, her painted fingernails pointing to a stainless-steel counter.

She had short, bottle-blond hair and a heavily made-up face. Balanced on top of her curls was a boxlike hat, its upturned brim standing stiffly to attention. A thick layer of foundation had blanked out any hint of blemish or freckle.

My smile was not reciprocated.

"Open your bag."

As I clicked open my suitcase, the lid sprang back, releasing a burst of cramped contents. It had been a tight squeeze.

Ten minutes later the guts of my case lay spread out across the counter—underwear, an emptied tampon box, a squeezed tube of toothpaste, socks, books, medication, a now unwrapped present of Scottish shortbread . . . Even the jar of Colman's mustard had been opened. I felt as if *I* had been opened up and emptied out too.

The khaki woman made an all-embracing sweep with her arms and stuffed everything back into the case, but made no effort to shut it. "Okay. Move along," she said, already heading for a young Indian man.

My face was burning and blood was pounding in my temples. "But . . ." I fought back tears as I struggled to close my case. Another official slouching against an X-ray machine looked on absently.

Eventually, my hands trembling and my blouse damp with perspiration, I heaved my bag off the counter and made for the frosted-glass doors marked *Exit*.

As I approached them, I faltered. They were about to slide open on a different world—a world of so many unknowns. I'd hoped to feel an immediate affinity with this land I so desperately wanted to call home, but I realized now it could never be that simple. This country did not want me either.

For two pins I'd have jumped on the next plane back to England—back to Dave and my job, back to Zelda and her kids, back to the life I knew. The country of my birth hadn't received me with open arms or clasped me to its breast. Instead, in just a matter of minutes, I had been deftly deprived of my dignity. Everything I'd learned and practiced in the study of the mind hadn't prepared me for the psychology of apartheid. How quickly it ensnared and undermined its prey. How quickly I had succumbed.

I was angry, mostly with myself for being weak in the face of these people, but also for foolishly believing the riddle of my life could be solved so easily. Where did I belong?

Then, like the Red Sea, the doors in front of me parted and I was looking into a busy arrivals area, the pathway bordered by a blur of faces.

*Miriam Mphephu.*

I spotted the whiteboard with red writing hovering above the crowd. It took a few moments for me to realize it was *my* name; I still thought of myself as Miriam Steiner. I traced the sinewy black hands holding up the placard back to their owner— a tall man standing in the front row of the crowd. I had the advantage of being able to inspect him before he knew who I was.

His hair, a mass of tiny French knots, framed a luminous, open face dominated by a prominent forehead, angled cheekbones, and wide, warm eyes. A scar pulled at one corner of his mouth as it tracked down over his jaw. He was wearing a casual cotton work shirt with the sleeves rolled up and collar unbuttoned. Faded blue jeans hung off his bony hips, big dents in the denim accentuating his skinny frame.

I maneuvered my trolley toward him.

"Miriam?" His voice was strong and deep and left me feeling flustered.

"Welcome, sister," he said, breaking into a huge grin that creased his eyes shut. I was about to put out my hand, when he leaned forward and pulled me into a tight hug. The smell of his shirt—wood smoke and soap—awakened in me a strange sense of déjà vu. Undeveloped negatives flashed through my mind.

"You must be Thabo," I said clumsily, as he released me.

He gave a deep, throaty chuckle and extended his hand in formal greeting. "So very pleased to meet you."

I giggled like a schoolgirl, embarrassed at my own stiltedness.

To my surprise a small sparrow suddenly alighted on his left shoulder. I screamed and Thabo ducked just as my handbag glided past his ear. He straightened and looked anxiously over to his shoulder. The bird was still there, its small body puffed up in fright.

Stroking its wings, Thabo smoothed down the bird's ruffled feathers. "Miriam, meet Zaziwe."

"Oh, I'm so sorry," I said, mortified. "I had no idea. Is it a pet?" This was one time I was glad of my dark complexion; otherwise I would have been the color of a tomato.

"Not really a pet," Thabo said, looking thoughtfully at the small bird. "That would imply some degree of ownership. No, we're just good friends." And with that, he nimbly wrestled control of my trolley. "Come, you must be tired and we still have a long journey ahead of us."

So we headed out of the airport building into a glorious morning—golden dry heat, still blue air, sharp white light. In the parking lot we stopped beside a rusty red VW Beetle bearing the scars of several skirmishes. It took numerous attempts to start the engine before the little car finally coughed and spluttered toward the exit.

At the ticket booth, a man leaned out of a small square of window. *"Skakel die motor af."*

Thabo switched off the engine.

"What are you doing?" I was mystified, considering the effort it had taken to start the car.

Thabo put a finger to his lips.

*"Goed,"* the man said, feeding our parking ticket into his machine. *"Twee rand."*

Thabo rummaged in his back pocket and handed over a crumpled note.

*"Ry aan.* Drive on."

Now free to move, Thabo made several unsuccessful attempts to start the engine again, before finally leaping out and, with the handbrake down, pushing the car past the elevated barrier into a running start.

"What was that all about?" I asked once we were moving again.

"A security measure," he said. "Many cars are stolen. They check to see you have keys for the vehicle you're driving, just in case you'd jump-started it." He gave an engaging chuckle. "Welcome to the Wild West."

The six-lane highway stretched in a straight line toward the horizon, the road bordered by strips of golden grass interrupted occasionally by bands of leggy pink and white cosmos. So this was Africa. Like a word on the tip of my tongue, I could nearly remember it.

"Open your window if you like," Thabo volunteered. "Natural air-conditioning."

I wound down the window and a warm, grassy breeze blew in. Zaziwe ruffled her feathers indignantly and took refuge behind Thabo's ear.

"You must be tired," he said, fiddling with the radio dials. "We'll have lots of time to talk later. Just sit back and relax."

I was grateful. It relieved me of the pressure to make small talk. I *was* weary, having slept for only a few hours on the flight. Strains of African music filled the small car, and it wasn't long before the deep bass beat, rattling car parts, and soaring morning temperatures lulled me into a mellow stupor.

When I emerged from my reverie, there it was in front of us—Johannesburg—a tall gray tower with a bulbous top dominating the skyline. The gouty finger grew larger and larger and soon our little red car was trapped within the shadow of this skyscraper.

We wove through a maze of flyovers and highways until a sign prompted Thabo to abruptly change lanes. A prolonged hooter blast from behind saw Thabo swerve sharply to avoid colliding with a minibus packed with people.

"*Ai!* Bloody taxi drivers!" he cursed. "They're a law unto themselves."

I laughed nervously, releasing my foot from an imaginary brake pedal. Thankfully we were soon veering away from the hectic metropolis.

Two mounds of yellow dirt rose up on my right like flat-topped dunes.

"Old Rand mines," Thabo said, answering my gaze.

The mines.

"I can remember my mother telling me my father worked on the mines," I said, this recollection coming as a surprise. "I remember her telling me how important his job was. Busy too, I guess, because he never visited us."

Where was this coming from? Had the landscape so effortlessly unlatched a box in my mind? My voice was shaking and I struggled to maintain my composure in front of this stranger with whom I was sharing my very personal history—history that felt new even to me. It was a shock to face such recollections—recollections that sprang uninvited from my unconscious. But memory was like that. Capricious.

"Gold," Thabo said. "*Black* gold."

I wasn't sure what he meant.

The countryside was changing, dry grass giving way to dusty paths littered with rubbish, overturned supermarket trolleys, and abandoned car tires.

"The ridge of ore discovered here was actually low grade. It was simply the sheer amount of it that gave it any worth."

I watched anxiously as his hands lifted off the steering wheel to accompany his script.

"Extracting the particles of gold was labor-intensive and required huge amounts of manpower and expensive machinery. If the mining houses were to make any money out of the venture, they had to have ready access to cheap labor; I mean *very* cheap labor."

He swung an arm out, as though inviting someone onstage from the wings. "Enter the black man. Forbid him from living in the cities. Put him in large reserves where the land is barren

and job opportunities poor. Offer him work and accommoda-
tion on the mines. And hey, presto, migrant labor is born!"

He slapped the rim of the steering wheel with the flat of his
hand. The horn sounded. I jumped.

"Then forbid his family from joining him. That way you
only need pay wages for a single man. And . . . wait for it . . .
this is the best bit . . . because the worker is a migrant, no need
to budget for illness or old age. Throw in hostel living with
appalling conditions; make it a crime for a worker to break his
contract; force him to carry a pass whenever he leaves the com-
pound . . . Your labor problem is sorted *and* you get rich. Very
rich."

I shook my head, unable to think of something worthwhile
to say.

"This African earth would not easily give up its treasures to
the white fortune hunters; it took the black man's pickax before
it finally succumbed."

We drove on in silence.

"Now you've really got me going." He winked at me, a wide
grin sweeping away his earnest expression.

"No. Go on, please." I wished I had something valuable
to say.

"Just be proud of your father," he said, taking his eyes off
the road to look at me. "Even if you didn't know him, I can tell
you he will have worked hard to build the wealth of this nation.
Our people are the true gold. The *black* gold."

For the first time in my life someone was claiming ownership
of me. I was a member of "our people." It was a heady feeling.

A lull descended again. I spotted a new blot on the horizon. My eyes narrowed, trying to make sense of it. As we drew closer, I could make out thousands of rooftops sprawling across a vast scape of grayness.

*Welcome to Soweto*, beckoned a dilapidated sign positioned where the tar road gave way to red dust.

I closed my window as the rust-colored particles settled quickly on our windscreen, conniving with the smog to shroud our view.

Thabo pushed down his doorknob. "Lock your door."

Characterless, square brick-and-corrugated-iron dwellings stretched for as far as the eye could see, one after another after another. Two windows, one door. Two windows, one door. Two windows, one door—like Lego blocks stripped of color. The only interruptions to this blanched monotony were the bright rags hanging limply on makeshift washing lines. Even the red seemed to have been leached out of the earth.

Smoke spiraled from crude chimneys to blend with the blanket of smog. Mangy dogs sniffed in upturned dustbins, while children dressed in shreds of fabric played in the dirt. Toddlers squatted on steps, oblivious to the flies feeding off their crusty noses. Rusty cars minus wheel or windscreen served as playgrounds. Scrawny chickens scratched in the barren earth.

I tilted my head back to take in the towering streetlights at every corner. They were more suited to prisons.

"Soweto," I said out loud.

Thabo nodded. "Stands for 'South-Western Townships.' Twenty-four townships clustered southwest of Joburg."

I sensed there was more to come. Thabo's amiable and easy-going exterior clearly belied a strong passion for the history of his people.

"The discovery of gold on the Witwatersrand saw a flood of black people into Johannesburg seeking work, and with time their labor became vital in areas other than just the mines; Johannesburg needed the black man. But where was he to stay? In desperation he built makeshift dwellings on empty lots out of anything he could lay his hands on—rocks, sacking, sheets of corrugated iron—and soon illegal shantytowns sprang up."

I saw the razor first, a glint of silver out of the corner of my eye. Then I spotted the barber. He cut a dapper figure leaning over his swathed client, in high-collared white jacket and neatly pressed trousers. An orderly queue of prospective patrons stood patiently looking on. On top of the bonnet of an old Toyota was a tray of the barber's instruments glinting in the sunlight. This barber's shop was the roadside; his barber's chair an upturned metal drum. All that was missing was a candy-striped pillar.

"These overcrowded and squalid settlements would quickly become a breeding ground for crime and disease, yet it was only after an influenza epidemic swept through the black population of Johannesburg, nearly decimating it, that a formal housing scheme was born, and with it, the concept of the township."

Thabo hooted as we passed a group of men playing cards beside the road. They looked up and waved.

"Townships are ghettolike areas positioned on the edges of white cities—an answer to the government's dilemma of where to house the black workforce servicing these cities."

It must have been break time. A group of children dressed in school uniforms milled around outside their classroom—an old shipping container. The girls looked out of place wearing their black school pinafores and white cotton blouses. Their busts were too big, their hems too high, and their exposed thighs too womanly. The boys seemed incongruous too—their expressions and body language jarring with the notion I held in my head of carefree schoolchildren. These schoolboys looked more like men, their eyes restless and hard.

"Houses began being built under a housing project, but far too slowly. Finally Sir Ernest Oppenheimer stepped in and loaned six million rand to the scheme to help ease the crisis." He turned to look at me. "Heard of him?"

I shook my head, embarrassed by my ignorance.

"The father of Anglo American—a corporation whose fortune was founded squarely on the backs of black miners."

We stopped at an intersection. The coins on the dashboard began to reverberate and the earth beneath us shuddered as a massive lemon-yellow vehicle rumbled past, leaving our car cloaked in another layer of grime. Rising up out of the dust, like an apparition, was a pimply white soldier standing on top of the vehicle, his R1 at the ready. He looked out of place, standing there in his khaki army uniform—too young, too fresh faced. School shorts and shirt would have been more fitting.

I twisted the flesh on my wrist. I needed to be sure I wasn't wading through a bizarre dream. It was all so surreal.

"And that, Miriam, is how this vast *city*, which is not classified as a city in any atlas I have seen, was born." Thabo swept a hand across the dashboard. "You know, it stretches for more than two hundred kilometers." The car veered slowly across the midline before he casually retrieved control. I don't think Thabo even noticed the army vehicle.

We drove through a labyrinth of streets with no names and, after a time, turned down a road that distinguished itself by houses boasting precast walls or small patches of lawn. Thabo pulled up outside a house with *7789* painted in black on the front door.

Behind a low wire fence was a threadbare strip of lawn. An elderly black woman was kneeling on all fours painstakingly trimming the grass with a pair of scissors.

"That's Patience, my brother's mother-in-law."

"You can say that again," I said in disbelief. "Cutting grass with scissors!"

Thabo laughed. "That is her name. I live here with my brother and his family. You'll meet them tonight. Everyone except Patience is away at work or at school."

Zaziwe jumped from the dashboard onto my shoulder, startling me.

Thabo smiled. "I think she likes you."

"Evidently not that much," I said, wiping a chalky blob off my blouse.

Thabo parked in front of a pair of lopsided old gates secured with a heavy brass padlock. I wasn't sure about the need for a lock; anyone could have leapt over the waist-high gates.

As Thabo climbed out of the car, the old woman stood up, flinching as her wizened body complained. He spoke briefly to her in his native tongue, then she shuffled over to unlock the gate, a warm smile creeping over her face.

I climbed out to greet her.

She took my hands in her callused ones and pulled me in, her sagging breasts the only barrier to her warm embrace. I could feel her dry, wrinkly skin pressed up against me. I inhaled deeply and a sweet earthiness filled my nostrils, then I closed my eyes, and for the briefest moment, Patience became my mother.

# CHAPTER TWENTY-FIVE

Thabo and Patience were seated at a table in the kitchen when I came in from the outside washroom—a lean-to shed swarming with flies.

He stood up and poured me a cup of *rooibos* tea from the battered aluminum teapot on the stove. He had strong hands—I always noticed a man's hands—with clean, blunt fingernails. I was looking around for the milk when he scooped up a spoon of sweetened condensed milk from an opened can on the table and stirred it into my tea.

This was a very different drink from the tea I was used to drinking in England. First, it was a rust-orange color and it had a sweet, smoky flavor. But I was an instant convert; a cup of char had never tasted so good.

"So our mission is to find your mother," Thabo said, pushing back his chair. His words were confident and reassuring, as if our success was a foregone conclusion.

"I'm so grateful to you for your hospitality and assistance." My words clunked awkwardly. I cringed at my own formality.

"Thabo Rhadebe at your service," he said, twirling his right wrist three times and bowing. He'd sensed my unease and made light of it.

The old lady couldn't speak much English, but she gave a hearty chuckle.

I felt so silly.

"As you know, I'm a journalist." Thabo's face was serious. "However, with all the recent unrest and the clampdown on media, my work has been severely restricted."

The old lady topped up my tea.

"The newspaper I work for has been under close scrutiny. The government considers *The Star* to be part of *Die Rooi Gevaar*."

I must have looked puzzled.

"Communism, 'the Red Threat.' All liberals are communist, didn't you know?" He winked at me and then crushed a biscuit in his hands, sprinkling the crumbs on the table. Zaziwe set about attending to the feast with short, sharp jerks of her beak.

"So, for the meantime I have to abide by my editor's directive and my pen is practically idle. But idle *out* of prison is definitely preferable to being idle inside." Thabo then proceeded to tell me how my visit would change things. He'd managed to persuade his boss to let him write an account of my search for my mother.

"I think your editor was instrumental in helping me get a visitor's permit," I said.

Thabo nodded. "*No politics* is what I promised him. Just a simple account of an adopted girl's quest for her origins. It has all the makings of a good story."

I shrugged. "I hope so."

"And who knows what I'll be able to slip in when no one's watching," he said with a mischievous glint in his eye. "What I'm trying to say, Miriam, is that I'm looking forward to the challenge and am most happy to be your guide."

My mind was spinning—the sights, the sounds, the smells, these words . . . Nothing felt real. A telephone started to ring.

It was David calling from England.

"Yes, she is safe and well, Dayyvid," Thabo shouted into the receiver. "We only got in about a half hour ago. Yes. No, right here at the table having a cup of tea."

Zaziwe cocked her head to one side as if following the conversation.

"Wait, I'll pass you to her. Uh . . . Just a moment, here she is."

I took the phone. It was like putting my ear to a windy tunnel, the line whistling and howling.

"Hi, darling-darling-dar . . ." Dave's voice echoed down the line. I could almost visualize his words navigating their way through the cable on the sea floor, the weight of water toying with his message.

"Hi."

"You okay-okay-okay?"

"Just a bit weary. It was a long flight—"

"What is—"

"What?"

"It's a bad line-ine-ine. What time did you get in-in-in?"

"Nine thirty. It seems ages since I left. Can't believe it's only been twenty-odd hours. So much has happened. What?"

"First —pressions?"

"Hot." I laughed. "And black faces everywhere. I'm not part of a dying breed after all! But listen, don't waste your money; it's such a bad line. I'll try to call next week. What you say? I . . . Look, I can't hear you, Dave. I'll write soon, promise."

"—you."

"What?"

"Love you-you-you. Miss y—"

"Me too," I said self-consciously.

"Me too?" He sounded hurt.

"I love you too," I said, cupping my hand over the receiver.

"Miriam, remember—"

"Sorry, Dave, I can't hear. Look—"

The line went dead.

I stared at the mouthpiece, then slowly replaced the receiver.

Thabo was sorting through mail at the table. He looked up. "All okay?"

"Just a bad line."

I felt unsettled. The call had been unsatisfactory. I fiddled with the locket around my neck. Open, shut. Open, shut.

"You have a picture inside?"

"No, not yet."


I had a fitful first night in my bed at the tip of Africa. I couldn't escape the oppressive heat; the toilet was outside and I was sharing a bed with Patience—not a very comfortable experience; the mattress was lumpy and the frame creaky.

The house had two small bedrooms. Thabo's brother and sister-in-law slept in one with their two older children. The three younger ones and the old lady slept in the other—the kids on a mattress on the floor. Thabo camped out in the living room. And now me, feeling like a real imposition.

I lay very still, anxious not to disturb anyone, listening to the breathing of my elderly bedfellow. Outside, the township wasn't sleeping either, and when I did eventually doze off, fractured voices and revving car engines intruded on my already cluttered dreams.

In the middle of the night I was ripped from my slumber by a chilling scream. I leapt out of bed and yanked open the curtains, my heart pounding in my chest. But I couldn't make out anything in the blackness, except for the luminous face of my wristwatch—1:13 A.M. Amazingly the others had slept through the disturbance. I slipped back into bed, my allotment of space further narrowed where Patience's limbs had spilled onto my side.

I was hungry. Thabo had told me to make myself at home, but I couldn't just help myself to their food. So I lay there hollow stomached, staring at the ceiling as the minutes and then hours ticked by.

At 4:30 someone stirred in the adjacent room. It was a relief to know someone else couldn't sleep. Then I realized the shuffling and scratching sound was more purposeful. I would later learn it was Thabo's brother and sister-in-law washing and dressing by candlelight. She worked at a drycleaner's in Johannesburg; he, at a shoe factory on the outskirts of the city. Both caught the train to be at their respective jobs by seven.

I heard the soft click of the front door. The eldest boy and his father, buckets in hand, were heading for the communal tap some blocks away, where they would be met by an already long queue and have to wait in the fading darkness for almost an hour before it was their turn to draw water.

By the time they returned, the second eldest would have made sandwiches for the entire household and left for her job at the local *spaza* shop, where she worked each day before school. Out on the table would be eight neatly wrapped peanut butter sandwiches stacked in a listing tower. Thabo would also rise early to help with the household chores. Only the old lady and the two younger children would be left to wake with the rising sun.

Thabo bowled into my room. "Rise and shine!"

I must have dozed off. Opening my eyes begrudgingly, I struggled to extricate myself from sleep. Sunlight streamed undiluted through a crack in the curtains.

Thabo was standing at the foot of my bed in a creased T-shirt and boxers, a mug of coffee in his hand and Zaziwe on his shoulder. The bird took off from its perch and started circling the perimeter of the room, tweeting a deafening wake-up call.

"So your first night was that bad, eh?" he said with a chuckle.

I was not a morning person.

"I've left a basin of water at the door for you when you feel like washing, and breakfast is ready when you are. We've got a pretty full day ahead."

I sat up. "I heard this awful scream in the middle of the night.

It sounded like someone was being murdered. Didn't you hear it?"

"Just one? That was a good night, then."

"But—"

"It's a war zone after dark. You'll get used to it." Then he was gone.

I sat in the already too-hot sunlight, gripped by a sudden loneliness and longing. I missed Dave cuddling up to me in the wee hours; I missed our tiny student flat in the middle of Cambridge; I even missed my troubled patients.

We climbed into Thabo's car. My seat was baking hot and the perished plastic stung the backs of my legs. The day promised to be a scorcher. I wound down my window a little, but the tepid breath of morning did little to relieve the unremitting heat, even when the car was moving.

The journey out of Soweto felt shorter than the previous day's trek through the sprawling township, and it wasn't long before we were drawing into a small town on the outskirts of Johannesburg.

"We need to refuel," Thabo said, slowing for a red traffic light.

A small pickup truck, or *bakkie*, as Thabo called it, pulled up alongside us. In the cab sat a white man and his dog. The dog was straining its head out the open window, hungrily swallowing the sluggish breeze. In the back, among farming implements and exposed to the elements, crouched a weathered black man. He saw me staring and his face crumpled into a toothless grin. I gave a self-conscious wave. Then we were moving again.

White men in safari suits strode purposefully down pavements. Women with big hair and high heels tottered about their business. From the heights of a banner strung across the local church, Jesus promised to save those who renounced their sins. A black boy struggled across the road under a load of animal feed. Shining farm equipment stood chained out in front of the local hardware store. Next door, lolly-colored Crimplene dresses hung off dusty, lifeless mannequins, while two shops down, a home-industries cooperative boasted crocheted creations and homemade carrot cake.

A delicious aroma of vanilla and caramelized sugar filled the car.

"Mm—that smells so good," I said hungrily. It was coming from a bakery advertising impossible-to-pronounce delicacies—*koeksisters*, *vetkoek*, and *melktert*.

"Traditional Afrikaans fare," Thabo said as we passed. "*Koeksisters* are plaited ropes of sweet bread soaked in a thick syrup, and *vetkoek* is a sort of fried dumpling filled with savory mince."

"What's the *melk* thing?"

"*Melktert*. It means milk tart—a simple but extremely delicious cinnamon custard tart."

"You're making me hungry."

"We've just had breakfast! You English have big appetites!"

It was strange to once again be lumped with a group of people, given a label, a presumed identity. I'd never thought of myself as English, yet I *had* spent most of my life in England.

We cruised on through the wide tree-lined streets until Thabo spotted a car park right outside Jacobus's Slaghuis. A blackboard at the door distracted the eye from the butcher's bloody window, guaranteeing the shopper a bargain. *Spesiale aanbod op boerewors. Special on boerewors sausage. Beef chuck for servants and boys only 60c.*

"Back in a minute," he said, hopping out of the car and darting into the butchery.

He was in the shop a long time. Through the window I could see him being bumped to the back of the queue each time a white customer walked in.

Across the road a handful of barefoot black urchins—all angled bones and gaping smiles—hovered around an overflowing dustbin promising treasure. *Recycled bottles 5c refund.*

"Have a piece of biltong." Thabo was at my window, his joviality undampened by the humiliating wait in the butchery. "It's a South African delicacy."

Gingerly I took the unappealing stick of dry, shriveled meat.

"Chew on it," he said, climbing back in the car. "It'll keep you going for hours. A great distraction on a long road trip."

I was reluctant at first, but had to concede it did actually taste good. The salty meat had a strong, spicy flavor.

Two blocks farther down, we pulled in to a petrol station beside a vacant pump. As soon as Thabo turned off the engine, a black attendant appeared, dressed in navy trousers, an emerald-green shirt, and a peaked hat with the BP logo on the front. He stood to attention at Thabo's window, his white teeth gleaming. He had the blackest face I'd ever seen, his features completely swallowed up by the darkness of his skin. Just the light bouncing off protuberances hinted at a nose, a chin, a forehead.

"Regula or supa?"

"No worries, brother, I'll fill her up. But the windscreen, she needs a clean."

In a few slick movements the eager attendant had sloshed soapy water over the glass then skimmed it off. Thabo thanked him, tipping him a coin for his efforts.

Another car was pulling up and the attendant once again sprang into action, volunteering his infectious smile in greeting.

"Fill her up."

As the pump ran and the driver went inside to pay, the attendant started uninvited to clean the car's windscreen. The female passenger in the front seat shifted uncomfortably as the BP man beamed at her through the glass. She looked away.

Once he'd completed the job, he lingered. The woman fiddled at her feet, then finally tossed something out of her window. It was a mangled toffee in a gold wrapper. The attendant leapt into the air to catch it, his smile never once leaving his face.

Petrol paid for, Thabo reappeared. "There'll be time enough to pay for things," he said, blocking my contribution.

Once back in the car, he pulled out a stained, bird-pecked map from under his seat and spread it across our laps. Zaziwe hopped about, chasing Thabo's finger as he traced our planned route to the Johannesburg suburb of Parkhurst.

"Out of the way, Zaziwe!" he cried. "I can't see a darned thing."

The bird hopped onto the steering wheel and then back onto the map.

"She's been really obnoxious lately. I think she's jealous of you." He grinned. "It's the first time she's had to compete with another woman."

I felt my face growing hot.

Then we were driving again, this time bound for the north of the city, to my mother's last-confirmed address. Even though my call to Directory Assistance had come up a blank, Thabo had resolved to pay the house a visit in the hope it might shed some light on my mother's whereabouts.

The city landscape started to change. There was more greenery—big trees, stretches of lawn, dense creepers, and shiny-leafed shrubs. I caught glimpses of magnificent homes on a scale I'd never seen before—stunning architectural creations hidden behind solid brick walls, intercoms and security cameras discreetly positioned on perfectly plastered pillars.

Less discreet were the signs. *Immediate Armed Response. Vicious dog—Beware. Enter at your own risk.* The signage and inconceivably high walls transformed these stately residences into fortresses. There were even sentries. I spotted a black man in official-looking gear standing guard outside one of the homes, a baton hanging idly from his waist.

"We must leave no stone unturned," Thabo said out of the blue. "You'll be surprised what you can find under a rock."

I decided I liked Thabo—his quirky, homegrown take on idioms, his passion and care, his easy laughter. It was just his driving that left a lot to be desired. Speaking of which, without any warning or use of indicators, he swung out of the traffic into a driveway, nearly leveling two black women chatting on the pavement. Then, still in gear, he released the clutch and we lurched forward, before coming to an abrupt halt.

"Nearly drove right past it," he said casually.

I released my grip on the armrest.

The two women on the pavement were shaking their heads and gesturing angrily. Thabo climbed out and strolled over to them.

"*Uxolo!* Sorry for the fright, mamas," he said, affectionately placing an arm around the chubbier one. She was the more irate of the two, the other expressing her anger in more muted mutterings.

Thabo tilted his head to one side and peered at the aggrieved women from under his thick black lashes. His enormous eyes were both apologetic and mesmerizing. Not surprisingly, the situation was quickly defused and when I ventured from the car, I stepped into a scene loud with laughter.

Twenty minutes on, the trio were *still* talking. I'd only been able to gather fragments of their lively discussion, gleaned from the few English words peppering their dialogue.

"It's the journalist in you," I said to Thabo later, when I discovered how much information he'd gathered. "You've got a knack for foraging, haven't you?"

After about a half hour, we were finally climbing back into the little red car. Images of Toad of Toad Hall's erratic driving flashed before me and I braced for the next leg of our intrepid journey, as Thabo wrote something down on a scrap of paper.

"So we're not going to call in at the house after all?"

"No point. The Rodrigues family, for whom your mother worked, has long since moved."

The reality of his words hit hard. So what had all the merriment been about? Only with time would I come to understand laughter was as necessary as breathing for black Africans.

"But," Thabo added slowly, the word fat with promise, "the

chubby one, she has worked as a maid next door for almost thirty years. She . . ." He scratched his cheek.

"She what?" I was impatient, especially since I'd already tolerated a half hour of indecipherable chatter.

"She knew your mother."

"She *knew my mother*?" My throat tightened and tears immediately blurred my vision. I swung around. The woman had gone. I wanted to say something, but nothing came out. I hadn't afforded her the import she was due. I hadn't studied her face or asked her a single question. I'd been a passenger for the entire conversation.

"They were good friends; however, she hasn't seen your mother in a very long time—many years, in fact."

He went on to tell me how my mother had fled the Rodrigues' employ, only to be arrested and thrown in prison on an accusation of theft. The two friends lost contact until, out of the blue, a letter had arrived from my mother. She was apparently working for a good family in Parktown North. The chubby one had visited her there once, before again losing touch.

"She's given me the address," Thabo said, pointing to the scrap of paper on the dashboard.

I grabbed it and scrutinized his scribble.

"So you see, it is not over till the fat lady sings," Thabo said, grinding the gears into reverse before we shot out into the busy road.

We drove for the next fifteen minutes in silence. I was oblivious to my surroundings and even Thabo's driving, and by the time we parked beside an imposing white wall in an avenue lined with plane trees, I had picked my thumbnails down to the raw, bulgy bit.

"Wait here," Thabo said, getting out.

I wound down my window.

He pushed the buzzer of an intercom positioned in the white wall.

"*Sawubona*," said a voice that crackled through the tiny holes.

"*Sawubona*," he said, speaking into the silver box. "Hullo."

Thabo leaned into the pillar, conversing earnestly with the device.

The voice at the other end went quiet.

Thabo straightened. My heart sank. What now?

I followed his gaze down the long driveway. A black woman in yellow overalls with a matching head scarf and frilled white apron was walking up the drive toward him.

Soon their intercom exchange had resumed in person, and once again there was much smiling, exclaiming, and pointing. The gentle pace and congenial preamble that seemed an integral part of any African interaction was beginning to frustrate me.

Unable to contain myself, I opened my door and made to get out.

I stopped. The woman was disappearing back down the driveway.

Thabo turned and held up a hand. I cursed and pulled the door shut.

Minutes passed. An eternity. My head was throbbing and Zaziwe, whom I was supposed to be babysitting, was being a pain, hopping excitedly about the car and leaving me dizzy.

Finally there was some movement again at the bottom of the driveway. I craned my neck to see two figures this time—the yellow overalls maid and someone else . . . a white woman—walking up the drive. Two small children followed in their wake.

Anxiety twisted through me. In England most of my patients had been white, but that felt like a lifetime ago. I'd only been in this country a short time and already I'd submitted to its edicts and pressures, to its beliefs.

I slunk down in the car, my determination now diminished and uncertain. I was just another black girl hoping this white madam would give me enough time to explain myself.

She looked about my age, with a shiny, rounded forehead, perfect complexion, and golden hair pulled back in a thick pony-tail. She was beautiful. A chunky gold chain drooped around her neck and slid effortlessly over her cream blouse. She stopped short of the gate, fingering a small black disk in her hand. Thabo would later explain it was a remote panic button.

Thabo's back excluded me from the ensuing conversation. Eventually he turned and beckoned to me. Suddenly running away seemed like the easier option. Did I really want to know the truth? And what if this was where the trail ended?

"Good morning," I said, approaching the gate. "I'm sorry to have disturbed you." I sounded out of breath, my words jerky and uneven.

There was a long pause, the woman obviously disconcerted by my Norfolk accent. I guess it wasn't what she'd expected to come out of a black person's mouth. She slipped the panic button into her cardigan pocket. A "white" accent had effectively bleached my complexion and lent me some credibility. "Not at all. Franscina tells me you're looking for a girl called Celia."

That word "girl" again. I'd heard it several times in my short stay. How could it refer to a mature woman in her sixties? How could "boy"—paperboy, garden boy, houseboy—refer to *any* black male, regardless of whether he was a *piccanin* or a grandfather?

One of the children started to pick her nose.

"We've certainly never had a girl by that name working here," the woman went on. "And we've been in the house now . . . Gosh, it's going on five years. We bought the place from a couple by the name of Eloff. Whether or not their maid was called Celia, though, I really couldn't say. They moved to the Cape."

"Do you know *where* in the Cape, madam?" Thabo asked.

"We forwarded their mail for almost a year. I think it was Knysna, or maybe George." She pulled her child's finger from its nose. "My memory fails me. I'll see if I can find the address. Give me a minute."

With that she turned and made her way quickly back to the house, her children scampering behind. The gate remained shut. My complexion had obviously not faded entirely.

Franscina was delighted with the new company and hung back to chat with Thabo while I stood aside, again a third wheel. After a time, the white woman returned.

"Franscina, go back down to the house, will you. I've left the children there and there's soup on the stove. I don't want it to boil over."

Disappointed not to be party to the rest of the saga, Franscina bid us farewell and headed dutifully back to work.

"Look, I can't find that address anywhere."

I felt myself plunging down the next dip on this roller-coaster ride.

"Leave me the details of where I can reach you if it comes to light," the woman said, a controlled smile moving across her face. Perhaps she felt she'd been too familiar and was now trying to claw back the appropriate boundaries.

"Thank you for your time, madam," Thabo said, jotting down his telephone number on the back of an advertorial he'd picked up off the pavement. "Here is my phone number in Soweto. You can leave a message there, for Thabo Rhadebe. That's me. Anything you think might be useful, anything at all, please call us."

"Remember," the woman added in a cautionary tone, "even if your mother *did* work for the Eloffs, she may not have followed them to the Cape."

I managed a courteous smile and moved quickly back to the car, tears not far off. I was embarrassed by my emotions. Lately they'd been all over the place.

Thabo caught hold of my arm.

"This is the very beginning of the journey, Miriam. You can't lose heart so soon." He wiped a tear off my cheek. "There will be other hurdles. This just the first of many."


The next day was Sunday—another perfectly clear and cloudless African day. Yet waking to the golden light did little to lift my spirits. I was trapped in a morose mood. How quickly I'd forgotten the grayness and gloom of the country I'd left behind.

In an effort to rescue me from myself, Thabo decided to take me on a drive to Zoo Lake—a man-made lake scooped out of the heart of the northern suburbs. It was a beautiful spot and strangely familiar—the colorful rowboats on the sun-drenched waters, the willows bowing over grassy banks, the swoops of undulating lawn; I felt like I'd been here before. We bought samosas and milk shakes from a small kiosk at the water's edge, then lounged on the grass while Zaziwe busied herself pecking off the crumbs trapped in the creases of Thabo's shirt.

Later, we hired one of the rowboats and ventured out onto the lake, for an hour splashing and fooling like children. I wanted the afternoon to last forever.

When our hour was up, we moored the boat and I bought a mango the size of a small soccer ball from an African woman peddling fruit. It cost me just twenty cents. In England a pitiful pockmarked one could cost anything up to two pounds!

Thabo peeled it with his penknife, and as I savored the sweet orange flesh, gates were opened in my mind, releasing flashes of another life and almost-remembered memories. *A black cloud of fruit flies hover over a cardboard box packed tightly with mangoes. I see myself choosing the biggest mango from the box. My mother . . . yes, my mother . . . puts it to her nose and nods. While she peels it for me, I suck on the sweet skins. Then I am chasing the slippery orange fruit around my plate, squealing with happiness and frustration. I also see a family of mango-pip dolls lined up on a concrete step. There's a big garden. The Ma . . . the Mam . . . the Mamelodi family! Yes, the Mamelodi mango family.*

*One doll has no hair. I remember cutting it off with blunt kitchen scissors. The others have crazy, stringy hairstyles . . .*

As the afternoon light softened and the day started to draw to a lazy close, Thabo and I reluctantly took our leave.

For a Sunday evening, the traffic was thick and slow, and soon our chatter had slowed too, until we'd settled into a comfortable silence. Just as we were approaching the silky haze of Soweto, the car began to judder and gasp for air in the evening smog.

"I'll need to get it serviced before we head off on any sort of long journey," Thabo said, breaking into my thoughts.

"This time you must let me contribute something," I insisted as we stuttered around a corner. Then I heard myself scream as I was catapulted toward the windscreen. Thabo threw an arm across me, arresting my momentum just in time and slapping me back into my seat.

"You okay?"

But before I could reply, I saw them—the crowd of people gathered in the middle of the road, oblivious to the fact that we'd nearly plowed into them.

"My god," I cried out, my words weirdly in unison with a bone-chilling wail that had risen into the evening air.

"Lock my door and stay in the car," Thabo said, getting out and making his way through the throng of people.

The crowd parted and I saw a boy lying in the middle of the road. There was a dark patch over the pocket of his denim shirt and another spreading in the dirt beneath him. His wide eyes told of a lonely fear. Thabo knelt down beside the teen and the crowd resealed around him. Then the group had burst wide open again and four men were carrying the groaning kid to our car. As they

laid him across the backseat, the car was filled with a meaty cocktail of blood, sweat, and alcohol. I felt bilious. Another youth
climbed in beside the boy, lifting the kid's limp legs onto his lap.
I kept staring straight ahead, for fear if I looked I would be sick.

As we drove away from the scene Thabo pointed out the
armored vehicle stationed at the corner. A white soldier was
standing on the roof of the Casspir observing us.

"Incident didn't warrant intervention," Thabo said cynically.
"A black stabbing poses no threat to stability."

With the horn blaring and hazard lights flashing, we sped
through the maze of nameless streets. Adding to the commotion
were the boy's deep groans, but as they started to dwindle, the
ranting of our other alcohol-fueled passenger grew louder.

Thabo put his hand over mine. It was warm and reassuring.

Eventually our headlights captured a lopsided green signpost
in their glare: *Baragwanath Hospital.* I breathed a sigh of relief.

At the emergency entrance Thabo jumped out and harnessed
a wayward gurney, and he and the other passenger hoisted the
boy onto it. I noticed the soles of the kid's feet were white. At
the end of a long corridor Thabo maneuvered the gurney
through a pair of stainless-steel doors.

"Surgical pit," he said to me over his shoulder.

A bizarre scene greeted us, an eerie sort of organized chaos.
Black patients were seated in rows on green plastic chairs, all
waiting their turn as if in some post office queue. One man, a
machete protruding from his skull, sat beside a woman gripping
her belly. A sullen schoolboy sporting two swollen eyes was
handcuffed to a black policeman. And an elderly man retched
quietly into an ice-cream container. The stench of fresh blood

and vomit swirled. Screams no one seemed to notice came from behind closed curtains, as black nurses and white doctors went about their business.

The sticky floor tugged at my sneakers. Looking down I saw I was making a line of red footprints as I walked. No one acknowledged our entrance. A doctor swept past us. He had an incongruously young yet unperturbed face, clearly already immune to the gore surrounding him.

Thabo caught a nurse's attention. She glanced cursorily over her shoulder at our patient, appraised him in an instant, then was shouting across the room. "Stabbed heart!"

Like magic, the scene before us transformed. Stitching was deserted and wounds left gaping as nurses calmly abandoned what they were doing. Two doctors and an orderly appeared, and the boy on the trolley was pushed into a vacant cubicle.

The curtains were left open.

I couldn't help but watch as the team worked to save the boy. It was like a well-rehearsed performance—every player familiar with his or her role. No prompting required.

A hush fell over the room when the principal walked in—a tall, unshaven man with tired gray eyes. A nurse unpacked a parcel on a stainless-steel trolley and assisted him to gown up. Once the green gown had been fastened, his gloves were meticulously applied. It was all happening so fast, yet nothing felt hurried, every detail calmly checked off.

Thabo wandered over to me. "You okay?"

"Is he going to be all right?" What a foolish question. How would he know?

He crossed his fingers and smiled.

"BP?" The gowned doctor was firing questions at his team.

"Sixty over forty."

"Pulse?"

"One-eighty, thready."

"Fluid?"

"Two fourteen-gauge lines. Haemaccel running. Blood sent for cross-match."

The doctor picked up a scalpel.

"He's the surgical registrar," Thabo whispered. "The consultants hardly ever come in after hours. Registrars deal with everything."

A metal blade scattered slices of light across the room as the registrar drew a thin white line down the youth's black body— a thin white line. Just one layer beneath the black was white. The white turned red, then yellow flesh sprang back.

My head began to spin.

A nurse stepped into my line of view, but the sounds of pulling and splitting and tearing worked closely with my imagination to complete the picture.

The registrar called for bone cutters.

*Kligh. Kligh.*

"He's cutting through the sternum," Thabo said. "They're going to pump the kid's heart by hand and force around the body what little blood is left, while they try to repair the laceration in the heart wall."

He was speaking like a medic. Was there nothing he didn't know?

"But surely they can't do open-heart surgery in a cubicle. I mean, shouldn't it be performed in a sterile theater?"

Thabo didn't respond. He was too busy watching. I followed his gaze. The nurse had moved aside and I could see a gloved hand reaching into the boy's chest. It grabbed hold of something. Tighten, release, tighten, release . . .

My knees were buckling and I felt myself falling.

When I came to, I was lying across a set of the plastic chairs with a towel propping up my head. The curtains of the cubicle were now drawn and I could make out two figures behind it in silhouette.

I looked up at Thabo. He was standing over me, frowning. He shook his head, answering my silent interrogation. At the same time an agonizing scream rang out—full of fury and despair. It came from the other youth, the companion of our man-boy. I watched as he thumped his fists against the wall, punching a hole right through the prefab partition. Then security had leveled him and he was being dragged from the room, kicking, screaming, biting, and ranting.

"He didn't make it." Thabo sounded almost guilty, as though he'd played some part in the boy's demise.

My eyes stung and my head throbbed.

He placed both his hands over mine. "I've got to make a statement to the police, then we can go. Lie here for now."

I lay there for what seemed like hours. Thoughts came and went; some stayed. What was the kid's name? Where was his mother? Was she happy the day he was born? What would he have looked like as an older man? And the doctor—what did it feel like to pump someone's heart? To hold a life in one's hands—the ultimate godlike act? Just a thin layer beneath the boy's black skin was white. White. White. White!

Zaziwe alighted on my chest and tilted her head from side to side. Thabo must have been nearby.

He supported me as I walked in a daze down the open hospital corridors, through pale fingers of moonlight. We passed patients in brightly checkered dressing gowns lounging in the spacious quadrangles of lawn, their drip stands and wheelchairs blending in with their silvered surrounds.

Suddenly a wave of the most beautiful sound I'd ever heard swept over us.

I stopped.

"The nurses are changing shifts," Thabo said. "They always sing with the patients at changeover."

We were outside the entrance to a ward. I peered in. At least a dozen beds lined each wall. All were occupied, and the overflow patients lay on mattresses on the floor. A horseshoe of nurses stood at the top of the room, their starched white uniforms hugging voluptuous figures, all bust and bottom. Every eye was trained on the matron. Fungating sores, amputated limbs, and debrided ulcers seemed to melt away as the heavenly voices caressed every crevice of this old ward.

I stood mesmerized by the music, and as the last healing notes of the African hymn settled, I realized the pain in my heart had eased.

We continued down the corridor.

"Baragwanath Hospital. If you've got a stabbed heart, this is where you wanna be." All that was missing from Thabo's advertisement was some corny jingle.

I didn't respond; I didn't feel like being lighthearted or silly.

"Seriously, they've got the best success rate in the world.

Doctors here do more thoracotomies for stabbed hearts than in any other hospital in the world."

A long, lean man crossed in front of us, pushing a drip stand connected to him by a lone translucent tube that burrowed into the back of his hand. He wore just pajama bottoms. Every rib on his spare torso was delineated, like ripples on a dark pond. And running down the middle of his trunk, from chin to navel, was a thick ridge of fleshy pink skin, freshly stitched.

"*Sawubona*," he said in greeting.

His eyes gave no clue as to what it felt like to have cheated death.

# CHAPTER TWENTY-SIX

## April

*My dear David,*

*I have sat down to write to you so many times, and each time, I've found myself unable to. In part, it's because I have so little to tell; I'm no closer to tracing my mother than when I arrived six weeks ago. In part, my delay has also been because I have so much to say and I don't really know where to start.*

*The last month and a half has been unbelievable—weeks, days, and hours crammed with new experience—I feel as though I've lived a hundred years. Finally I've managed to fill some of the holes in my life with "living" that feels real. And I've certainly been changed. Like a clay figurine first pummeled into a shapeless ball, I am now being remodeled. I can't yet see the whole, but already I catch glimpses of a new me.*

*Living in this country with a black face has been indescribable. In every way I'm handicapped by my color. Sometimes being black has made me feel so worthless I've found myself apologizing for just existing. It's terrible to feel so without worth and so inherently bad.*

*What I can say in favor of the lawmakers here is that at least they're honest. There's no pretense. They tell the world we're second-class citizens and treat us accordingly. Growing up in England was more confusing. I was encouraged to believe I was like everyone else, so my disappointment was all the greater when I realized I wasn't. Equality for all—that's such a farce. Here in South Africa you quickly learn to curtail your expectations, because there are no false promises.*

*Thabo has been my salvation. One day I hope you two meet. He reminds me a lot of you—principled and practical. He's kept my hope alive. It's extraordinary how he manages to keep his self-esteem intact, his morale high, and his vision so clear in the face of such adversity. He also has a great sense of humor, which definitely prevents life from getting too serious. In fact, most of the black Africans I've met do. When I think of them I think of easy smiles, genuine goodwill, and infectious laughter. Amazing, considering the regime they live under.*

*These past weeks I've tasted African life at its most raw. I've sung in churches. Yes, me in a church, can you believe it! I've danced in a* shebeen *(a local illegal drinking house)*

*and hidden under floorboards when the police raided it.
I've met people in the dead of the night who risk their lives
and sanity every day, to fight this government. I've eaten
mielie pap and gravy with my fingers (thick cornmeal
porridge), I've drunk home-brewed millet beer (a heady
experience), and I've picked at chicken giblets in a meal
shared with twelve other hungry mouths. I even got to
wring the bird's neck. Apparently an honor!*

*I've watched a young man, a boy really, bleed to death
from stab wounds. I've seen an alleged police informer
"necklaced"—burned to death by a mob who placed a car
tire filled with fuel around his arms and chest and then lit
it. (This horrific image will live forever in my head.)
Yesterday, a clerk in Pretoria spat in my face. I'm getting
used to being ignored in shops until all the white customers
have been served. I could go on.*

*Dave, I've lived like an African, and laughed and
cried like one. But strangely, wait for it, I don't feel as if I
belong here. Maybe I'm destined to straddle the two
worlds, fitting into neither.*

*Most importantly I haven't yet found my mother.
We've explored every avenue and followed up on almost
every lead, even resorting to pinning up random signs
around Soweto, asking for any information on my
mother's whereabouts. The replies I've had have all been
from "tsotsis"—criminals only after the reward.*

*I guess I've come to accept there is a good chance she is
dead. What is so frustrating is that I'm sure, considering*

*this is a country where the black population is so heavily
regulated, information about her must be held by at least
one government agency. Yet all my visits to government
offices have been futile. Without exception, civil servants
here are obstructive. They've thwarted my efforts at every
turn, and failed to deliver anything despite some having
extracted a hefty bribe first.*

*Days have been spent getting to places, either in
Thabo's car—a hair-raising experience in itself—or by
train and bus. Then there's been the waiting in eternal
queues before being redirected from one department to
another, only to eventually reach a dead end.*

*The infuriating thing is that I know she is out there
somewhere, even if she's lying in a box under a mound of
earth. I suspect I won't find her. Maybe it wasn't meant to
be. At least I tried.*

*So unless I make some miraculous discovery, I plan to
return to the UK in a fortnight. My funds are running low
and my permit will soon expire. I'll call when I've
finalized the details. In the meantime, can you please let
the university know I'll be back to resume my clinical
attachment.*

*Dave, I know we left the future open. Just know I miss
you and love you.*

*Miriam xxx*


A white and green blob appeared beside my name where
Zaziwe had decided to leave her calling card.

The telephone pierced my dreams. I was loath to open my eyes, preferring the blankness of sleep, the faded lines and muted realities, the escape. The ringing continued.

I opened one eye. The room was awash with bright yellow light and there was a definite midmorning feel in the air. I sat up and reached for the alarm clock on the box beside my bed: 10:30 A.M.! How had I slept so late? The phone was *still* ringing, drilling holes through my head.

I swung my legs over the side of the bed, found my balance, then stomped through to the kitchen. "Hello?" My tongue was thick and furry. "Rhadebe residence."

The line crackled, then a woman's voice. "Is Tayboe there?"

"Who? Oh, you mean Thabo. Look, I don't think he is. I've just woken up and—"

"Never mind," came the crisp, tailored voice. "Could I leave a message?"

Something in the voice sounded familiar. "Aren't you the lady from Parktown North?"

"Yes. And you're the British girl? The one looking for your mother. Have you had any luck?"

"Do you have something?" I couldn't pace myself. I had no restraint left for courteous preamble.

"As a matter of fact I do."

My heart cartwheeled inside my chest.

"I was clearing out my desk last night and found the Eloffs' address. You know, the people from whom we bought the house. Got a pen handy?"

"Hang on." I put the receiver down and darted about the room in search of a pen, eventually finding one in the cutlery tray.

"Sorry. Okay. Go ahead."

There was nothing, just a hollow tinny silence.

"Hello. Hello?" I tapped the receiver, but there wasn't even the reassuring hum of a dial tone. The line was dead. I slammed the receiver down and stood staring at the instrument, willing it to ring. Every few seconds I lifted it to check, but still there was no dial tone. I fiddled with the jack, tipped the telephone upside down, shook it . . . Nothing!

When Thabo swung through the front door an hour later, he found me pacing about the room in a crazed state. He put down his parcels on the kitchen table. "Morning."

"Where have you been?" I demanded.

"Is everything okay?" Concern clouded his face. "I thought I'd let you sleep in while I went to buy some milk and bread. Were you worried?"

"How come it took you over an hour just to buy milk and bread?"

Thabo looked at me bemused.

"That woman rang, the one from Parktown North," I shouted. "Something about my mother. Then the phone went dead and . . . and I've lost the only lead we've had in seven bloody weeks!" I started to sob.

Thabo walked over to the phone and lifted the receiver. He shook his head. "Murphy's law. They must have cut us off."

"Who?" I said, wiping my nose on my sleeve.

"Murphy," he said. "Only joking. It will have been the phone company. I haven't paid last month's bill. I'm sorry."

"You haven't? Why?"

Then I realized. I sank down into a chair, overcome with guilt and embarrassment. The phone bill would have been hefty, due to all the calls I'd made. I felt so ashamed, I didn't know where to look.

"I'm so sorry," Thabo said again. "And just at a break-through."

"I'm the one who should be sorry. God, how rude of me! It was just that, it was the first time we were going to get some useful information, and now we . . ." I buried my head in my hands and tears took over. I couldn't stop them. I was crying as much for my own appalling behavior as for the terminated phone call. I was crying for Dave—I missed him so much—and for the emotional seesaw I'd been on. I was crying for Thabo and every other black person living in this forsaken country. It all poured out, weeks of pent-up emotion.

Eventually I felt a soft, warm hand on the nape of my neck. "Don't worry, I'll go over to her today and hear the news in person. Thabo Rhadebe will not rest until he is victorious."

And later that day I learned the Eloffs had moved to Knysna in the Cape—some one thousand miles south of Soweto.

# CHAPTER TWENTY-SEVEN

The Transvaal Highveld receded behind us. As we crossed the willow-lined Vaal River and ventured into the Orange Free State, the landscape started to change, as if the artist had been left with just two colors on his palette—gold and copper. The road we took cut through fields of wheat and corn, then valleys bounded by sandstone cliffs, which rose up starkly to greet us. There were turmeric-tinted poplars, sunflowers, and the surprise of green at the foothills of the Maloti Mountains.

We crossed another immense waterway—the Orange River—to find ourselves in the Cape Province. As we left the lushness of the river in our wake, the fertility of the land gave way to more barren surrounds. The Great Karoo—"land of thirst"—stretched endlessly in front of us. Now and then boulders cluttered a corner of the vast opus and flat-nosed mountains disturbed the emptiness, casting long shadows. Our small red car was dwarfed by the infinite space of this wider canvas, on which, toward the close of day, was painted a magnificent sunset.

Throughout the long journey, Africa wooed me, tantalizing my every sense. Its breath was sweet, its touch warm, its beauty astounding. Southern Africa wrapped itself around me and held me. And I surrendered to it, my heart soaring with this new love affair. I was home at last.

Thabo told me secrets guarded by the soil we were traveling over, and as we covered hundreds of miles, we traversed years of the black man's struggle for self-determination and freedom in his own country.

"We are traveling in the opposite direction to the Boer farmers when they set off on the Great Trek away from the Cape many years ago," Thabo began. "A bit like you, they were on their own personal journey. As they crossed the Orange River with their ox wagons they were forming part of a deliberate movement to cast off British governance, as well as any notion of black equality. They were headed for the largely unexplored Western Transvaal, Orange Free State, as we now know it, and Natal, where they could establish an independent society founded on the notion of white supremacy."

He took a long swig from the bottle of Coca-Cola we were sharing.

"You know, just as this journey will impact on your future, the Voortrekkers' expedition in the 1800s determined your past, for as the Boers pushed back the African tribes they met en route—an assegai no match for a gun—the native people, your forefathers, soon found themselves tenants on what they'd always considered to be their land."

I felt a deep sadness as I listened.

"The Voortrekkers' ideology of Afrikaner nationalism would, in time, be expanded into the doctrine of apartheid."

The parched desert of the Karoo was disappearing as the geography made way for the Land of the Outeniqua.

"A Khoikhoi name," Thabo explained, "meaning 'man laden with honey.'"

It was breathtaking—the lush forests, sagging creepers, and staggering gorges.

And just when I thought this kaleidoscope of beauty would never end, we were there, at the tip of Africa, where land and sea vied.

We had just passed through a small seaside settlement, when a policeman waved us down. I could see my reflection in his sunglasses as he peered into our car.

"*Dompas.*" His voice was rough and abrasive.

Thabo leaned forward, stuck his hand into the back pocket of his jeans, and pulled out his worn green passbook. He put it into the policeman's hands.

"Far from home, hey."

"I have permiss—"

"What is the nature of your business?"

I could see Thabo's teeth were clenched under the taut pull of his cheek. "I'm a journalist. I'm researching a story for *The Star.*"

"Communist trash!"

Another policeman made his way around to the rear of the car. *"Maak oop,"* he said, banging a fist on the boot. "Open up."

I licked my lips. As Thabo ducked down to reach the boot lever in the footwell, he appeared to startle the policeman at his window.

"Get out! Get out! Put your hands on your head!" the man yelled, panic exciting his fury.

Blood was pounding in my head. A gun was at my temple, the cold ring of death pushing into me. Then we were both being forced up against opposite sides of the car, our hands behind our heads.

"Any firearms, weapons, hand grenades?"

The car's metal burned into my front, and I could feel the heat of the body behind me.

"No . . . noth-nothing," I stuttered.

Something hard was pushing into the small of my back. At first I thought it was the policeman's R1, but it was throbbing. Then a hand was on my breast and fingers were squeezing my nipple. I felt the coolness of air on my legs as my skirt was lifted. A hand grabbed at my crotch and a knee forced my legs apart. I knew Thabo couldn't see what was happening from his position on the other side of the car.

"And where are *you* hiding your passbook?" the voice snorted.

Perhaps it was my pained expression or the leering tone of the policeman's words, but I saw Thabo's countenance change — a fury I'd not thought him capable of suffused his expression.

"Leave her!" he cried. "She's a British citizen. Her passport is in the car. Touch her again and your face will be on every front page here and overseas!" Not once did his voice falter.

I closed my eyes and counted time in breaths. I'd already inhaled three times when, like magic, the roving hand stopped and my skirt hem swung back down.

"Keep your hair on, Kaffir boy. Just a standard road check."

I couldn't believe it. A white man obeying a black man. The taut line of my fear slackened. But it was short-lived. How could I have been so stupid?

I watched the face of my molester as he circled the car—a scavenger eyeing its prey. His expression was that of a child chastised and humiliated in front of his peers. I felt an impending sense of doom. I looked into the darkness of Thabo's eyes.

Time slowed. I could smell the ocean. I could smell sweat. I saw the blunt bristles of the policeman's mustache and the ripple of leaves on a roadside tree. I saw the thousand tiny bumps on Thabo's skin acknowledge the breeze. I saw Zaziwe ruffle her feathers, puffing out her small body into a gray-brown ball. And I saw Thabo's big, strong hand caress her.

I saw the policeman take this all in.

"*Kyk die voel.* Look at the bird," said the smarting policeman, taking a swipe at Zaziwe and missing. For a moment Thabo's dearest companion remained suspended in mid-air and then . . .

A deafening bang reverberated through the valley. Two meerkats scurried across the road, a pair of Egyptian geese took to the skies, and a rabbit darted into its warren.

"Nooo!" rang out in synchrony with the explosion, as feathers, blood, and spattered sparrow flesh splashed across the gun-blue sky.

We drove for twenty minutes, neither of us speaking. Zaziwe's bloodied head rested on Thabo's lap, her glassy eyes dulled by death and dust. Eventually Thabo slowed and we pulled up under a *keurboom*, next to a hillside of wild watsonia. He turned off the engine and just sat there, staring into the distance, his eyes navigating a different landscape.

I put my arm around his trembling body and fingered his wiry hair.

His tears were silent, unlike my hiccuping sobs.

Eventually our weeping gave way to calm as we were transported through the day on the conveyor belt of time. The shade from the tree was the only thing to move as the late-afternoon sun found its way patiently inside our car.

"Tell me about Zaziwe," I said.

His words arrived with ease, as though they'd been ready for some time. "I was detained last year for four months. Kept in solitary confinement on suspicion of inciting subversive activities." He swallowed. "It was a black hole in my life about which I choose to remember very little. I was a broken man, except for . . ." He glanced at his blood-drenched trousers and smiled.

"Each day Zaziwe would land on the ledge of my cell window. I started to leave bits of dry porridge for her, and soon we had a date every day. She never let me down. Every time I was taken from my cell to be tortured and interrogated, when I was thrown back, she was waiting. When I awoke in the black of night, petrified by dark dreams, she was there, silhouetted against the moonlight. When I needed to talk, to keep my mind calm, she listened; and when I left that godforsaken place she came with me. I called her Zaziwe. It means 'hope.'"

We buried Zaziwe on the hillside, the long stems of watsonia bowing to a breeze that muddled the whites, pinks, and purples into a mash of mauve. After Thabo had fashioned a small cross from some twigs, we stood at her grave while he said a prayer. Then the heavens roared and opened, and big, cool drops of water fell to the parched and thirsty earth.

Thabo turned to look at me. At first I looked away, unable to bear the strength of his stare. Then I looked back. Inside the loud thunder and lightning, our silence was intense and our anticipation tightly sprung. Like magnets, our bodies leaned toward each other, ignoring the invisible restraints of our cautious minds. When he touched my hand I gasped. Then he touched my face—tracing my features like a blind man. I closed my eyes. Electricity crackled across the sky. He pressed his lips to mine.

My nipples rose up through my sodden blouse. Thabo acknowledged them carefully. He undid my bra and my breasts swung free, settling full and round in front of him. He lingered there, touching and kissing, caressing and tweaking. His smell, mixed with the scent of rain, was intoxicating. I'd only ever had teasing hints of it before, but now, close up, I inhaled deeply, losing myself in his bare torso.

The storm raged around us. I licked away his salty tears and sucked at the sweet raindrops that gathered on his jawline. A sense of urgency overtook us, and Thabo lowered me onto the wet earth. He was leaning over me, strong and black, and I was aching for him. As the sequence unfolded, he sought wordless permission at every step, yet there were no pauses in this dance. I took his hand and guided it, my arousal seeping onto his fingers. His head moved down my body and he played in my lap, driving me to the brink of ecstasy. Then it was I bent over him.

He entered my warmth and together we traveled beyond the confines of our lives.

## CHAPTER TWENTY-EIGHT

It was Sunday when we drew into Knysna. We'd spent the previous night with a friend of Thabo's in a township on the periphery of the seaside town. It had been a subdued evening and Thabo had gone to bed early.

After a breakfast of tea and warm doughy bread smeared with peanut butter and apricot jam, we set off for the town center. A holiday atmosphere prevailed. People in summer prints and wide-brimmed hats meandered down the streets—black, white, and brown bodies blending with apparent ease. Shop windows boasted all the trappings of recreation and relaxation—hammocks, surfboards, arts and crafts. Restaurants spilled patrons onto umbrella-lined sidewalks, and flower sellers enticed with their beautiful blooms. It felt good to be in the middle of all this positive energy.

We bought pies from a local baker and sat on a whites-only bench to eat them. But after a few minutes I lost my nerve, so we found a spot in the shade of an old plane tree overlooking the ocean. They were the best pies I'd ever tasted, the pastry rich and crumbly, the curried-meat filling delicious.

I looked up into the branches. The leaves had just started to turn; summer's green was making way for the orange of autumn.

"Funny how something as superficial as color can be so important," I mused. "Imagine if this poor plane tree was subject to apartheid. What a dilemma it would pose for the officials. *Well, tree, you can only reside in Knysna during the spring and summer months. In autumn you must move to the townships, and in winter—well, in winter you won't belong anywhere.*"

We fell back onto the spongy grass laughing. Thabo was so close, but we didn't touch. The previous day two damaged and lonely individuals had offered themselves to each other in consolation. Now guilt and the confusing complexity of real life intruded. Strangely, my mind wandered back to Rita. For the first time some of her actions seemed almost understandable.

"I feel so happy-sad," I said.

"Yes, this *is* a land of paradoxes." There was a small bare patch in front of Thabo where he had mindlessly picked away the grass. "South Africa has been the arena of my life," he said. "It's where the best and the worst have happened to me. A place of great beauty and ugliness."

We looked at each other.

"I feel so alive-dead," he said after a while.

Still we didn't touch. We couldn't.

Later we went to a service station to get directions to the Eloffs' house, and within fifteen minutes found ourselves sitting in Sylvia Eloff's lounge awaiting the coffee she was preparing for us. One entire wall of the room was glass, confusing the boundary between inside and out—the rugged carpet of fynbos, the stretch of glittering sand, and the teal-green waters all invited into the room, itself a trove of maritime treasures and curios.

I counted seven shell ashtrays. A stuffed marlin drove out of the wall above the fireplace. A driftwood chandelier—its gnarled arms bearing six globes—hung suspended from the ceiling. There were bottles of sand art and balls of tumbleweed . . . A second wall told another tale. Devoted entirely to books, from floor to ceiling, it told many stories—*Travels to India*; *War and Peace*; *Cry, the Beloved Country*; *Driving Routes through the Lake District*; *Birds of the Cape*; *Fifty Ways to Cook Chicken*; *Healing Hands*; and *Lord of the Flies*. Nadine Gordimer, Alan Paton, and Saul Bellow rubbed spines with Chaucer and Shakespeare and Wilbur Smith.

On the coffee table stood a vase holding a solitary protea—South Africa's national flower. With its thick woody stem, tough gray leaves, and furry pink petals, it was clearly equipped to survive the harshness of this wild continent.

"Here we are." The woman's voice was round and reassuring. She put down a wicker tray bearing a coffeepot, three mugs, and a plate of buttered date loaf.

She had a youthful appearance, light reflecting off her forehead to give her complexion a pearly translucency. Her eyes were half-hidden beneath soft hoods of skin, and her hair, cropped short and cinnamon in color, was interrupted by bold streaks of gray. Her long fingers trailed after graceful sweeps of expression, and a skew smile worked to hide her slightly overlapping front teeth.

"What a thing! Celia's daughter—just incredible!" Like a chameleon, she had started to adopt Thabo's accent, as if to put us at ease. "How do you take your coffee, black or white?"

"Well, seeing we're in the suburbs it'll have to be white," I jested, surprised at my brazen familiarity.

We all laughed.

"Celia and I still keep in touch," she said.

I covered my mouth to catch the strangled sound of my surprise. My thoughts started to tear around inside my head like a child left unchecked at a birthday party. After waiting months to hear these words, my mind would not be still for long enough to fully appreciate them.

"Celia was my right-hand woman. In the latter years, especially after Jo died, she was an invaluable friend." She swallowed a mouthful of cake. "We met under awful circumstances—she needed admission to hospital, and I—" She stopped, perhaps checking herself as she considered what details I could cope with.

I sat on the settee that afternoon at the tip of Africa, hearing about *my* mother. Sylvia Eloff paused every now and then to give me time to absorb what I'd heard, and throughout this uncharted journey of emotion, Thabo clasped my hand tightly.

"Did I miss her when she retired and went back home last April! No one can make shortbread like Celia. Most of all, though, she was an outstanding companion."

She stood up to catch a praying mantis that was climbing up the vase. In cupped hands, she took it over to an open window and released it. "Celia used to travel home each year to Venda, her homeland, where she was rebuilding her house. It was a very slow process. A couple of years back I gave her something to help get the project completed. But then her heart started plaguing her, and I decided it was time for her to go back home for good and let her children look after her."

*Her children.* The words hit me in the stomach, winding me. I'd forgotten . . . had not considered . . . Of course! I had siblings! The news was overwhelming. I couldn't remember, or could I? Had I simply expunged this fact from my childhood mind?

"She had a heart attack last March. Her heart had been broken for some time; the attack was really just the physical manifestation of her inner pain."

I sat still, not daring to interject with any one of the hundreds of questions jamming my head, just in case a crucial bit of information was lost. After years of living with an incomplete puzzle, I couldn't afford to lose a single piece.

"Celia was in hospital for almost two weeks, and after that, well, between us, we decided it was time to let her boys take care of her."

Thabo squeezed my hand.

"Three boys. Lovely lads," Sylvia Eloff continued, brushing the crumbs off her lap. "The eldest, Christian, was training to be a doctor when he became caught up in politics. He suffered terribly at the hands of the police; died in detention. His death changed Celia. She was never the same."

I felt the loss and grief immediately. I had gained and lost a brother in seconds.

Sylvia Eloff continued. "Nelson, the middle boy, he's a builder in Pretoria. Then there's Alfred, the youngest and short-est," she said with a chuckle. "He's a teacher in Dzanani. More coffee?"

"Thank you, no," Thabo said, answering for both of us.

I could only shake my head. Brothers. Siblings. These were still just words—words to be kept at bay. They led to possibili-ties and places I wasn't yet ready to visit.

"And then there was Miriam." Sylvia Eloff smiled fully, for the first time revealing her skewed front teeth. "Celia told me about the beautiful daughter she had lost. She never elaborated, though, and to be perfectly honest, I assumed she meant you had died. I'm sorry."

We spoke of many things that afternoon, that perfect after-noon. But as light fell and nature started to fold away the glisten-ing sheet that had been draped over the ocean all day, we took our cue and said good-bye.

Under my arm I held a bulky brown parcel secured with string.

"How can I ever thank you?"

Sylvia Eloff leaned in and held me in a gentle hug. Her fra-grance of linen and lavender enveloped me and stayed with me for years to come, merging with the memory I would always guard of those flawless few hours.

"I am just so pleased for Celia," she said, finally letting go. "She's in for one big surprise. Do be careful," she cautioned. "With her weak heart. And don't forget to give her that." She tapped the parcel in my hand. It felt heavy. "I've had it in the back room for ages. I keep meaning to post it. It's just some things she left behind in the upheaval of the move. I found them when I got around to clearing out her room. I've let it to a student. Some company, you know, and a bit of rent."

We drove through the night, stopping at about 2:00 A.M. on the side of the road so Thabo could snatch a few hours' sleep. I fell asleep beside him, my arms wound tightly around the brown paper package marked *Celia Mphephu* in bold black ink. Below was an address—my mother's address.

# CHAPTER TWENTY-NINE

"Stop! There's something in the bushes," I cried.

The Beetle screeched to a halt.

Hovering above a large tuft of grass was what looked like a gray pipe cleaner that had been twisted into a trembling spiral. The tuft wavered. The spiral disappeared. Then the golden grass parted and out trotted one truncated body, four stubby legs, and a snout that looked like an ice-cream tub. The creature passed in front of our car, clearly unperturbed by its audience, and disappeared into the long grass on the other side of the road.

"It's a bush pig," Thabo said.

"A bush pig! I've never seen one before," I squealed. "In fact, it's the first bit of wildlife we've encountered—except for those stray policemen."

"Then you must have a picture." And with that, Thabo veered off the road and into the scrub after the animal.

Completely ignoring my protestations, he negotiated the unforgiving terrain, shaking up every bit of loose plastic in the car. I grabbed for the hand rest as I was bounced off my seat.

The tail we were chasing came briefly into view. "There!" I screamed.

Several crazy minutes in pursuit of the elusive pig followed, then the car came to a sudden stop, the smell of burned rubber in the air. Our hilarity instantly evaporated and we turned to each other like two naughty schoolkids who'd just crashed the parents' car.

"Have we broken down?"

"It's probably just overheated."

He leaned over the back of his seat to retrieve a plastic lunch box. "Might need to take an early lunch break, while the engine cools down."

I climbed out of the car into a sea of golden grass, which swept from my feet to the horizon, uninterrupted except for an occasional rocky outcrop. I looked around. "Where's the road?"

Thabo pointed behind us. "It'll be over there somewhere."

Anxiously I followed his finger to a giant billboard rising absurdly out of the veld to advertise Coca-Cola. I stared, incredulous. But it wasn't the advertisement that had captured my attention; it was the colossal tree beside it.

"We can lunch in the baobab's shade," Thabo said, following my gawking gaze.

Approaching the tree, we started to shrink and soon we were standing directly beneath the tree's enormous canopy, Lilliputians dwarfed by Gulliver. The tree dominated the landscape, leaving no doubt as to its status as king of the African vegetation. Its gnarled trunk straddled meters of earth and its twisted branches writhed and reached out in every direction.

"According to San legend, the baobab didn't grow on earth," Thabo said, patting the rutted trunk. "The Bushman believes that one day the great tree just appeared, dropped from the heavens." He sat down and leaned back against it. "You know, it can live for over a thousand years."

"A thousand years?" I fingered a knot of bark.

I plonked myself down next to Thabo, so our shoulders grazed each other. We'd not made love again, nor would we. It was a mutual understanding—our minds and souls in silent agreement. All the same, I was glad we were comfortable with each other again.

Sheltered from the shimmering heat, we ate day-old Peck's Anchovette sandwiches (not my favorite) and fistfuls of cold *mielie pap.*

I stopped chewing, emptying my head of all noise, so it could fill with the mewling cry of birds overhead, the swish of wind through the grass, and the scratching of a dung beetle foraging in the dirt.

An hour later, we were on the road again.

"Nearly there," Thabo said, slapping my knee. "We'll head to a hostel and then tomorrow visit your mother."

The landscape was changing. Mountains, forests, and rivers now defined our new vista, while the sweet smell of pine needles, eucalyptus, and damp clay infused the air. As evening settled, a fine mist rose up from the deep lakes and dark forests to shroud everything in a haunting beauty.

The night was hot and muggy, the smell of rain strong. A

thunderstorm had threatened all afternoon, but the underbelly of cloud seemed impenetrable; the day remained trapped beneath the sagging gray canopy.

I could just make out Thabo's angular contours on a squab on the floor as I tossed and turned on the dormitory bunk, the air unbearably dense and close. Around me figures shuffled and snored and grunted, these sounds punctuating the long dark hours. At length I fell into a fitful sleep and began to dream. I hadn't dreamed in so long.

*A woman stands alone in a vast desert, her arms outstretched. Each time I try to reach her, a group of pale freckly boys hurl mangoes at me. Just as I succeed in getting past them, the woman vanishes like a mirage. I see a baby crying on a dune. I call out to the infant, but I make no sound. One minute the baby is white, the next brown, then I see it is actually blue. Frantically I try to climb the mound, but the sand keeps giving way and I slip back down. A wiry Indian girl jumps out from behind a baobab and picks up the dead child.*

*"Zelda! Zelda! I'm here. Bring me my baby!" I scream, but my voice is lost in a stampede. The earth shakes, sand swirls, and men wearing hard mining hats tear past me on the backs of lions. In their bloody hands they are carrying pieces of black rock, which they are holding up like trophies.*

*"No. Not gold, I want my baby. It's in Sixth Street . . . Sixth . . . Not Second . . ."*

"Miriam!"

I stared wildly into the darkness. Thabo was leaning over me, his face gleaming in the blue moonlight. "You were having a nightmare."

I sat up, my shirt damp with perspiration. "It was awful, I was trying to—"

"Shift over," he whispered, and he edged onto my narrow bunk. Outside, the clouds finally relinquished their treasure and rain started to clatter noisily onto the tin roof. Thabo lay facing me. He was so close I could feel his warm breath on my face. His strong hands stroked my head until I found myself falling down a deep black hole to where dreams don't venture.

When I woke, sunlight was streaming through the small squares of window. Thabo was still asleep, his head resting awkwardly against the wrought-iron headboard. A comforting aroma of coffee, paraffin, and porridge wafted into the room. I looked around. People were quietly busying themselves packing up their bedding and gathering their belongings.

I climbed carefully over Thabo and made my way outside into the crisp, clean morning. Steam was rising from the red earth and birds were singing in a post-storm cacophony. I filled a bucket with rainwater from the tank at the back of the building and knelt down on a bed of damp pine needles to wash my face. The icy water stung my cheeks.

Suddenly there was a warm hand on the back of my neck.

"It's such a beautiful day for you, Miriam," Thabo said, rubbing the sleep out of his eyes. He was still in his boxer shorts and vest, sunlight bathing his toffee-brown body.

We joined the circle of hostel dwellers perched on old tomato crates around a single Primus stove. Breakfast here was a communal affair—everyone's offerings placed in the middle of the circle on a small square of tarpaulin. It was a cheery gathering of strangers.

I had two triangles of bread smeared with butter, and a mug of coffee sweetened with condensed milk.

As I sat there in the pine forest, surrounded by the gentleness of people and place, I felt a deep sense of belonging. I couldn't have explained it and dared not analyze it too deeply, for fear of it being lost in translation, but it was the perfect mix of everything—a strange, tentative sort of homecoming.

## CHAPTER THIRTY

The car shook up our bones as Thabo negotiated the uneven ground and numerous potholes. Hills of gray-green scrub and patchy red dirt undulated around us. Dwellings dotted haphazardly across the countryside boasted great ingenuity—mud and wire, bricks and branches, all held together somehow—and falling fences demarcated small sections of cultivated land. Scatterings of chickens scratched busily in the earth; mangy donkeys strained as they hauled lopsided carts; children in bright rags with backs as straight as poles balanced pails of sloshing water on their small heads.

Thabo slowed as we drew up behind a woman bent under the weight of a bulging hessian sack she was balancing on her head. She swayed as she walked in a sort of perpetual motion, which worked to keep her load righted. She appeared to be talking to herself, but when I wound down my window, I heard her words ring out across the veld.

"Gr-ee-n *m-ie-lies*," she cried.

"What's she saying?"

"She's selling green *mielies*."

"*Green mielies?*"

"It just means they are freshly picked, their sheaves still green."

As we passed the old woman, she carefully extricated a hand from her load to wave. I waved back.

Thabo stopped the car a little farther down the road and walked back through the dust toward her. The old lady had already undone the rope sealing her sack by the time he reached her. As I'd come to expect, there followed some signaling and pointing, then the shaking of hands. Was this it? Surely not! Was *this* my mother?

Thabo climbed back in the car with five heads of corn. He pulled down the green sheaf of one to reveal plump golden beads of corn. "Now that's fresh." He lifted it to my nose. It smelled sweet and grassy.

I was relieved the *mielie* lady wasn't my mother. I didn't want to just find her on the side of the road by chance.

We were moving again and soon we'd turned off the main road onto a narrower, even bumpier track. After some way, Thabo pulled up under the sparse shade of an acacia tree. My eye followed his down a track to a hut nestling in a shallow valley.

The house stood alone, with no other dwelling nearby. The walls were fashioned from a variety of bricks, the roof a patchwork of blackened corrugated iron. Two ill-fitting windows toyed with my sense of alignment and proportion, as if in a photograph taken on a slight angle. A couple of branches, bowed like an old man's legs, supported a small thatched vestibule. Some *piccanins* squatted in its shade. To the left of the dwelling was a sagging clothesline, its vibrant passengers twisting in the breeze. To the right was a green patch of corn.

"Are you ready?" Thabo rested a hand on my knee.

"This is it?"

"I'll go in first if you like."

I nodded.

Thabo got out and walked down the red-dirt path. At the bottom he pushed open the dislocated gate that stood alone—no fence attached to either side. The *piccanins* leapt up from their game to crowd around the newcomer; their jumbled chatter and laughter transported back to me on the breeze. Then they were pointing in the direction of the *mielies*.

My heart started hammering in my chest, my throat, my mouth. I turned my gaze to look where they were pointing. As I squinted into the sun, I spotted a bent black figure working in the maize patch—a woman. I watched as Thabo approached her. She stood slowly, supporting her back on one side. They greeted one another and conversed, silhouettes against the sun. Then Thabo was putting his arm around her and together they started to walk toward the car.

I opened my door and stepped out. The earth seemed to move beneath me and I had to steady myself against the hot body of the car. Then I was putting one foot in front of the other as I made my way across the clearing. Dry grass poked through my sandals and pricked my feet; red grit worked its way between my toes.

Thabo stopped a short way off. The woman and I kept walking.

As she drew closer I saw that on her head she wore a brown felt beret and around her neck hung a string of bright wooden beads. A floral pinafore was gathered at her solid waist, and beneath it, a faded orange T-shirt hugged her sagging bosom. The sleeves defined strong, muscular arms. Her ankles were thick, and her feet cracked and hardened, but not her face. She had the loveliest face I'd ever seen, and a peaceful, almost regal, countenance. Her chin was pulled back in on itself, and her curly eyebrows arched evenly over eyes that were gentle and wise and shining with tears. They hungrily took in my face, my frame, my features.

She would have seen my hair was a mass of loosely woven knots and my face, a light milky-brown color. She would have noted the frayed jeans hugging my long limbs and the crisp white T-shirt outlining my tiny breasts. Around my neck was a simple gold locket. She would also have seen my brown eyes were awash with tears.

We stopped. Two meters and twenty-five years separated us. She stretched out her arms—matte black skin robbed of its gloss by age; hands crusted with the earth she'd been working.

I faltered.

No dune collapsed. The figure before me did not melt away. I took her hands in mine, fingering the residue of crushed African clay between our palms and inhaling *that* heady cocktail of Sunlight soap, wood smoke, and freshly toiled earth.

Memories rushed in.

"Miriam. *Mbila.*"

I was caught off guard. I'd heard my name countless times before, but never had it sounded like this. It encircled me and said all the things that could not be said.

"*Mme.*"

And then she was kissing me on my cheeks, my eyelids, my head, my arms, my hands . . .

# CHAPTER THIRTY-ONE

Inside my mother's hut it was cool and dark and smelled of the compacted dung floor, of earth and grass and cooling embers. The table was set as if we'd been expected—three tin mugs and a plate of assorted cream biscuits arranged on a plastic tablecloth decorated incongruously with Christmas motifs. A fine net had been draped over it all to keep off the sluggish horseflies, which droned around the room in lazy flight.

"I sent word to your mother," Thabo said, answering my puzzled expression. "I didn't want it to be too much of a shock."

A dented and blackened kettle began to rumble and shudder as the water came to the boil. Celia—my mother—carefully lifted it off the fire and set about making us tea. I recorded every movement she made. Years of agony, doubt, anger, and hope were concertinaed into this unlikely reality. She was standing in front of me, *my* mother—her bent body no apparition, her soft eyes no mirage. The importance of the task at hand—making tea for her daughter—weighed heavily on her.

But her solemnity was punctuated with joyous exclamations of disbelief. "*Hau*, my Miriam! I can't believe it!" Then she would clasp her hands and look to the heavens, and we'd all laugh.

Tea made, she sat down on the chair beside me, and for the entire afternoon held my hand, never once relinquishing her prize. We drank tea and ate countless biscuits as music from a crackling radio lent the atmosphere a festive air. The four *piccanins* danced excitedly around the room, while we talked and talked, filling in the missing years.

"This is my dear friend David," I said, pulling out a picture from my purse. "He should have been here too."

My mother screwed up her eyes and held the photo at arm's length, scrutinizing it. Milky cataracts clouded her eyes. After a time she nodded. "He has a good face." Then she looked across at Thabo. "You have a good face too."

We conversed in simple conversation suited to my mother's English and the vastness of the years and culture that separated us. With a university degree on my wall, business clothes in my wardrobe, and London—with all its tubes and taxis, theater and sophistication—woven into my heritage, I was sometimes unsure of what to say or how to say it. Thabo periodically rescued me, using his native tongue to fill in the pictures I tried to paint. They sounded beautiful—the words—in that velvety, melodious language.

"These are your brothers," she said, pointing to a long, narrow photo frame. "Nelson and Alfred and . . ." Her face darkened. "Christian."

"I know." I squeezed her hand. Three unknown faces smiled back at me, one I would never come to know.

After tea, she took us around her small plot. We admired her crop of corn, the sheaves robust and strong despite the arid earth. We stooped under the sparse branches of her pawpaw tree and inspected the limp leaves of her diseased tomato plants. She insisted on collecting me some eggs from the chicken run, and she spoke excitedly of electricity coming soon to the area.

"But what do you use now?"

She was puzzled by my question and frowned, deep ruts crumpling her forehead. "Fire, my child, and kerosene, of course."

As the afternoon wore on, all barriers dropped away and our interactions were as effortless as the love between a mother and child. "The parcel!" I exclaimed, suddenly remembering. I darted out to the car to retrieve the square brown package.

My mother opened it slowly. I'm not sure if it was her arthritic fingers or apprehension that delayed her. Inside was a note from Sylvia Eloff, a bag of cashew nuts, a crocheted table-cloth, a small tray of dried peaches, and two bars of Peppermint Crisp. There were also some odds and ends my mother had unwittingly left behind when she'd left the Cape—a woven grass coaster, a scarf, nail scissors.

"Chocolate!" cried the *piccanins*. These happy urchins were my brother's children, and *I* was their aunt. I closed my eyes and drank in their giggles and exclamations.

"There's something else," Thabo said.

My mother was lifting out a book from the bottom of the box; its cover was faded, its spine torn. She held it with great care so the pages wouldn't fall out. I was intrigued. Written in a big, childlike scrawl under the title was a name. *My* name. Miriam Mphephu.

I looked at the title of the story the book seemed to automatically open to—"The Gift of the Magi"—and in an instant the years disappeared and moments that had been lost were magically retrieved. Once again I was five years old, sitting excitedly in the dip of a sagging mattress recounting the tale to my mother.

"I loved that story so much," I said to Thabo. My mother nodded. As I paged slowly through the book, great holes in my mind were filled. "It's exactly as I remember it!" I looked up at Celia. "Do you remember Michael would tell me stories at supper? He was such a good storyteller. I loved his stories."

My mother smiled, but her eyes told a different tale. She was in some other place.

"Why don't I read it to these scalawags," Thabo said, taking the book off me. "I'll translate it. I'm keen to find out what happens in this famous story."

Neither my mother nor I took the hint.

"Go on, you two. Outside! Have some time alone together."

So we headed out and sat down on a rickety bench beside the front door. A bee trapped in an empty Fanta bottle was buzzing around its plastic prison, disturbing the stillness of our afternoon.

After a long pause my mother began to stroke my hand. "Master Steiner, he was good to you?"

I looked across the hills, nodding slowly at first, but with more conviction as I summed up Michael in my mind's eye. I was no longer angry with him. "Yes. He always was, and still is, very good to me."

She smiled, and I saw in her smile several different stories. I saw relief that I'd been cared for and the residue of exhilaration at our reunion. I also saw a mysterious coyness.

Then she told me she'd met Patrick when she was just fourteen. They'd lived on adjacent farms, walking the same road every day to fetch water. On one of these trips they promised one another that when they were older they would marry. I listened closely to this piece of unexpected history, unsure of where it had sprung from or where it was leading, but I sensed its importance.

"When Patrick is fifteen, he leave Louis Trichardt to find work in Johannesburg. After he find a job on the mines, he write to me and tell me to come and be with him in the city where the jobs are many and there is much money too."

She'd followed him to Johannesburg and found work as a maid, cleaning white people's houses. But they couldn't live together because Patrick was forced to live in the mining hostel and she in the suburbs.

She started to cough. What initially sounded like a tickle in her throat grew into a prolonged gasping rattle that for a few moments hijacked her whole body and wrestled her into breathless submission.

Eventually, after several sips of water, she continued. She went on to tell me how she and Patrick missed each other very much, but only got to see one another when their annual leave coincided. Then they would meet back in the homelands for a week. And nine months after each meeting, a baby was born—first Christian, then Nelson, and finally Alfred.

"After that, I don't know why, Patrick stop coming home. The mines, I think they made him wrong."

I waited for more.

One day when she was already working for the Steiners, she overheard them having a terrible fight. A door banged and she found Michael outside in the yard, crying quietly. She had never seen a man cry before. "He is very sad, so I make him tea and he sit on the steps, talking for a long time." He spoke of his mother and father—good people who had died in a car crash when he was at university. He spoke of meeting Rita soon after, and his rush to marry her to fill the emptiness. "But when he talk about her, his eyes are empty. I think his heart is empty too. Then he tell me it is too hard for the Madam to have babies."

She shook her head and stared into the distance as though watching the scene she was describing to me unfold again before her—the scene where Michael kissed her.

I couldn't hear the trapped bee any longer, nor did I notice the hills stenciled against the burnished horizon. I was floundering in my mother's words.

"He is a very kind man and we make much happiness, but always in secret and always scared for the police or Madam Rita to find out. Then . . . then I am pregnant and we worry too much because a colored baby is no good in South Africa." She dragged a hand over her eyes. "We pretend Patrick is the father, and when the child is born we are lucky because it is looking more like a black baby than a white one. So we pretend, and we make a promise never to tell anyone."

My mind danced on the periphery of comprehension.

"You mean . . ."

"Yes, *Mbila*. Master Michael, he is your father."

I gasped. Michael, my father? I turned and looked my mother in the eye. I expected to find regret there, and shame, perhaps an apology. But all I saw was forbidden love and an indomitable strength. Then my mind was turning back the pages, trying to reinterpret my life—my adoption, Rita's infidelity, Michael, the pull of two cultures, two colors, two places, two people.

As the sun started its slow descent, slipping gracefully behind the hills, my mother and I sat in silence, holding hands and letting the evening wash over us. It had been an unbelievable day. Words were inadequate.

Eventually Thabo and I took our leave. Our little red Beetle would soon disappear in a cloud of dust sent on its way by the self-appointed farewell party of *piccanins*. I would not get to meet my brothers this time. Alfred was in Johannesburg for a long weekend and Nelson lived in Pretoria. And I had a plane to catch in less than forty-eight hours. But I would be back.

My mother kissed me good-bye, tears driving new tracks down her dusty cheeks. Then she turned and moved slowly toward her *mielie* field. With about twenty minutes of half-light left, there was still work to be done.

We'd been driving for almost an hour when I broke the silence.

"He's my father," I said, a smile creeping across my lips.

Thabo turned. "What? Who?"

"Michael. He's my father. My mother told me."

I pulled down the sun visor and looked at myself in the tiny rectangle of mirror. The amber light of dusk, which had lit up the car, was falling on my milky-brown complexion and spongy curls. The last piece of the jigsaw had slid into place. The picture was complete.

# CHAPTER THIRTY-TWO

"This is the final boarding call for British Airways Flight 0034 to London. Please make your way immediately through customs to gate number five. *Hierdie is die laaste aankondiging om aan boord te gaan . . .*"

Still we lingered outside the opaque glass doors. In a moment I would have to walk through them and they would shut behind me—one chapter closing, another about to begin. People and places would become names, photographs, and marks on a map.

An image of the baobab tree flashed before me, its roots traveling deep into the ground, its branches reaching for the heavens. It would remain like that for many more years, but everything around it would change. Time and people would keep moving on.

"I hate good-byes, so this isn't one," I said, fidgeting with my locket. "Just know a different person is leaving from the one who arrived eight weeks ago, thanks to you."

"It's been really hard having such a difficult and awkward visitor," he teased. "Now how am I to describe you to my editor? I'd say . . ." His cheeky smile vanished and his dark eyes were staring into mine. "Soul mate."

We hugged. One last moment of soap, aftershave, and wood smoke. I leaned down and lifted a green cardboard box off the trolley where it had been carefully wedged between my bags. I handed it to him. "Don't tip it upside down, whatever you do."

I turned and moved quickly through the doors toward customs.

"Papers," the thick accent barked.

Once through passport control, I had to take a long flight of escalators down to the departure lounge. As I descended, someone tapped me on the shoulder.

"Look," the woman behind me said. "Someone's trying to catch your attention."

I turned.

Thabo was standing behind a thick pane of glass, knocking on the soundless barrier. As he caught my eye, he lifted my gift out of the box and held it up for me to see. The stairs kept moving, relentlessly transporting me away from him and the baby cockatiel with orange beak, tomato-red cheeks, and charcoal feathers. He was waving my note in the air. I could see it had already been shredded at the corners and was no doubt sporting a couple of chalky exclamation marks.

At midday another bird—a huge metal one—rose into the sky. Africa grew smaller and smaller and eventually disappeared beneath a cloth of clouds. I was leaving it behind, but my roots were deep in the dry red earth; they could never be severed.

I was ready to grow.

# EPILOGUE

"Push! Come on, you can do it! One more push!"

"Aaaah!" The pain was intolerable—the burning, tearing pain.

"Come on, love. Give it all you've got. I can see the head. I can." Dave kept encouraging me, his strong hands caressing my forehead. I wanted to clobber him.

The midwife bent down and grasped something in her hands.

"Nooo!"

As my flesh tore, I screamed; then, as if a vacuum sucked up all sound, the room held its breath.

A faint cry filled the void, growing louder and louder as if someone was turning up the volume.

"It's a girl, Miriam. You have a bonny baby girl," said the midwife.

I lay back in wet exhaustion, bathed in an overwhelming, indescribable feeling of warmth and elation.

Dave, his eyes dancing with tears and joy, held the bundle proudly in his arms. "Miriam, she's beautiful."

The pink lilies in my room had filled the air with a gentle scent, reminding me of Sylvia Eloff. Dave was asleep in the La-Z-Boy chair beside my bed. Across his chest our baby slept, her perfect little fingers peeping out from under a furry white blanket. I couldn't stop smiling—I was so happy my cheeks ached.

I glanced at the TV set in the corner, its volume muted. A man's face flashed across the screen. He had proud shoulders, an open face, and sloping eyes full of wisdom and gentleness. I reached for the remote control.

"—reporting. Yes, Susan, the first images of a man whose face has not been seen for over a quarter of a century. On this warm and cloudless day on the outskirts of Paarl, in the lush wine-growing region of South Africa, one of the last bastions of apartheid has come tumbling down. Who would have believed it could ever happen? Nelson Rolihlahla Mandela released from Victor Verster Prison, having spent twenty-seven and a half years of his life behind bars for his part in the struggle to end apartheid. It is certainly a new chapter in his life and in the lives of all South Africans—black, white, and colored. He is expected to address—"

I leaned over and carefully eased the sleeping bundle from David's grasp. He stirred, gave me a dreamy smile, then dozed again.

As I looked down at the parcel in my arms, two big brown eyes looked back at me—deep, dark pools in which I saw reflections of many things. I saw my mother's immense love; I saw Dave's fortitude and generosity. There was Zelda's jollity, Rahini's wisdom, and Michael's kindness. And Thabo's unwavering convictions too. All branches of an immense baobab tree.

I leaned forward and placed a kiss on my daughter's crumpled forehead. She smelled like a puppy—of new life and warm skin.

"Hello, Baby Celia," I whispered. "I've been so waiting to meet you."

# ACKNOWLEDGMENTS

The act of writing might be a solitary one, but the process of bringing a book to publication is most definitely collaborative. Every chapter of this book holds something of the time, expertise, and experience so generously shared with me. While there are too many to name individually, I am ever grateful to you all.

A special mention for my dearest husband, Luigi, whose love and unwavering support got me to the finish line, and my beautiful children, Nadia and Andrew, who never once stopped believing in me. Thank you.

To literary agents Glenys Bean, Heidi North, and Hannah Ferguson—I am indebted to all three of you for backing my book and working tirelessly to find it a home.

To Susie Dunlop of Allison & Busby, and Julie Mianecki of Berkley Books, Penguin USA—thank you for embracing this book with such enthusiasm. It is a privilege to have been invited into your respective folds.

Lesley Marshall, thank you for your sage input early on, and Lorain Day, for your exacting editorial eye at the end. Thomas Maraheni, Agnes Tshivhula, and Andries Liswoga, for your assistance with the Tshivenḑa translations; and Dario Dosio, Christine Dimitriou, Pat Scott, and Helen Stewart for facilitating this. And of course my book club ladies for all the laughter and cake on a Wednesday night, which sustained me.

Thank you to my brother, Peter, whose splendid childhood theatrical productions and boundless imagination introduced me to the magic of stories, and to my late father (publisher and person extraordinaire) and dear mother (chief bedtime-storyteller and confidante), who both brought the wonder of words into our home, and that, of course, is where it all began.

Finally, to authors Nadine Gordimer, Athol Fugard, Alan Paton, Doris Lessing, Herman Charles Bosman, and J. M. Coetzee, whose brave works stirred and inspired me.

# SOURCES CONSULTED

While *Another Woman's Daughter* is not a factual account, and the characters in it fictional, I am indebted to the authors of the books and websites below whose works supplemented my knowledge of the world my characters would inhabit.

Connew, Bruce, and Wright Vernon. *South Africa.* Auckland, New Zealand: Hodder & Stoughton, 1987.

Fugard, Athol. *Tsotsi.* New York: Random House, 1980.

Mandela, Nelson. *Long Walk to Freedom.* Randburg, South Africa: Macdonald Purnell, 1994.

Omer-Cooper, J. D. *History of Southern Africa.* London: James Currey, 1994.

Powell, Ivor, Mark Lewis, and Mark Hurwitz. *Ndebele: A People and Their Art.* Cape Town: Struik, 1995.

Reader's Digest. *South Africa: Magnificent Land.* Cape Town: Reader's Digest, 1988.

South African History Archive (SAHA), Google Cultural Institute. http://www.google.com/culturalinstitute/collection/south-african-history-archive.

South African History Online (SAHO). http://www.sahistory .org.za.

Venter, Paul C. *Soweto: Shadow City.* Johannesburg: Perskor, 1977.

Wannenburgh, Alf, and J. R. Dickson. *The Natural Wonder of Southern Africa.* Cape Town: Struik, 1987.

# ANOTHER WOMAN'S DAUGHTER

## BY FIONA SUSSMAN

# DISCUSSION QUESTIONS

1. In the author's note, Sussman acknowledges "the challenge of writing in the voice of characters whose life experiences and culture [are] so different from [her] own," and ultimately draws on her "experiences as a mother, daughter, wife and sister" to tell her story. Can we look to our shared humanity to understand each other? How?

2. Why did the Steiners want to adopt Miriam? Do you think it was the right decision? Discuss the ups and downs of Miriam's life in England and the life she might have led in Africa.

3. Miriam describes how she "worked hard to make [herself] invisible." Later on Celia feels invisible to the white family she works for. What does invisibility mean to each character? Why is it sought after by Miriam, yet so hurtful to Celia?

4. As Celia observes, "These township kids had looked down the barrel of the future and seen little hope. They had nothing to lose." Do you see any parallels between

apartheid and current events? Are there lessons we can draw on for today?

5. What effect does Sylvia Eloff have on Celia's mindset and self-image, and on her life in general?

6. Why does Rita scold Miriam for cleaning when they first arrive in England? What does this act of cleaning signify to both Rita and Miriam? What does the scene tell us about Miriam's adoption?

7. Rita is clearly a flawed character. Do you sympathize with her? Why, or why not?

8. Discuss Michael. Is his love enough, or should he have been more proactive, and interfered in Rita's treatment of Miriam? Why does he allow the deceit—about their marriage and the adoption terms—to perpetuate?

9. In the book we see three instances where love is sought outside a prescribed relationship—Michael is unfaithful to Rita, Rita to Michael, and then Miriam to David. How do these three instances differ? Can any or all of them be condoned?

10. "At least they're honest. There's no pretense. They tell the world we're second-class citizens and treat us accordingly. Growing up in England . . . I was encouraged to believe I was like everyone else, so my disappointment was all the

greater when I realized I wasn't." What do you think of Miriam's assessment of England as a kind of apartheid in disguise? Which unfortunate truth would you choose in her place?

11. Dave says, "Miriam's past is integral to who she is. For her to move forward she needs to explore her past. It's her history, her connectedness." How does this apply to your own life? Is your past intrinsic to your identity?

12. What advantage do you think a work of historical fiction might have over that of nonfiction in causing a reader to acknowledge and reflect on human behavior? Has reading *Another Woman's Daughter* led you to ponder wider issues?

31901056873278